THE MORTICIAN'S APPRENTICE

W · W · NORTON & COMPANY

New York · London

THE MORTICIAN'S APPRENTICE

Rick DeMarinis

A portion of this book first appeared
in the magazine *GQ* in somewhat
different form.

The text of this book is composed in Bodoni,
with the display set in Poster Bodoni and Eve.
Composition and manufacturing by The Haddon Craftsmen, Inc.
Book design by Antonina Krass.

Library of Congress Cataloging-in-Publication Data
DeMarinis, Rick, 1934-
The mortician's apprentice / by Rick DeMarinis.
p.   cm.
1. Teenage boys—California, Southern—Fiction. I. Title.
PS3554.E4554M67 1994
813′.54—dc20 93-45969

ISBN 0-393-03662-6
W. W. Norton & Company, Inc., 500 Fifth Avenue, New York, N.Y. 10110
W. W. Norton & Company Ltd., 10 Coptic Street, London WC1A 1PU
1 2 3 4 5 6 7 8 9 0

THE MORTICIAN'S APPRENTICE

I am sitting in the dark backseat of the Packard reading comic books and thinking about Death while my folks take a breather in a roadhouse called the No Tomorrow. We are in Gallup, New Mexico, 1948, on our way back to California after a year in Texas. We took a restless, circular route, as if trying to throw someone off our track. Fort Worth to New York to Michigan, then back down to Texas through Kansas and Oklahoma, and now we are on Route 66, seven hundred miles from Paradise. That's what Mitzi calls it, meaning California. San Diego, to be exact. This time, Mitzi says, we will definitely put down roots.

Roots. This makes me think of the ground and the ground makes me think of graves and graves make me think of Death. Death as Idea. And it seems to me that Death is also circular, just like our looping travels through America. Fred is willing to go along with me on this, at least for the time being. Fred is someone I have invented, or maybe Fred has invented me. It's possible. I've read enough comic books to believe that anything is possible. Fred says maybe you start where you end and you end where you start, like hopscotch or Ferris wheels. Death is where you get off and get back on again. I think of it as a huge halo, big enough to loop the universe. One small piece of the halo, an arc that is about one-tenth of an inch long in this trillion-mile circumference, is rainbow-bright. Like a diamond in a wedding ring. That bright diamond is Life. Anyone's Life. Mine. This little wink of light in the endless ring is me. I am thirteen years old and so the flicker of light is fairly small. When I am an old man, say forty or fifty, it will be a little bit bigger. When I die, say at age eighty or ninety, it will still be small, but big enough now to be seen by a Distant Observer. Wait a minute, what are you talking about? Fred wants to know. What Distant Observer? But my grip on the idea loosens up right there. No one said anything about Distant Observers. Even so, it is hard to think that no one at all was ever interested enough in these billions of temporary lights to wonder what they were going to do next and if what they did was ever going to make sense. Hard for you maybe, Fred says. Fred can be sarcastic at times. I don't know where he gets that from, or what he thinks it will do for him.

How did I come to see Life and Death in this way, sitting in the ovenlike backseat of that Packard Clipper in Gallup, New Mexico? I was trying to remember who I was before I was born because in one comic book an Egyptian magician, Magus the Great, dies and is reincarnated as an American who grows up to be the mayor of St. Joseph, Missouri. But I couldn't remember ever being someone else, and Fred was no help. The idea of being somebody else before you were born was a brain-buster. It seemed more likely that I was just plain dead forever before I was born, and that I would be dead forever again after I died, and that forever looped on and on. Somewhere in that loop I popped up. But this was a scary idea, because loops are continuous and that meant I'd keep popping up, and I'd be here again and again, waiting for my folks to come out of the No Tomorrow while I talked to a sarcastic creature of my own imagination who had nothing better to do than poke holes into my ideas. But it was a perfectly fine idea, I thought. And a fine idea, even if it's scary, is still a fine idea, and something to be proud of. I imagined this was some future duplicate of Now, 3948 A.D. say, as I flipped through my comic book, following the magical adventures of the mayor of St. Joseph, Missouri. You don't make sense, Fred said. It's always going to be 1948 for you, if you believe what you're saying. There is no future. It's like a phonograph needle that skips, riding the same dumb groove over and over until the groove wears out. Wears out! Was that possible? I pictured a big hand (the Distant Observer's) picking up the tone arm and saying, I am sick and tired of listening to this worn-out piece of junk! and sailing the record and all its tired grooves out of his house and into a furnace of stars. Then he'd put a brand-new record on his phonograph. You're goofy, said Fred.

It was too hot to think and I had confused myself. "You think too much," Mitzi often says. Mitzi is my mother. She had married her latest husband, Wes Caulkins, in Fort Worth after knowing him for only two weeks. And now they were going to California to get defense-industry jobs after having tried their luck everywhere else. But things between them had gone sour on the long hot trip. First of all, the Packard, which belonged to Mitzi, vapor-locked every hundred miles or so, and Wes would have to pour water on the fuel lines and fuel pump and intake manifold so that the air bubbles that blocked the gas from getting to the carburetor would go away. We carried our own water in one-gallon canvas bags that hung from the Packard's fancy hood ornament and rode against the grille. It took about a half hour for the vapor lock to break loose. We'd wait in the blazing heat, sitting on the running boards, or under nearby trees if there were any. All this made their quick tempers quicker, even though Wes doused water from the canvas bags over all of us just so our brains wouldn't fry.

What happens next happens fast. The door of the No Tomorrow flies open and Wes and Mitzi come spilling out. Wes has a man's arm wrapped around his neck and Mitzi is yelling at me to start the goddam car. This has been going on for a while now, since Enid, Oklahoma, to be exact. Practically every time we stop for a breather, Wes and Mitzi get into a jam with the locals. I'm tired of it, but what can I do? Wes likes to drink and fight, Mitzi likes to drink and flirt.

I climb into the front seat and switch on the ignition. The radio comes blaring on to some local jamboree, guitars and banjos jangling the air. I press the starter button, and Mitzi piles in next to me. "Git, git!" she says, breathless, and I slide the shift lever into first gear and ease out the clutch. I'm not old enough to drive but I'm big enough and I can. Wes is on the ground, rolling away from a big man's boot. "What about Wes?" I say. "He can DDT!" she says. "He's just another bad apple." DDT means Drop Dead Twice. It's something people in California say. California people

are always coming up with neat new things to say, like Hey
bob-a-rebob! when they are excited, or Let's make the
scene! when they want to go someplace special. I like it
when things are new. It makes me believe that you don't
have to stay in the same old rut, over and over. If you keep
making things new, you beat the trap of having to live the
same things again and again. You can jump from one
groove to another. California would be a new groove for
both Mitzi and me. Another dopey idea, Fred says.

After we get back on the highway, Mitzi says, "They're
all bad apples, Ozzie. I hope you break the mold, kid."

I'm not sure what she means, but I say, "I will, Mitzi.
Cross my heart and hope to die."

1

The bodies were arranged in neat rows on metal tables. Colleen dared me to look at them. We were in the "cold room" of her father's mortuary. Her father, the mortician, had gone downtown on business, so there was nothing to worry about. "Kiss me, Ozzie," she said. We French-kissed next to an old woman. The old woman was covered with a sheet, but wiry strands of her dead, yellow-streaked hair spilled off the table. Her feet were also uncovered, the gnarled arthritic toes, the waxy gray nails. "Don't," Colleen said when I groped under her sweater. She broke away from me and ran around the old woman and then along the row of bodies. I went after her. When I reached her, she pulled the sheet off the head and shoulders of a middle-aged man. His jaws were clenched as if he had died refusing to utter his last words, but his eyes were open and fogged with confusion. "Touch him," Colleen said. "I double dare you." This was her idea of a game.

I touched his white shoulder. He was room-temperature, but felt like ice. "Jesus, Colleen," I said.

"It isn't so icky, is it?" she said. "I mean, once they're dead, it isn't as if they're actual people anymore, you know?"

She held my hand and I was grateful for the living heat of her body. We kissed again. "You got some pennies?" I said.

"What do you mean?"

"Pennies. We should put pennies on his eyes. Or a twenty-dollar gold piece on his watch chain. Like in the song, 'St. James Infirmary.' But I don't think this guy died standing pat."

"Whatever are you talking about, silly boy?"

Actually, she didn't want to talk. She flitted away from me again. I was doing my best to stay cool, but I was beginning to feel a little sick. She was different, but she was good-looking, and she was hot.

I kissed her again by the embalming table. By now we were both trembling from excitement and from the clammy dead air. "Let's go to the beach," she said. "I'll pack a lunch."

We'd met at a sock hop for seniors. "Colleen Vogel thinks you're neato," Denise Linstead had said.

"No lie?" I said, surprised.

Half the seniors were already engaged, a month shy of graduation. There was a kind of frantic desperation in the air, you could almost taste it. Graduation and marriage were linked topics in a lot of people's minds. I danced three dances with Colleen. We danced poorly with each other. But our mistakes threw our bodies together often. Sparks crackled in the fuzz of our sweaters with each collision.

A few nights later we double-dated with Denise and her boyfriend, Art di Coca, in Art's lowered and chopped '41 Mercury. Art was my best friend. We went to the Aztec Drive-in to see *Human Desire,* starring Glenn Ford and Gloria Grahame. Art and Denise slumped out of sight in the front seat as soon as the opening credits started to slide up the screen. Colleen and I watched the movie through the fogged windshield, which was only about six inches wide. The actors moved through a narrow panel of fog that got denser and denser. I couldn't tell Glenn Ford from Broderick Crawford. Then Denise's moans drowned out the sound track, and the air in the car got warm and heavy. I was embarrassed, but Colleen wasn't. She leaned her head back into the seat cushion and waited for me. I was a little slow on the uptake, and when I finally pressed against the soft, weighty curvature of her upper body, she said, "You're quite the moody one, aren't you?"

She had mature, forward-thrusting breasts and long, slender—almost skinny—legs. She had high fine cheekbones and strong jaws. Her generous nose was busily freckled and her blue eyes were self-consciously playful and always up to some small mischief. She was aggressive, but not as popular as some girls who were not nearly as pretty. Normally she held her mouth thoughtfully pursed, like a hard button, but it bloomed into a large loose O as I turned to kiss it. When our tongues flexed into action, she began to make the same helpless moans Denise was making. It was as if they'd practiced these sounds together the way cheerleaders practiced their yells.

It took me an hour to inch my fingers past the tight band of her jeans and into her panties. By then, Broderick Crawford had killed Gloria Grahame, or Glenn Ford had done it. Or Ford had killed Crawford. They might have been on a train, but it could have been a boat. It was hard to tell.

When I reached the fine scrub of pubic hair and the hot wet cleft it hid, my excitement betrayed me. I'd been in control, but now I began to self-destruct. I didn't think of stopping the pulsing eruption until it had gone past the point of no return. This was the farthest I'd ever been with any girl. I had just turned eighteen. It was 1953—a forgotten card in history's stacked deck.

I crossed my legs against the rampaging traitor and leaned back into the seat cushion, thunderstruck but playing it cool by trying to whistle "The September Song" in the mellow way Gerry Mulligan would have blown it on his baritone sax. Colleen, patting my hand, saw this as more evidence that I was a complicated man of many moods. A thinker. I excused myself and climbed out of the car, saying that I was going for Cokes. I went to the concrete-block building that served as a projection room and concession stand and headed for the men's room, where I got rid of my soggy shorts.

We went to the beach in her MG roadster. The sun had not yet burned the fog out of the air. We had the beach to ourselves. "Let me bury you," she said. I dug a pit with a little beach shovel

she kept in the car. I got into it, arms folded across my chest. She
covered me up with cool sand, then flopped down on top of me.
"Rest in peace," she said. She gave me a feathery widow's kiss,
teasing me with her darting tongue. "You like this, Ozzie? You
like being buried alive?"

I didn't much. My trapped crotch pulsed against her weight
and the weight of the sand. I wanted my arms. "Dig me out, Colleen," I said.

"Be nice," she warned. Her lips compressed to a severe line.
She looked like a cross pixie. She twisted my hair in her fingers.
Gulls walked up to us, eyeing our lunch bag. "Look, the souls of
lost sailors," she said, inventing a playful mythology on the spot.
She ran down to the water and splashed in the waves for a while,
then ran back to me glistening like a pink seal.

"Are you nice?" she said.

"Come on, Colleen," I said. "Dig me out. I'm getting pissed
off." My lungs felt small. I couldn't get enough air. There was
sand in my mouth. I wasn't nice.

She freed my arms and I did the rest. Her lips puckered in a
mock pout. "So, is this one of your famous 'moods,' Ozzie?" she
said.

I brushed myself off and sprawled out on the beach blanket.
She stroked suntan lotion into my shoulders and back. It felt
good. I got drowsy. The ridges on either side of the spine are
packed with fine nerves that love to be stroked.

"Oh, Ozzie," she said, her voice honeyed with confidence. "If
we ever have children—or should I say *when*?—I think they will
be significant additions to the human race, don't you?"

"Our children?" I said. I felt my back muscles stiffen.

"Peter, William, Rosemary, and Deirdre," she said, jabbing the air with a matriarchal finger, as if counting little heads. "I've named them already. I mean, subject to your approval. We shall have four. Oh darling! We'll be so happy!"

The sun began to disperse the late-morning fog but the wind gusting off the ocean was still cool. We both had goose bumps. Mine were left over from the mortuary. The cold room where the bodies were kept was connected to the Vogel house by a hallway. As you walked down this hallway from the comfort of the house, the air got damp and wintry. It was springtime in the house, dim January in the cold room.

I pushed myself up on one elbow. "Excuse me?" I said.

"You'll make a wonderful father, Ozzie," she said, rolling against me, her aggressive breasts trapping my panicky chest. She looked like a rising pink wave, ready to break. "Daddy will take you into the business—after we graduate, or whenever. You'll be his apprentice, and we can live in the apartment above the garages. It'll just be *super*. Can't you just *see* it, honey?"

I stared at her, stunned mute by that claustrophobic "honey." Daddy was Morris Vogel, owner of the Vogel-Darling Funeral Home. Frank Darling, his partner, was long dead. His heart, Colleen told me later, had stopped while he was closing the deal on a top-of-the-line six-thousand-dollar funeral for a former Congressman.

Her eyes narrowed, sly with significance. "I mean, after last *night*, and all," she said. "*You* know. I mean, about what we *did*. In Art's *car*. Remember?"

I felt pinned down by shame and guilt. "Hey, Colleen, we were
just . . . you know, messing around." The words wormed out of
my dry throat.

"No. It was not just messing around, as you so crudely put it."
Her lips tightened. She looked wounded. Her eyes got misty as
they searched the empty western horizon.

"I mean, I *like* you, Colleen. I like you a lot. But . . ."

"Some people don't. They think it's creepy that Daddy's a
mortician." She lowered her eyes and blushed. She drew careful
circles in the sand.

"Geez, Colleen, that's not it. I mean, I'd never . . ."

"Two souls were linked last night, Ozzie." Our eyes met. Hers
were bright with conviction. Mine danced in their sockets like
caged lunatics. "Do you believe in destiny?" she said. "*I* do. I'm
extremely intuitive about such things."

"Destiny," I said.

"You know, silly, *fate.*"

I glanced at those aspiring breasts. They seemed like twin dec-
larations of victory. There was no argument they could not
smother. A tiny silver crucifix was pressed between them: Christ
asphyxiated for good measure.

"We'll have a nice car, honey," she continued, her voice se-
rene again with visions of our future. "A Studebaker. No, no, a
DeSoto, I think. And we'll go camping every summer in the Yosemite Valley with the children. We'll take a camera and have
slide shows for Mom and Dad when we come back. I mean, *your*
folks can come watch the slides, too. I mean, I don't see why they
couldn't. They'd *want* to, wouldn't they?"

I sat up abruptly and pointed at the water. "Jesus, look at that crazy surf!" I yelled.

I got up and ran, bellowing, into the Pacific Ocean. The cold surf of La Jolla Shores knocked me down. It took my breath away. The water temperature wouldn't go up until June and this was early May.

I swam out past the breakers and into the kelp beds. The effort warmed me up. I rolled over on my back and floated, black tendrils of kelp winding around my arms and legs. Swimmers had panicked and drowned in this kelp. I could see Colleen on the beach, a substantial patch of impatient white against the gray sand.

"I don't want to be a mortician's apprentice!" I yelled, knowing she could not hear me. I worked my way out of the kelp and kept moving out to sea, on my back, only my head out of the water. From her perspective it must have seemed that I'd been caught in a riptide. I waved my arms as if in distress to complete the illusion, then drifted into a patch of immature jellyfish. I took multiple stings along my legs and back but kept moving west.

I was a good swimmer. I'd been on the Melville High swim team, until I got kicked off for having a bad attitude. "Uncooperative, undependable, inattentive, and does not understand what the word 'team' means," said the coach, in a note to Mitzi. "Ozzie doesn't seem to know what side his bread is buttered on," he added, puzzling both Mitzi and me.

I drifted past a jetty, past a rocky spit, and all the way to Mission Beach, where the surf was huge and breaking far out from

shore. I rolled over and started swimming toward the roller
coaster and Ferris wheel of the amusement park.

I reached the heavy swells in about twenty minutes. Then I
crawled up the back of a giant breaker and sank into the valley
behind it and waited for the next one to rise. It came up fast,
steep and green-black. I flailed my arms and legs, swimming hard
to match its speed. As it swept me up in its flying tonnage, I yelled
again, "I don't want to marry you, either! I don't want to have
any damn kids named Rosemary or Peter or whatever else!"

The big wave hammered me toward shore. Bodysurfing was my
way of putting things into perspective. The power of the ocean
made you understand your place in the natural scheme of things:
If you had one, it didn't amount to a hell of a lot. The wave rose
up and pounded the beach, with you or without you. It would still
be doing it ten thousand years from 1953.

This was a favorite notion of mine. It put distance between you
and the disasters—past and present, and even those to come—of
your life. It turned you loose in the same way jazz turned you
loose, especially bop, when it was hot. Hot bop was wild and irre-
sponsible and without purpose, a way the world would never let
you be because the world couldn't admit *it* had no purpose. The
world, as I saw it, was chained to ideas of itself. Gray purpose
nailed almost everybody to one cross or another. Hot bop muffled the hammer strokes and the awful whimpering with happy
noise.

While riding my motorcycle, I would get this same feeling—the
low roar of my single-cylinder BSA erased everything from my

mind except the solid rush of wind and scenery until the machine, the rush, the pulse of the engine, and I were one perfect thing that didn't need to be explained or justified.

The giant wave gave me a thundering pile-driving ride that crushed the air out of my lungs. When it was over, I stood up in thigh-deep foam-sucking wind, three miles south of Colleen Vogel and her blueprint for my future as a baby-making, DeSoto-owning mortician's apprentice. A sand shark knifed between my legs. It nosed around in the shallows—an aquatic rat. I kept wading and gulping air.

I found a beachfront real estate office and told the secretary that I'd been caught in a riptide and my car was up in La Jolla. She let me use the desk telephone. I called Mitzi.

"Is that you, Stupka, you *shit*?" she said, before I'd said a word. "I've been dying for you to call, darling. Damn you, you *bastard*, don't you know what I go through when you don't call? Who was it this time—Dolores? That Chula Vista whore? You son of a *bitch*! Was it Inez Watson? No, don't tell me, darling. I don't want to know." Her voice wavered between wheedling desperation and whipcrack rage. I could hear her stamping her high heels into the oak floor of our house.

"Whoa, Mitzi," I said. "It's just me."

"Ozzie?" She sounded confused, as if it wasn't supposed to be me calling just then. "I thought it was that goddam bohunk. Why are you calling me? It's Sunday. I never see you on Sunday. Where are you?"

"I got caught in a riptide at La Jolla and wound up in Mission Beach. I don't have a ride home, and I don't have bus money."

The line seemed to go dead, but she was only lighting a cigarette and thinking things out. "Can't you hitchhike?" she said. "I'm expecting a call, Ozzie."

"I don't like to hitch rides in my swimming trunks. People won't pick you up. They think you live under a rock or something."

"All right," she said. "Tell me where you are and I'll get there as soon as I can."

Half an hour later I saw her gray, smoke-belching Nash careening down Mission Boulevard. She drove with both hands high up on the wheel, her face up close to the windshield, the ever-present cigarette snagged in her teeth. The car drifted eerily on its bent frame in front of a cloud of blue smoke. When she saw me, she reached over and opened the door while the car was still rolling. "Get in," she said, her cigarette bouncing furiously. "That snake Stupka finally called. He's coming over for dinner tonight."

"What about Dad?" I said.

She glanced at me through her cigarette smoke. "What's that supposed to mean, smart-mouth?"

I shrugged. The truth was, she was getting tired of Dad, my fourth stepfather. Dad was Nelson Glasspie, a blueprint maker at Convair. He was twenty years older than Mitzi and half blind from all the close detail work he'd had to do most of his life. They'd been married a year and a half. A record for Mitzi.

"Screw off," she said, answering my silence. I was born when she was barely fifteen and we looked more like sister and brother than mother and son. I guess we acted that way, too.

"Just asking," I said. I took a cigarette from her purse and lit up.

"*Dad*," she said, "is working the swing shift, just like every stupid goddamn Sunday. They're going to work that poor old man to death."

I lived in the dark side of the house, where the windows were high and small and shaded by a thick, untrimmed oleander hedge. Mitzi had the other side, along with Nelson Glasspie, number four. I kind of liked number four, a mild-mannered guy with a college education who had the careful and neat ways of a watchmaker or engraver. He wore thick, square glasses. They looked like ice cubes. His eyes darted nervously behind them, minified and confused. Mitzi was nice to him, but it was hard to understand why she'd married him. She was beautiful and could marry anyone she wanted to, but she usually went for knob-knuckled brawlers, like Wes Caulkins or Emile Stupka. Nelson was fifty-three but looked more like sixty-three.

Mitzi had always been restless, as far back as I could remember. Boredom got her down. She'd pace the floors, the perpetual cigarette between her lips, tears cutting through her makeup. It always seemed as if the love of her life had just run out on her, but it was only boredom, the constant wish for something else, something better. Sometimes she'd jump into the Nash and go rattling up and down the coast highway at high speed, as if she could outrun it or scare herself into accepting what life had dealt her with peace of mind, if not gratitude.

I understood it. I often felt the same way. I guess I inherited it from her. I'd rather walk barefoot on rusty razors than sit through five minutes of a boring lecture. That's why my school record wasn't so hot. I was a senior, barely pulling a C-minus average. I had a bad attitude when it came to studying. Reading stuff just to memorize it and cough it up on a test struck me as an idiotic way to waste your life. I thought of life as something that was easy to use up carelessly, like so much high-test gasoline. You got one free tank, no refill.

Art di Coca never had enough money for gas. We'd scrape up loose change until we had enough to cruise the neighborhoods of east San Diego, listening to L.A. rhythm-and-blues stations, nursing the few gallons we were able to put in the tank. On hills, Art would switch off the ignition and coast. Now and then we'd siphon gas from cars parked on dark streets.

I coated my jellyfish stings with calamine lotion, then went to my room and played my Gerry Mulligan record. When I got tired of Mulligan's controlled style, I put on the blasters: Big Jay McNeeley, Illinois Jacquet, then my favorite, Charlie Ventura. Music—jazz—put me into another frame of mind. It was like being drunk. McNeeley's, Jacquet's, or Ventura's tenor sax could blast holes through your brain. Light, like the headlight of a train, blew through the holes. The Doppler-like shifts of those jackhammer honks and moans and gutty rebops were boiling with love, hate, misery, and unapologetic fun.

My door opened. "Jesus, turn it down, Ozzie!" Mitzi said. "Emile's here."

Whenever Emile Stupka came over he brought his own records. Mitzi and Emile would smoke cigarettes in the dark, drinking slivovitz, and listen to depressing songs on our Stromberg-Carlson console. Even when the music was upbeat you could hear the sound of mourning in it. No wonder the people of eastern Europe were in the fix they were in. I pictured them sitting in cold-water flats staring at their hands while listening to that shit and nodding to each other saying, yes yes, that's how life has always been for us.

Mitzi had fixed pork chops and yams for dinner. There was a place set for me at the candlelit table, but I just grabbed a pork chop and took it outside. I made Emile nervous, and he made me nervous, so no one objected. I wheeled my bike out of the garage and rode it over to Art di Coca's house, which was only five blocks away. I kept it in second gear so that the big, long-stroke, torquey engine would shake the windows of the neighborhood. Now and then I'd twist the throttle and let the front wheel rise off the pavement.

Art was contemplating his exhaust manifolds. "I've decided to get headers," he said, barely acknowledging my arrival. "Headers and glasspacks."

"Bitchin'," I said. Headers would increase the engine's output by eight or ten percent, and glasspack mufflers would produce a mellow tone, like twin trombones. "But where you going to get the bread?" He'd done all the bodywork on his car himself, piecemeal, but the engine, a '50 Ford V-8 Art had bought for thirty dollars from a wrecking yard, didn't have the torque a chopped and lowered street dragster should have. Souping it up with high-compression aluminum heads, dual carbs, and dual ignition was financially out of reach.

Art didn't like to be questioned. He was tall and well-built, except for his legs. From the waist up he was built like Mr. California, but his legs wouldn't respond to the weights. He squatted every day with two hundred pounds on his back, did hamstring and quadriceps curls, yet his legs stayed scrawny as a polio victim's. He had a narrow face with heavy supraorbital ridges that canopied his small black eyes, making them opaque and sinister.

He closed the hood. "I've got a job, shit-for-brains," he said.

"Right. At a car wash," I said. The Toltec Car Wash paid seventy-five cents an hour and he worked only on weekends.

The di Coca family was not rich. Benedetto di Coca was an old-country stonemason with strong Communist sympathies. Now and then an olive-drab Chevy with a whip antenna on its bumper would park across the street from the di Coca house: some FBI agent in a hat, reading a paper, wishing he was back in Washington keeping track of real threats to national security.

Art and his father were always arguing about something—loud music, noisy cars, Art's obsession with bulking up his muscles, the old man's radical rantings—but it was all rooted in their different outlooks on life: Benedetto, the immigrant leftist bricklayer, and Art, the American teenager.

"Sit on this, bug fucker," Art said, showing me a black-knuckled middle finger. "We graduate in a month and then I'm going to get a job at Convair. Denise and me are getting married.''

"Come down, man!" I said. "You fracture me! *Married?*"

"It's either that or the Army. Wake up, man. That war is going to kick in again. They'll draft your useless butt unless you get married or go to college.''

The Korean war was stalled, two armies facing each other across the 38th parallel, but they were still drafting people who didn't have better things to do with their lives.

"I just hope my old man's stupid politics don't shaft me with Convair,'' Art said. "Man, I'd love to work on those B-36s.''

The B-36 was the world's biggest airplane. It was an intercontinental bomber with six huge radial engines and four jets. "Six turnin' and four burnin' '' was how the pilots described it. It was a strange-looking plane that made so much noise the dishes sometimes fell out of the cupboards when it flew overhead. B-36s flew low over the rooftops of our neighborhood at least twice a day as they prepared to land at Vultee Field—one of three landing fields in the entire country with landing strips hard enough to accept the huge bomber. It could fly ten thousand miles without refueling, delivering atomic bombs to a dozen enemy cities from altitudes so high the citizens of those cities would only see its vapor trails before they were turned into hot putty. Convair's production line was in Fort Worth, Texas, but a lot of work was going to be done at the San Diego plant. Jobs were easy to get and the starting pay was $1.67 an hour, the best in town.

Art got in the car and started it. I got in beside him. He gunned it, his ear cocked for abnormalities. We sat there, listening to the engine rev, then took a spin through the neighborhood, Art speed-shifting deftly, making the tires bark and fishtail slightly as we hit each gear. He pulled back into his driveway and revved the engine to its red line and held it there.

"If you had another brain it would die of loneliness," he said. He could change subjects like that. Or start a new one midstream.

"It's cutting out," I yelled, nodding toward the engine.

He got a strained look on his face. He revved it higher.

"No," he yelled back. "Just some shit in the fuel line." He took his foot off the gas and leaned back into the seat.

"You calling me stupid?" I said.

"I *am* calling you stupid. Soon as you graduate, they're going to draft you. If I didn't already have Denise, I'd marry Colleen myself. She's a fine quim, Oz. Jesus, what a classy set of head-lights. And her old man's loaded, or haven't you made the con-nection yet. Girls who drive MGs have fat dads."

"He's a fucking *undertaker*," I said.

"So what? It's just a job. Somebody's got to deal with dead people. Colleen's hot for you, man. You could nail her in a min-ute. But listen, she's no Rosy Rottencrotch. She's a damned nice kid. I don't want to see her get hurt."

He gave me a menacing look that held the promise of extensive bodily injury. He could be a badass when he wanted to. I'd seen him tear up a football player who had made a joke out of his name. "Coca di Nut," said the football player, a mean-looking slob with a crew cut. Art drove his fist into the slob's guts, drop-ping him to his knees. The fight was over, but Art wasn't satisfied. He pulled the football player up to his feet, leaned him against the gym wall, and pounded him until two coaches pulled him off.

"You could tangle assholes with her every night of the week," he said. "Or you could sleep in your own shit in Korea. Only a fuckin' moron would think that was a real hard choice."

"She's even named our kids, for Chrissakes," I said.

He laughed. "So she's hot to trot. So what?"

"That's a little too hot, I think."

"No such thing as too hot. Too cold, now that's a well-known problem. Hot never is. Hot is what you want."

I opened the car door. Art grabbed me by the shirt. "She wants kids, shithook," he said. "That's normal in a woman. A woman who doesn't want kids, now that's *not* normal. That's *abnormal*."

"You're not hitting on all eight, Art," I said. In fact, I always thought Art had a screw or two loose.

"Hope you dig Korea, Oz," he said.

I straddled my BSA and kicked it over and twisted the throttle wide, sending shock waves of unmuffled roar through the neighborhood. Art, to make sure I knew he wasn't impressed, yawned.

I waited for the principal, Mr. Flooding, to call my name: Osvaldo Santee. He'd stumble on it, of course, because he always stumbled on it. He had the learning ability of a moth. But I was far down on the list of graduating seniors—two hundred and twelfth out of two hundred and fifty—and I'd be hammered by then and wouldn't care how he screwed it up. Art had a pint of Seagram's hidden under his graduation robe. We passed it back and forth and up behind us to "Monster," Brian Crutchfield, and waited out the speeches.

A Marine Corps major who'd seen action in Korea gave the opening speech. He electrified the audience with nostalgic accounts of combat: bayonet charges, grenade attacks, the wonders of napalm and white phosphorus, the flesh-shredding power of a .50 caliber machine gun. He wanted us boys to join up so we could get in on killing the Commies when the truce talks broke

down. "These politicians aren't going to settle things at the nego-
tiating table when both sides are still willing to settle them on the
field of combat, muzzle to muzzle," he said. He spit out the word
"politician" like it was a bone chip he'd tongued out of a hamburger. He was a thick-necked, crew-cut bulldog of a man. He
flashed his short mean teeth every so often for punctuation.
"Then you boys will have to wait around for the next little so-
called police action." He looked like he'd caught a whiff of ran-
cid fart. "War is war is *war*," he growled. "We're not giving the
little yellow sons of bitches traffic tickets! We're killing them!"
He made a bayonet lunge with an imaginary rifle. He stunned Mr.
Flooding by stepping toward him, offering a boxer's feint and a
brutal smile. "Hey! Excuse my jarhead French, Professor!" he
yelled. Everyone laughed and then applauded politely as Mr.
Flooding, searching his poorly stocked mind for an appropriate
gesture, took the major's hand and raised it in victory.

Crutchfield belched. Belching was one of his talents. You could
hear his vile eruptions across the quadrangle during lunch hour.
Teachers thirty rows down from us turned and scowled at
Crutchfield. If pure evil had tried to paint a picture of pure inno-
cence, Crutchfield would have been the result. Blond, blue-eyed,
rosy-cheeked, tall, fleshy—but only the gullible would miss the
depraved curl of his cherubic lips, or the mockery behind his
sleepy-eyed smile.

The major was followed by a stuffed-shirt bureaucrat from the
school district. Then the vice principal gave a pep talk, painting
our futures in bright primary colors. This was followed by a rous-
ing rendition of the school fight song by the pep band.

It seemed the crap would never end. All this was the school's last chance to bore us to death before handing out our tickets to freedom, our diplomas. We would soon be bona fide graduates of Melville High School, ready to take the world by the balls and make it dance to our tunes. We were the Melville Whalers. Our cheerleaders threatened opposing cheerleaders with hard rubber harpoons, and the football players had helmet-wearing cartoon whales stitched to their letterman jackets.

Osvaldo Santee, harpoon master, prepared now to skewer every whale of opportunity and make something of myself. But I had learned nothing useful in four years, and had no desire to make something of myself. Mr. Flooding, who had trouble with names like Yarborough, Villareal, Horowitz, and Rigetti, could not get past the first syllable of my name.

"Oss, er, Oss-valve-oh?" or "O-O-Oval-Dough?"—the question mark always trailing after this verbal mauling, as if to shift the blame from his aboveboard righteous American simplicity to an underhanded foreign deviousness, before he settled for "Oslo" or "Oshkosh," or once, in the grip of an inspired jocularity, "The Wizard of Oz!"

"Why don't you trade in that Eye-talian monicker for a good old-fashioned American name, Mr. Santee?" he once advised. "Wouldn't you like to be called 'Teddy' or 'Bobby' or 'Stevie'?"

Mr. Flooding was a witless backslapper. He was credited with having a great sense of humor by people who didn't know what to make of his shameless ignorance or of his insulting, ham-handed manners. He had three sons. Their names were—I am not lying—Tom, Dick, and Harry.

Osvaldo Santee. My name, my self. Me. The Santee who fathered me was Carlyle Santee, a lanky A&P stock boy with a carefree smile. Mitzi met him in Hershey, Pennsylvania, where she worked at the chocolate factory in violation of the child labor laws. Carlyle took off when she gave him the bad news.

"Carlyle, you've done it now," Mitzi says she said. "Done what?" young Santee asked, the carefree grin losing track of itself as his suspicions became aroused. Mitzi patted her hard round belly where I had recently taken up residence. Carlyle's face drained. He was, in spite of his dashing manner, given to sudden, inwardly violent sulks. I guess if I am moody at times, it is because I inherited the tendency from Carlyle. He was a grade-school dropout. I guess he was more bored by school than I was. He had no prospects or ambitions, and he didn't want Mitzi and her surprise passenger. So he packed his bindle and headed for the rail yards to start his life adventure anew, with a clean slate, in the grievously depressed U.S.A. of 1935. Often, when Mitzi got mad at me for one reason or another, she'd say, "You're just like him. You're just like that no-account stock boy, Carlyle Santee."

Osvaldo. That came from a movie magazine, Mitzi says. A new actor from Buenos Aires who went by the intriguing single name of Osvaldo, a mysterious-looking leading-man type with eyes that burned divots into the female soul. The magazine promoted him as the Latin Gary Cooper and the "heart throb of the future." He only made one picture in Hollywood, a South American oater called *The Gaucho and the Princess*, a stormy romance that galloped and warbled across the dusty pampas. Mitzi liked his looks and she liked the appearance of "Osvaldo" in print, though she didn't know how to pronounce it either. She settled for Ozzie.

Osvaldo: Spanish for Oswald. Osvaldo, the failed actor, wasn't from Argentina, it turned out, and his name wasn't Osvaldo, either. He was Casimiro Lechuga from El Paso, Texas, via Juárez, via Chihuahua City. I often wondered what became of him. I thought of him sometimes as an abstract absent father, no less real to me than the disposable men Mitzi ran with.

"Don't hog the panther piss, you homos," Crutchfield said. He slapped me on the shoulder, then put his hands around my neck. He squeezed hard enough to make bright spots float in front of my eyes. I grabbed his wrists and broke his grip.

"Sphincter lips," I said. Heads ten rows down turned to see what the commotion was all about. Crutchfield cut a lengthy belch at them. It sounded like a plank being ripped apart lengthwise. A teacher monitoring our section of the bleachers rubbernecked the blue-robed crowd, half rising out of his seat. He pointed at us, his arm stiff as a rifle.

"Frantic," Crutchfield said, guzzling booze as soon as the teacher turned away. Crutchfield was graduating in the top ten percent of our class. He was good in math and science, and was dedicated to defacement, sabotage, and ruin. He wanted to get an advanced degree in math or physics and enter the atomic energy field. He was a great fan of the just-tested hydrogen bomb. "It's unbelievable how much *shit* one of those bombs can blow away," he once said. The glitter in his eyes was strange enough to be real. "You're fucked up, Crutchfield," I told him. "No, man, I'm a fucking visionary," he said. He drove a natty little English car, a

Hillman Minx, and the trunk (he called it the "boot") was full of tools—tools not meant to fix things but to wreck them. He'd spent a day in jail once for rewiring the traffic signals at a busy intersection so that all four lights showed constant red. His parents were doctors. They lived in a posh house on Mount Helix. His father was a gynecologist, his mother a pediatrician. They were dismayed, I think, that fine people such as themselves, who had dedicated their lives to the health and well-being of mothers, infants, and children, had produced a child who had the social conscience of a squid.

"Your turn, Oz," Art said, nudging me with his elbow.

Mr. Flooding was struggling with my name. "Oss—Ossval—Ossvo—oh heck! Ozzie Santee! Come down here and get your diploma, boy!" He held the mike too close, generating a squeal of feedback. The crowd laughed. I got up, shuffled toward the aisle. The floor under my feet twitched. I sat back down, suddenly smashed. It wasn't the first time I'd been drunk, but I was still amazed at how booze sneaked up on you, how one minute you felt normal, the next minute you were in the bag. I giggled. The crowd around me laughed. But it was nervous laughter instigated by something more than my buffoonery. The dead weight of a witticism tractored toward the conscious rim of Mr. Flooding's tired brain, but before he could get it out the auditorium gave itself a mighty shake, like a giant wet dog. The silence of collective breath-holding stopped the graduation ceremonies. I felt vindicated—it had been the earth's faulty crust that had tripped me up, not booze. We were having a little old *earthquake*.

Crutchfield stood up, his big face split in a radiantly evil grin. "Go daddy-o, *go!*" he boomed across the silent auditorium. "Get *on* it, man!" he yelled, as if he were at a bop concert and the tenor man had cut loose on a solo with reboping riffs that sent powerful spasms of joy through the crowd. Not that Crutchfield ever went to bop concerts. He thought bop was a fraud, an attempt to be different just to be different. "Un-American," he sneered, when I played Charlie Ventura's version of "East of Suez" for him once.

There had been a rash of earthquakes all over the southern half of the state recently. Most of downtown Bakersfield had been demolished the previous summer. Art, Crutchfield, and I drove through the wrecked town on our way to a weekend in Yosemite. Crutchfield acted like a kid in a candy factory. "Shit oh dear," he said, full of righteous approval, as Art steered carefully through the partially blocked-off main drag. For Crutchfield, lover of big bombs, this was a holy event. "One little shake and half of this shit-ass little Okie town is *gone*. Terra ain't so fucking firma, man." Bearded men with THE END IS NEAR signs strolled through the debris, talking to themselves. "Not near enough, you fucking pea brains!" Crutchfield yelled at them.

Crutchfield was hard to figure out. It didn't seem very likely, but it had to be true: There were people who loved disaster. Something in their personalities hated the tidy, self-satisfied world. Anything that came along that had the power to turn the whole works upside down and inside out was as welcome to them as the return of Jesus was to others.

This trait of Crutchfield's expressed itself in minor ways, too. Contrariness was automatic with him. Even so, I'd never seen him get into a fight. This was kind of miraculous, since he liked to irritate people and wasn't too selective about it.

He could get waiters tongue-tied by speaking to them in a believable English accent. And though he didn't like bop, he knew it well enough to point out unintentional slurs in Charlie Parker recordings. "Bird couldn't get fixed that day," he told us, and we had to nod with understanding—it would have been uncool to ask what he was talking about. But he saw through our fake understanding and explained: "See, he was on the pin, man, a mainline shooter, and if he didn't make his connection on the day he was going to record he got the heebie-jeebies. This is something you can actually hear, if you know what to listen for."

He said older women loved French ticklers, and before we could scoff he produced one out of his wallet and we marveled at the red rubber ring with the dainty claw reaching up from it. "I fucked a forty-year-old woman in Paris with one of these little doodads on my hammer," he said. "She fucking near screamed herself out of her little froggy mind." Seeing our blank looks, he said, "The older ones are loose from abuse and overuse, see, and they need a little extra stimulation to get their stones off. You don't know what gratitude is until you've laid one of those gray-haired charity cases." We knew he had been to France with his parents, and so we were half inclined to believe him. In private, Art and I would tell each other what a lying sack of shit Crutchfield was, but when we were with him we lost the power of doubt.

A B-36 passed overhead, its deep rumbling roar adding to the general atmosphere of destruction. The foundations of the oldest buildings of Melville High were all cracked from decades of quakes. But the auditorium was new and designed to be earthquake-proof. This meant that the building rocked and rolled with the seismic punches, and this dramatically exaggerated the power of the quake, which was probably only a 5.5 on the Richter. By the time the screaming began, the quake was more or less finished. That's when panic took over.

The need to maintain social status kept the boys artificially calm. The girls were free to scream and carry on, but the boys had to be cool or pay the price later. If a boy bolted, he'd be called "pussy" from that point on. ("Did you see that pussy Alton split for the door? What a *pussy*.") So we sat, scared, but unwilling to risk humiliation. *Death* was the more attractive alternative. I lit a cigarette. A few others laughed like maniacs or howled like dogs as the ceiling tiles popped loose and helicoptered into the bleachers.

The teachers, who had no social status at stake, sprinted to the doors. Mr. Flooding, clutching his chest, staggered out a side exit, the school district bureaucrat one step behind. The Marine major stood his ground. He grabbed the mike and started giving battlefield commands. He saw me take a drag on my cigarette. "Put that thing out!" he yelled. "The gas mains might be ruptured!" I cupped the weed and held it down between my knees. No one paid attention to the major. Some flipped him the bird, some stood up on the benches as if riding surfboards. When a ceiling tile hit the stage next to the podium, the major yelled,

"Screw you asswipes! You punks are on your own!"

"Duck and cover!" someone yelled.

"Fuck your mother!" someone answered.

Art passed me the bottle. I took a long pull, then passed it back to Crutchfield. An aftershock made the building shudder again. "I'm going down there and get my diploma," I said.

"You're too bombed to bop," Crutchfield said.

"Eat it, Monster."

Crutchfield didn't like this private nickname Art and I had given him. I think he saw himself as a kind of Hero of Darkness, cool as Dracula. "Monster" suggested a weirdo victim of society who destroyed things because of hurt and rage, not because of underlying philosophical differences. In senior English, when we had to read *Paradise Lost*, Crutchfield argued that Satan was the best character in the epic. The teacher, like all the other teachers, hated Crutchfield and was afraid of his perverted intelligence. "Why do you think so, Brian?" he said carefully. "Because Lucifer is just like we'd like to be if we had the *cojones*," Crutchfield said. "Remember what Voltaire said?" He paused cruelly while the stumped teacher fought to recall Voltaire. "He said, 'God is a comedian playing to an audience that is afraid to laugh.' " The teacher, a nice man and a devout Catholic, turned toward the blackboard and crossed himself surreptitiously. Crutchfield sat down, wagging his head in stagy disbelief, chuckling softly, vastly amused by the quaint failures of human beings.

I stepped through the rubble and made my way to the abandoned stage. The few remaining diplomas were on the floor, next to the podium. I sorted through them until I found mine. My name was misspelled. Oswaldo. I tossed it back into the pile. The mike was still working. "Ladies and germs," I said. "You have wasted four years of your young lives. Four years you won't get back. And what do they give you? A piece of paper. Might as well be candied cat shit." My audience was small. Most had drifted outside now that the quake was over.

"Ingrate," Crutchfield growled.

"No, I'm serious," I said. This surprised me, because I realized that it was true, I *was* serious. "Four years of coming to this place and what do you have? A piece of paper."

"Jesus, you already said that," Art said.

"I mean, what have you really learned?" I said. "Being able to name the Great Lakes, or all the Presidents, or that A squared plus B squared equals C squared, or that the major export of New Zealand is wool? What good is that?"

"What about Health and Hygiene?" Crutchfield said. "You learned what can happen to your future if you fucked diseased women in foreign countries."

"Okay, okay. There *were* a few things."

I remembered that movie, *Joe and Mary*, about the soldier returning from Europe with a venereal disease he didn't know he had, then infecting his lovely young wife, Mary, and destroying her chances to have children, after which Joe takes to the bottle and Mary is committed to a mental ward. The movie ends with a shot of Mary staring blankly into her dead future. A profound moral lesson. The teacher, Mr. Rygard, who was also the football coach, stepped in front of the screen and said, "You boys want to beat the *odds*, then stick to the straight and *narrow*." He nodded, eyebrows raised significantly, toward the frozen-frame image of poor insane Mary as the credits rolled over her broken-hearted face.

"And what about auto shop?" Art said. "You learned how to gap spark plugs, didn't you? You learned how to change your filters, didn't you? You learned to tell piston slap from rod knock, right?"

"Okay, I'm wrong. These four years have been a joy. I'm a lucky man."

"You're not a man," Crutchfield said. "You're a boy until you've had a dose of the clap."

A few more ceiling tiles dropped into the seats in front of me. They were made of some kind of lightweight material and not really dangerous. Their spinning motion caught my eye, and my eye transferred the spin to my guts, and suddenly I was sick.

"But you've missed the main point, Oz," Crutchfield said. "You didn't spend four years here to soak up knowledge. You spent four years here to learn how and when to kiss ass. The people who learned this best are the ones who are going to the top, you wait and see."

"You're cynical, Monster," I said. Then I puked next to the podium.

"He's repeating himself," Crutchfield said.

We went outside. The sun was painfully bright and the air was hot and still. Earthquake weather—one of southern California's folk myths. Meteorologists dismissed it, yet quakes always seemed to happen when the weather was like this, hot and dry and very still, like the earth itself was holding its breath. When it got like this, people became tense with anticipation. Strangers would look at each other and say, "Earthquake weather," and half the time they'd be right.

There wasn't much evidence of the quake outside the auditorium. All the buildings of Melville High were still standing on their foundations. But if you studied them, you could see a missing roof tile, a new crack in an old stone foundation, or a bike on the ground that had been in a rack.

A crowd had bunched up on the quadrangle. "Fight," Art said. But it was too quiet for a fight. If it had been a fight, there would have been a lot of shoving and yelling and side-taking. Someone would have been yelling, "Fight! Fight!" announcing the festive event to the entire campus.

We pushed into the crowd. I found Colleen and took her hand. She squeezed my hand hard—we'd made love for the first time the night before, and this hand squeeze was the reminder—but then I saw that she was upset.

"What's going on?" I said. Then I saw Mr. Flooding. He was stretched out on the grass, his face gray as wet paper. The Marine major was kneeling next to him, holding his wrist.

"What happened to him?" I asked.

"The major is afraid it might be cardiac arrest," Colleen said. The drama of tragedy-in-the-making, coupled with the fading bloom of first sex, gave her voice the solemn authority of a concerned adult.

"No *shit*?" I said.

Colleen frowned at me and sniffled. She touched my lips. "Shush, honey," she said.

I put my arm around her and pulled her against me hard.

"Oh God, you've been *drinking*!" she whispered, pushing me off.

An ambulance wailed in the distance. I felt for her breast through the heavy fabric of her graduation robe. My drunken hand took possession of it.

"Don't!" she said out loud, and heads turned toward us.

"But honey," I said. "I *wuv* you." There was a deliberate flippancy in my voice. It was ugly. I grabbed her again. She shoved me away.

"Knock it off," the Marine said. "This man is dying."

I looked down at Mr. Flooding again. The fall he'd taken had broken his nose. It went off to one side, but it wasn't bleeding. Which meant his heart had stopped pumping blood. His eyes were open, but they weren't seeing anything. He looked calm, even wise. For a moment I reversed my low opinion of him.

"He's gone," said the Marine.

Girls and boys held each other and wept. I looked at them, amazed and ashamed. I felt as if I'd missed something. Maybe I'd been missing it for years. Their tears were real, not hypocritical. But how could that be? Had I been wrong about everything?

"But he was a *jerk*," I said, mostly to myself.

The crowd looked at me with undiluted scorn. Colleen, frowning like a troubled elder, moved as far away from me as she could and still remain with the crowd. I turned my back on them. I dropped to one knee and retched quietly into the grass.

I was sorry for Tom, Dick, and Harry, and maybe for Mrs. Flooding, but the fact remained that Flooding himself had been an incompetent and a fraud. Which didn't mean he deserved to die. It just meant that once he was gone he was easy to forget.

"We'd better haul tail out of here," Crutchfield said, "before they get a rope."

We went to the parking lot and got into Art's car. "Let's cut out to Mexico and celebrate," Crutchfield said.

"Celebrate what?" Art said. "Flooding kicking off?"

"No, man. You've got to be alive before you can kick off. Flooding didn't make the qualifying heat."

"Earthquake," I said. "He wants to celebrate the earthquake."

"Give me a break," Crutchfield sighed. "What did we just do? We just graduated. We're out of this candy-ass snake pit. We're entering the big, twat-infested world."

The ambulance for Mr. Flooding was coming up the road. "Maybe he's not dead," I said.

"Like I said," Crutchfield said, "no one's going to notice, either way."

Art slammed it into second, leaving streaks of rubber in the pavement. Art's new glasspack mufflers tromboned farewell.

3

The half-million-watt transmitter of XERB was too much for the radio. Which was too bad, because they were playing solid R&B that day. Joe Turner's "Midnight Special" hammering through the speaker sounded more like surf during a storm than music. Big Jay McNeeley's "Texas Turkey" was a train wreck in progress. The closer we got to Rosarito Beach, the worse it got. The sexual beat of "Night Train" was thunder trapped in a barrel. Mexican radio, with unrestricted power, could be heard in Canada after the sun went down. So we had to listen to some tame San Diego station. We sang along with Vaughn Monroe's "Racing with the Moon," Frankie Laine's "Lucky Old Sun." Les Paul and Mary Ford, Teresa Brewer, Patti Page. When Johnny Ray sang "Cry," Crutchfield rolled down his window and pretended to vomit. His retching howls were infectious. He made me sick again.

"Pull over, Art," I said.

"The old hotel is only a couple of miles farther," he said. "We'll stop there. You can puke up your rectum if you want."

"Fine, it's your car, man."

"You puke in the car, it'll be the last time you puke anywhere, turd-knocker."

I forced back the urge by thinking about my big mistake. I'd taken Colleen for a ride the evening before on my motorcycle. We went up the coast as far as Carlsbad, then came back on the inland highway through Escondido, and headed for the mountains. We rode all the way to Palomar, where we walked around the giant telescope dome. The sky was black and clear and the mountains were chalky under a fat gibbous moon. You could see the city lights gleaming like costume jewelry all the way to Mexico. It was a romantic moment, timeless yet urgent. The two of us motorcycling to the top of the mountain was like a pilgrimage. When I killed the motor we were buried in a hush thick as cotton. "The silence of the soul," Colleen said, and it didn't seem corny. "We were destined for each other, Ozzie." None of this seemed stupid; it seemed true. "Looks like it," I said. And we made it official in the long grasses that grew on the mountainside. We were both virgins, and the first attempt ended quickly and without a sense of having committed anything at all. The second attempt was a convincing welding of hearts. It was so purely romantic, so true, that we both wept afterward, exchanging hundreds of I-love-yous.

"We'll be so happy, darling," she said.

"I'm happy now," I said.

"You *know* what I mean, dear."

In the milky glow of the lopsided moon I was afraid I did.

We rode back through the sleeping mountain towns of Descanso and Jamul, and then back home. She could barely walk to her front door—five hours on the back of a hard-sprung BSA Victor had taken its toll. We kissed and groped, long and athletically, but already with the anticipated moves of veteran domestic coziness. A sudden cavernous depression made me break it off. She saw my long face and said, "Here comes old Mr. Moody." I rode home slowly, taking streets I'd never been on. But the same yellow light fell like squares of butter from every tract-house window: lighthouses calling me in, away from freedom's rolling seas.

I had acted like a jerk at the graduation ceremonies, and out on the quadrangle afterward, thinking I could derail the machinery we'd set in motion the previous night. But had I? In any case, I was hell-bent on keeping the act alive.

Art pulled into the parking lot of the Rosarito Beach hotel. I got out and puked between two parked cars. I grabbed my graduation robe out of the car and wiped off my shoes with it.

"See, your education wasn't a complete loss, Oz," Crutchfield said. "As old Miss McHenry used to say, 'Be neat at all times, for a book *is* known by its cover.' It does my heart good to see that you learned that much at least."

We went into the hotel. It was an elegant old place that catered to American tourists and wealthy Mexicans. High school kids and sailors were discouraged by snotty desk clerks and arrogant waiters. But we'd worn dress shirts and slacks under our graduation robes, and so they had no real excuse to give us a hard time. We marched through the lobby and out onto the beautifully tiled patio that overlooked the beach.

I'd been here before with Mitzi and number three, Wayne Duchesne. He was a machinist at the Navy air base on North Island. He was a nasty drunk, and we were thrown out of the restaurant because he insulted the people sitting around us for no reason other than his need to make trouble. It was his hobby, the way he entertained himself. "Oh Christ, it's the *Rock*efellers," he'd said when a well-dressed couple took the table next to us. But he was only warming up; it got worse.

I was only fifteen at the time, but the old hotel impressed me with its high-class atmosphere. I felt out of place then, and I felt out of place now.

The patio was nearly empty. A few people sat at tables drinking beer or margaritas, as strolling mariachis passed among them. A good breeze was coming off the ocean. I loved that smell, briny and slightly foul, like rot. I felt like going for a swim—the shock of cold water would clear up my booze-sick guts in a flash.

"Let's get some eats," Crutchfield said, flapping open a menu. "I am too fucking starved, man. Look here, they've got clams and oysters. That'll fix us up."

"Shut your hole, Crutchfield," I said. I hated clams and oysters. Just the thought of them made me want to puke.

"Would you please stop using that indecent language?" the man a few tables over said.

"Eat it, dork," Crutchfield said, not looking up from the menu.

He *was* a dork, a guy in his twenties wearing a cheap black suit. He had no sideburns. His hair was short and spiked with cowlicks. Gray-edged teeth slightly bucked, zit farm for a face. Mr. Harvey Peckerwood's Mexican adventure. The woman sitting with him was touching her throat and sucking wind. Mrs. Peckerwood. They were drinking nonalcoholic *atoles*, taking their chances with native refreshment. A pair of Bible readers from Dull City.

"I'm sorry," I said. "Didn't mean to be an asshole."

"But see," Crutchfield said to them, his tone conciliatory now, "he can't help himself. Assholes run in his family."

Art buckled over laughing. "Assholes *run* . . . in his family!" he sputtered.

The couple got up and moved to the far side of the patio, followed by indifferent mariachis.

I hadn't started out to spoil anybody's day, not even dorks'. I decided to apologize to them. I walked over to their table. "My friend didn't mean anything personal," I said. "See, he's just been discharged from an insane asylum." I tapped my forehead, cut a secret glance at Crutchfield. "The poor guy flipped his lid in the Army. But not before killing a dozen Reds."

They looked over at Crutchfield, wide-eyed, awestruck. It was their turn to be apologetic. I waved them off. "You couldn't have known," I said. "It wasn't your fault."

My guts roared and a thread of acid crawled into my throat. I walked over to the seawall separating the patio from the beach, hopped over it, stripped down to my shorts, and sprinted toward the surf. I heard Crutchfield bellowing at my back but couldn't understand him. I dove into a wave and came up in the trough behind it and began swimming. I swam out to a bell buoy and held on to it.

I was a couple of hundred yards out and the water was cold. A Portuguese man-of-war big as a tire drifted by. The world's strangest fish: a dome of transparent gel crosshatched with red stripes, trailing behind stinging tentacles that could disable a swimmer. I gave it wide berth. A little farther out a small boat full of tourists bobbed toward me, appearing and disappearing in the swells. I waved, they waved back. I blew them a kiss, they blew kisses back.

I swam out toward the tourists, then ran into the reason for the buoy: black volcanic underwater rocks waiting to tear the bottom off a boat. The tourists looked like Midwesterners, so square in their Hawaiian shirts and billed caps. *Buenos dias*, one of them yelled, thinking I was a local. He thumbed through his phrase book. *Tienes algunas perlas, muchacho?*

They thought I was a pearl diver. They'd have to go another eight hundred miles south to find one of those. But I played along with them. "No mon, no hab any porls today," I said. I stood up on a submerged ledge. The water here was ankle-deep. They must have believed that I had been given the power to walk on the sea. Water lifted and hissed around my legs. They waved happily, yelling, "*Vaya con dios*, buddy," as the boat chugged off. I swam back to shore on my back, slow and easy, filling my head with a million acres of blank blue Mexican sky.

Mr. Flooding emerged in the blue field, like an image on photographic paper in developing fluid, detailed and motionless, gaining clarity by the second. His sky-blue eyes rested on me, a neutral stare that seemed to be coming from across all space. A couple of summers back I'd worked with Art's father as a hod carrier. I went to bed at night seeing hods of mortar shimmer against the backs of my eyelids. This was like that. I saw Mr. Flooding dead and staring, as if I had been paid to imprint his face in my mind by gazing at him for a full eight-hour shift. My heart skipped a beat and I rolled over and swam hard until my feet touched sand.

I pulled my clothes on and hopped over the patio wall.

"Plant your young shitter down here, man," Crutchfield said. "I want to show you something."

I pulled out my chair and sat. The table was covered with food. Not clams and oysters, but *carne asada*, chicken *mole*, refried beans, *gazpacho*, warm sweet bread, and margaritas in giant frosted glasses.

"Jesus, who's paying for all this?" I said.

"Gramps," Crutchfield said. He showed me a roll of twenties. "Gramps is cool, unlike my folks. He made his coin in oil, up in Long Beach. Gramps said, 'Kid, you only graduate once from high school,' and he stuffed five hundred bucks in my pocket. And he's right, man. This is a fucking occasion. Who knows what dismal crap lies ahead?"

That bothered me too: the crap, dismal or otherwise, that lay ahead. I didn't want to get married. I didn't want to work for a mortician. I didn't want to work for anybody. I didn't want to go to college. I didn't want to get old, wear suits, and say important

things to important people. I didn't exactly want things to stay as
they were, but I didn't want them to change drastically, either. I
could picture myself living in a shack on the beach forever, swimming and listening to bop.

"Looky here," Art said. He pointed at Crutchfield's lap.
Crutchfield tilted his chair back. He patted his belt buckle. I
hadn't noticed it before—a wide silver oval, like a cowboy
buckle, but with the head of Jesus engraved on it.

I believed in jinxes. This looked so bad to me that I wanted to
head back home. Putting Christ's head on a belt buckle was bad
enough, but on Crutchfield it looked totally depraved. First the
earthquake, then Mr. Flooding dropping dead, and now this. We
were in trouble. I felt it.

"Aren't you going to ask where I got it?" Crutchfield said.

"I don't want to know anything about it," I said. I sipped my
margarita.

"The dorks over there drinking ten-cent *atoles* are mission-
aries," he said. "He thought I was a Korean vet. He wanted to
give me his belt, like it was a lucky charm. 'This will help you in
your illness,' the guy says."

"I told the guy that nothing could help Crutchfield's illness,"
Art said. "But the guy just smiles that sad little Jesus smile people like that have—you know, like they've got your number. But
they were flat broke, it turned out. So Crutchfield here buys
them a meal and slipped the guy twenty bucks for the Jesus belt.
They're on their way to some little fishing town near La Paz to
convert the pagan Catholics. They can't even speak Spanish. I

guess they're going to draw pictures in the sand. 'This here is God. This here is you. This, heaven. This, hell. And this, your spaghetti-chokin' pope burning up.' "

We laughed, but Art was always a little on the pissed-off side of funny. Humor for him was an unplanned side effect. He was almost always serious. Even though you swore he *meant* to be funny, he'd look at you, surprised and suspicious, when you laughed.

We knew he didn't have much use for religion. His old man had been thrown off his stony patch of land in Abruzzi by priests with the aid of Mussolini's Blackshirt thugs. That's why the old man sympathized with the Reds. Art had no use for the Communists either, but he had a strong sense of injustice.

We ate and drank. I got a little drunk again, but my stomach had settled down. We headed south then, to Ensenada. Crutchfield had bought a bottle of Cuervo at the bar and we were taking hits. Tequila, once you got used to its smoky flavor, went down a lot easier than blended whiskey. You knew you were going to be sick after a half-dozen shots of whiskey, but tequila was sneakier. It made you think you could drink it nonstop, getting higher and higher, never peaking, never paying the price. I didn't want to trust it, and took guarded sips from the bottle, just wanting to maintain. I'd been sick enough for one day.

We turned east into the mountains and drove the rest of the way to Ensenada on the back roads, away from the main highway. These roads were not meant for tourists. They were twisty and narrow, and all the curves were blind. Art kept his foot on the gas as he snapped the gearshift from second to third and back again on the roller-coaster terrain, and the twin tailpipes roared.

The radio, now that we had hills between us and XERB, was able to deal with the half-megawatt station. They had finished their R&B selections and were now playing bebop. In fact, they were playing a record I owned, Charlie Ventura's 1949 concert at the Pasadena Civic Auditorium. Charlie was introducing a Benny Green number: "Bennies from Heaven." The hip audience laughed. My mood climbed out of whatever dump it had fallen into. Charlie said, introducing the next soloist, "Here's the Count—Conte Condoli—with a head arrangement of—a head arrangement means—we just make it *up*—and put a little *back*-ground in. Here's Conte Condoli—with 'Fine and Dandy.' "

"Like life," I said. I wouldn't have normally said anything decisive like that. Some things are better kept to yourself. Blame the tequila and music.

"Like life *what?*" Crutchfield said, instantly annoyed.

"Like life is a head arrangement."

"For you, maybe," Crutchfield said.

"For everybody." I squirmed a bit.

"Not for me. For me it's scored, note by note. Otherwise you're in the shithole, man."

"I mean, you make it up as you go along," I said, "but when you finish, it's like it was all arranged, like every move you made was planned even though it couldn't have been, you know?"

"Rave on, fool. That's called self-delusion."

I clammed up. You couldn't argue about such things, even if you knew what you were talking about. Ventura was soloing now and I didn't want any interference. He was so sly, tiptoeing along with those pure tones, a kind of fake humility, then like it was all a joke, like modesty in a tenor man was ridiculous, he cut loose with a raunchy riveting jackhammer riff of mind-bending sound that told you life *was* a head arrangement, from go to stop. No argument against held water.

"Ventura, man. He's the best," I said, when it was over. They were playing something ultracool now. Too cool for my taste.

"His name's Venturo," Crutchfield said. "If you like that crap so much you should at least know the man's name."

"Come off it, Monster," I said.

"No lie, Oz. His name is Venturo. He changed it to Ventura because he liked the sound of it. Thought it would give him more public appeal."

"So what? He still plays the best bop in the country."

"So, it was a career move, him changing his name. The man was thinking ahead. Maybe he makes head arrangements when he plays, but not when he's running his life."

"You're bringing me down, Crutchfield," I said.

"Both you guys are boring the living shit out of me," Art said, as he jammed it into second to pull a long grade.

When we pulled into Ensenada, Crutchfield told Art what streets to take. It dawned on me then that Crutchfield had a plan. He had Art park on a narrow side street behind a pre-1930 Buick taxi cab. Crutchfield got out and walked over to the cab. He and the cab driver talked for a few minutes. Then Crutchfield gave the man some money. When he came back, he said, "Lock up the wheels, Art. The ladies are waiting for our nasty young bodies."

"I'm not leaving my car," Art said.

"You have to," Crutchfield said. "The cab ride is part of the deal."

"I'll follow the cab."

"The place we're going to is way out of town and the roads are bad. You'll drag your shackles, maybe tear up your undercarriage."

"What do you think will happen to my car if I leave it *here*?" Art said, glancing up and down the narrow street.

"Shit," Crutchfield said. "I've got us all fixed up. Man, they're *waiting* for us."

Art leaned against the car, arms folded against his chest.

"Maybe this isn't such a great idea anyway," I said.

Crutchfield looked at me as if he couldn't believe his ears. "*What?* Did you say what I think you said, Oz?"

"I mean, Art and me, we're already pretty serious about our—you know—girlfriends."

Crutchfield laughed viciously. "Jesus, you guys kill me. Any freak can have a girlfriend. This hasn't got diddly-squat to do with *girlfriends*. We're talking *whores* here. Bitchin' whores from Mexico City. These are definitely not *girls*."

"You know what I mean, Crutchfield," I said. "Why pay for it when you can get it free?" This was a sorry effort on my part. I had a serious case of cold feet.

"You're not paying for it, Grandpa is," Crutchfield said. He was full of mock wonderment, as if seeing us for what we were for the first time. "You guys are too much. Here's your chance to experience something you couldn't even imagine during your wildest pud-pounding daydreams and you're chickening out. I'm beginning to think you both still have your cherries."

Art took a step toward Crutchfield. "Watch your mouth, Monster," he said. "Oz is right. We've got girls. Why should we take a chance with gonorrhea?"

"You feel that way, Oz?" Crutchfield said.

I shrugged. "Yeah, I guess." This was a bad moment for all of us. We'd been friends for four years.

"Look, man," Crutchfield said, subdued. "They'll give you a rubber if you're worried about catching something. But listen, this is a high-class operation. These aren't two-dollar waterfront whores. These women are class. Twenty bucks each. They usually deal with businessmen types—bankers, cannery managers, government people, dentists—you know, *family* men who can't afford the embarrassment of having their prongs turn into green cheese and crumble off inside their good wives. This is your chance to learn something you won't learn anywhere else. You'll probably have better marriages because of it, seriously."

It was quite a speech. "Okay," I said.

Art grabbed my shirt. "Think twice, Oz."

"I did," I said.

The cab took us to a two-story adobe building on the side of a hill. Crutchfield paid the driver, asked him to come back in an hour. We walked up a steep rocky path to the front door and went inside. A new-looking bar made of knotty pine ran the length of the room. The bartender, a gray-haired man with an enormous stomach, was reading a newspaper. He didn't look up when we came in. Some tables and chairs were scattered around the saw-dust floor, but no customers. Too early, I figured. A half-dozen girls were lounging at the tables drinking what looked like colored water—amber, green, blue. Even though it was still bright out-side, the bar was dim. The small square windows on either side of the front door were covered with heavy canvas curtains.

"*Buenas tardes, señoritas!*" Crutchfield boomed.

"Gee, he speaks Spanish," one girl said in unaccented En-glish.

"*No hay escuela hoy para los señoritos,*" another one said, and they all laughed.

Two whores pushed themselves wearily out of their chairs. The one who took my arm was pretty, but kind of sour-looking. She had fine features—so fine they looked brittle. Her hair was the color of iodine. She was close to my age, maybe younger. The four of us climbed a narrow staircase to a loft. There were several rooms off the loft. My whore opened one of them and pulled me in after her.

The room was neat and smelled of incense and disinfectant. Religious icons covered the walls: Jesus looking nine-tenths dead with his bloody thorn-wrapped heart exposed; wooden crosses with tin *milagritos* tacked to them; various forms of *la Virgen*, one with a colorful three-headed fish swimming out of her stomach. Three candles burned on the dresser. The atmosphere was churchy.

She unbuttoned her blouse and stepped out of her skirt and opened herself to me on the narrow iron bed. Naked, she was indisputably choice. My heart punched my ribs so hard I was sure she could hear it. I pulled off my pants and shorts and crawled into the silky yoke of her twenty-dollar thighs.

But she wouldn't let me kiss her. She dodged her head from side to side when I tried. Kissing was not part of the deal. Just fucking. Kissing was too personal. But without kissing I couldn't get myself ready. She took care of that by grabbing me in her educated fingers, which transformed my reluctance into rebar. *"Andale,"* she hissed, guiding me in.

She lay very still with her eyes closed, as if trying to forget her life. I worked hard, as if trying to discover mine. She was dead as Jesus, but now I didn't care. When I came she opened her eyes, but they were distracted, distant. Maybe she was counting pulses in her head, like a child doing mental sums, as if there was a well-established maximum number of throbs per twenty-dollar gringo orgasm. When it quit she pushed me away and jumped up.

"Veinte," she said, as if she was a bargain at twice that amount. I gave her the twenty Crutchfield had given me. I would have rather had a sick waterfront girl for twenty pesos.

I went back down to the bar. Crutchfield was already there, lifting a mug of beer to his lips with studied nonchalance.

"Have a good time, Crutchfield?" I asked.

"Go fuck yourself," he said glumly.

"Next time I will."

"You're a riot, Oz. I'm laughing so hard I'm pissing all over myself."

We waited for the cab and drank beer. The whores from Mexico City looked at us with casual contempt. They were used to a better class of trade.

"How was it?" Art asked when we got back to the car. He looked a little bleak.

"Oh, man, it was something *else,*" Crutchfield said. He shot a glance at me, daring me to say otherwise.

"It was so *bitchin',*" I said, shaking my head slowly as if unable to believe what had happened. Which was true enough. "You don't know what you missed, Art."

We let it go at that, and went to Hussong's, a bar owned by a German immigrant. After a few sixty-cent tequilas there, we went down to a waterfront cantina that sold it for ten cents a shot. Sometime during the night I got adventurous and wandered outside on my own. It was dark and a pungent west wind hummed off the ocean. I walked past a pair of squat Quonset huts that were dimly lit by an overhead bulb suspended from a pole between the buildings. Girls in the doorways of narrow cribs waved and called to me. I stopped and a fat madam in a housedress and carpet slippers approached.

"Two *dolarucos*, just for you, baby," she said. I dug into my pocket and came up with two quarters, a nickel, a bus token, and six pennies. Full of hope and resurrected lust, I showed them to her.

She scoffed. "Cheap *pinchi gringo!*" she said.

"It's all I have, señora," I said.

She spit at my feet and waddled away. The girls in the doorways waved and called, but they might as well have been Sirens in the Aegean Sea.

I kept walking until beach sand filled my shoes. I watched the Mexican moon kiss the water, becoming liquid itself. Then I curled up on the cool sand and passed out.

I woke next to a dead seal, still traveling with a dream. The old Packard was running again, and I watched it from altitude as it rolled down the highway. Then I was in the car with Mitzi and a man I didn't know. He winked at me as if we were insiders in the midst of people who habitually missed the point. Mitzi and the man were singing, "California here I come, right back where I started from." I recognized the man but could not remember who he was. I liked him but felt uncomfortable, and when he started to turn around to look at me again, I was afraid.

The seal smelled of rot and diesel. I was near the docks. The small tuna boats were chugging out of the bay. It was gray and

cold, the horizon silvered with fog. I rolled to my knees and vom-
ited lime-green bile.

The cure was a hundred yards away. I stripped and walked
toward the weak surf. My legs were shaky and my knees buckled
a few times. The water was cold, exactly what I needed. I flopped
down into the low waves and rolled over and over in the shallow
foam. The pain of cold water canceled the pain of hangover. I lay
there, blanketed by foam, staring straight up into the weak light
of early morning.

I tested my legs again. Tremors still buckled my knees, but the
pain was nearly gone. I still felt a little drunk. When I pulled on
my clothes, something fell out of my shirt pocket. It was a Benzedrine inhaler. I picked it up, uncapped it, took a long sniff. I
half-remembered buying it for a dollar from an American woman
who needed to make cab fare back to her hotel.

I walked back to the main drag, hoping to find Art and Crutchfield. I found Art easily enough. He was sleeping in his car,
around the corner from Hussong's. He was in the backseat, knees
up, his arms pillowing his head. I climbed into the front. "We got
to find Monster, Art," I said.

His eyes snapped open but he didn't move. "Why?" he said,
staring straight up into the headliner. "Is he lost?" There was
nothing behind his eyes. He closed them again, stone to the world.
I inhaled another lungful of Benzedrine.

It was six a.m., Saturday morning. I walked from one end of
the main drag to the other, but saw no signs of Crutchfield. I
checked out some of the side streets with no luck. I found the jail-

house, but hesitated. Mexican cops could be unpredictable. If they were looking for a gringo kid who'd stuck a knife in someone, you did not want to present yourself to them while they were complaining about the shortage of suspects.

I didn't go in. Besides, even if Crutchfield had been there, I didn't have the money to get him out. Unless someone took it away from him, he had enough money to pay his own bribes. And if he was being held on serious charges, what could I do for him anyway, other than offer myself to the cops as a possible accomplice?

I had all the answers. I felt disgusted with myself.

I went back to the car and shook Art awake. "I can't find Crutchfield," I said.

"I know where he is," Art groaned. "Said he was going back to that cathouse on the hill. He had a couple of Marines with him."

Art drove up the bad road in low gear, at about one mile an hour. Now and then a shackle would bang into a rock. Art gritted his teeth when this happened but said nothing.

We didn't have to go all the way up the hill. We found Crutchfield alongside the road. The side of his head was blue. Art honked and Crutchfield rose up. His eyes were swollen shut. He began to run away from us on his knees, belly-flopping every other step into the weeds.

"Someone fucked him up," Art said.

I got out and grabbed Crutchfield's arm. "Come on, man, it's us," I said. "We're going home."

Crutchfield roared something, but it was weak and unintelligible. I stuffed him into the backseat.

The Marines had kicked his ass. He wasn't in a mood to talk
about it, but we got a few of the details out of him. Crutchfield
usually pissed off people who wouldn't, or couldn't, retaliate
physically. He'd made a big mistake with a pair of MCRD recruits. They'd gotten into an argument on the way up to the
whorehouse. Something about Korea, of all things. Crutchfield's
cynicism didn't go over with the Marines. They were a couple of
farm boys from Indiana, and cynicism was as alien to them as the
Pacific Coast. Crutchfield claimed to have nailed one of them in
the nuts, but the other one sucker-punched him. Then they took
off their canvas belts and wrapped their fists in them, Marine-
style. They took turns working Crutchfield over, knocking out
three front teeth and breaking his nose. His lips looked like split
sausage. I couldn't see his eyes.

The customs inspectors at the border looked us over hard, but
let us through the gates. One of them was a wit. "Our nation's
young heroes return," he said.

We got aspirin and ice in San Ysidro. Crutchfield swallowed a
dozen aspirins with beer, and rode the rest of the way home lying
down with ice on his face.

I thought Crutchfield should go to a hospital, but he wanted to
go home. "My parents are doctors, for Chrissakes," he said. He
spoke without moving his blood-caked lips.

"You're going to have to be more choosy about who you piss
off, Monster," Art said. "Jarhead recruits aren't exactly your
average social studies teacher. They tend to be a little on the
eager side."

"Oh, thanks so much," Crutchfield said. "Gee, I really treasure your genius, Art. I mean, now I can live a full and rewarding life.''

Art pulled over to the side of the road. He turned and glared at Crutchfield.

''Listen, pissant,'' he said. ''You want me to take the rest of your teeth out just say so, okay?''

Crutchfield shut up.

Art slammed it into first and laid fifty feet of rubber.

When its transmission went out, Mitzi had the old Packard towed behind the house. It was left to decay under an eighty-foot euca- lyptus tree at the far end of our yard. The tires went flat and weeds surged through the gaps in the floorboards around the brake and clutch pedals. The fenders were freckled with rust, the hubcaps stolen, long strips of rubber were peeling off the running boards, and the hood ornament—a chrome-plated winged lady— had been attacked by hammer-swinging vandals. A wingless, headless figure with corroded breasts now topped the noble grille of the Packard. Mitzi thought she'd get the old car worked on someday, but kept putting it off. Now it was too late to do any- thing but watch it rot and settle. I was sure the engine was frozen with rust and could not be turned over anyway. In the meantime she'd bought a used Nash, and it ran well enough even though it burned oil and the frame had been bent in a wreck so that it reeled down the street at a tipsy angle.

When I was younger I used the Packard as a kind of stepladder to get into the lower branches of the eucalyptus. I climbed with a hoop of copper wire over my shoulder, a claw hammer in my belt, nails and insulators in my pockets. My object was to attach the far end of a long-wire antenna near the top of the tree. The higher the wire, the better. At sixty feet, the wire could loft shortwave signals to Europe and Africa.

Mitzi had just married the brawler, Wayne Duchesne. We were still new in the neighborhood. I didn't know anyone yet. Shortwave radio had always interested me, and so I crammed for the FCC license exam and passed. I was almost fourteen and fascinated by electromagnetic radiation. How strange and unlikely it was, to be able to send Morse code into the shortwave-reflecting ionosphere with nothing but a few vacuum tubes and wire, and receiving them the same way.

The tree, at sixty feet off the ground, was slender and fragile. It swayed dangerously with my weight, but I didn't come down after my work was done. I stayed up there for an hour or more, gliding back and forth with the Pacific breeze, half hypnotized, the sun a smoky red ball in the west. Mitzi and Wayne were in the house, arguing. The rasp and grind of their loveless voices kept me treed.

I walked out into the backyard and climbed into the mildewed backseat of the Packard. It was nearly dinnertime, and Mitzi had

fixed my favorite meal as a graduation present—roast beef and
mashed potatoes and gravy. My shortwave antenna had snapped
in a storm years ago and a sagging strand of corroded twelve-
gauge wire scraped the hood of the car. The breeze pushed it
back and forth, making birdlike screeches.

Nelson Glasspie knocked on the window. It was Sunday, but
he'd gotten the swing shift off, just for this special occasion. I
opened the door for him.

"Hi, Dad," I said. Nelson liked to be called Dad. It was easy to
do. It didn't feel phony, even though we hardly ever talked.

"Mind if I come in?" he said.

I slid over. "What's up?" I said.

He took off his heavy glasses, squinted at the prism-thick
lenses, then hooked them carefully over his ears again. "Mitzi's
made a fine pot roast for supper," he said.

"Yes, I know."

The wind gusted and the wire hissed across the windshield.

"That's your old radio antenna, isn't it?" he said.

"Yes."

He drummed his skinny thighs with his fingers, impatient with
himself. He wanted to say something to me but was having trouble
mustering the words. He reached into his pocket and took out his
wallet. "Look here," he said.

He showed me a snapshot of a young man sitting in front of
old-time radio gear.

"That's me," he said, "in 1921."

A curly-haired kid sat in front of a bank of old amperage meters bolted into a steel panel. He was wearing earphones and holding a telegraph key and staring into the camera lens as if he'd been caught stealing.

"You were a ham, too," I said.

"You bet I was!"

This bit of enthusiasm stopped the conversation for a while.

"Thought about State College?" he finally said.

"No. I don't have the grades. I also wouldn't know what to study."

"They'd let you in on probation," he said. "If you wanted to go."

"But I don't."

"I think you should give it some thought. The next few years, I mean with the Cold War and all, there are going to be good jobs. Especially in defense. Convair always needs engineers. You could take electrical, or mechanical. You'd be good at things like that, don't you think?"

I'd never heard him say so many words all at once before. His speech was clipped and he ran the words together, almost chattering. I had to unscramble them as if he'd spoken in another language that I could barely understand.

"Maybe," I said.

"You should give it some thought."

It struck me then that he was giving me fatherly advice. He was doing his duty by me. Mitzi had made a fine dinner, and now Nelson was helping me plan ahead. I was being launched into the future.

"Thanks, Dad," I said. "I will. I'll give it some thought."

"Electrical or mechanical," he said. "That's the ticket these days. I wish I had gone electrical."

"Electrical," I said. "Electrical sounds good."

We sat in the backseat of the Packard listening to the old wire dragging itself back and forth across the hood as the wind began to buffet.

"Looks like rain tonight," I said.

"We could use some rain."

But he'd said what he came to say, and now couldn't find the words for ordinary chat. His dutiful speech had left a tight vacuum suspended behind it.

Nelson was intensely shy and private. He was a little strange, too. Once I surprised him admiring his feet. He had just gotten out of the bathtub and thought he was home alone. I was in my room, listening to records with the volume turned down. I came out to get a Coke but stopped short because there was Nelson, in his bathrobe and bare feet, sitting in the kitchen, splaying and knuckling his toes. His long narrow feet were white as china. He rotated them vigorously on his thin ankles, admiring the fine articulations of his immaculate toes. I slipped back to my room, unnoticed. Some time after that I heard him say to Mitzi, "You know, dear, a man—with some training, of course—could learn to dial a telephone, or even learn to play the piano, with nothing but his feet." It seemed like a casual remark, an interesting observation about human feet in general, but I knew he was talking about himself.

I had stopped trying to figure out why he and Mitzi had gotten married, but now and then the implausibility of the two of them together made me shake my head in pure wonder. Nelson had never been married, and that went a long way in explaining his poor judgment, but nothing explained Mitzi's. Security may have been part of it, but Mitzi had always taken pride in her independence. She knew she could always make a living. Besides, even though Nelson brought home a good paycheck, he was just an hourly wage-earner, not a man of means.

After another few minutes of painful silence, we left the Packard and went into the house. The roast was on the table, sending threads of fragrant steam into the candlelit air. A bowl of mashed potatoes sat next to it, and next to the potatoes a gravy boat. A one-layer chocolate cake with "Congratulations Oz!" scrawled across it in pink letters sat on the counter between the stove and the refrigerator. Mitzi wasn't around. The house seemed abandoned.

"I guess she went out to the store to pick up something she forgot," Nelson said.

I pushed the kitchen window curtains aside. "No, the Nash is out front."

Then I heard Mitzi's voice. It rose in anger, then fell to a hiss. "Yes!" she said. "But not *this* Sunday!" A telephone receiver banged down into its cradle. Mitzi was in the bedroom, using the phone. I heard the dial whir, and the furious hiss of her whispers started again.

Nelson heard it too, but said nothing. He poked the roast with the big carving fork. "Very tender," he said. He began to cut slices. He filled three plates with meat.

We sat down and helped ourselves to the potatoes and gravy. I

poured myself a glass of milk. Nelson opened a can of beer. Mitzi
had cooked some canned green beans, for color. None of us liked
green vegetables.

"Well, we might as well start eating," Nelson said.

"Or feed it to the hogs," I said.

Nelson forced a smile. Candle flame flickered in his glasses. He
sipped some beer. I cut a piece of meat. It was perfect—well-
done, dry, spiced with garlic. I spooned a crater into my mashed
potatoes and filled it with a lake of dark brown gravy. Mushroom
bits floated in the lake. I sprinkled salt and pepper on top, then
added a square of butter. The butter sank into the hot, gravy-
filled crater. Mitzi came in. She was in her robe and slippers.
Rags of Kleenex hung from the pockets of her chenille robe.

"Well just *look* at you two," she said, like the beaming mother
of ravenous boys. But this was a hard act to pull off. Her eyes
were red and swollen. Mascara leaked from the corners. She
opened herself a beer and sat down.

"Do you like your dinner, dear?" she said to Nelson.

"Oh, gosh yes," he said. "Very much so."

"It's great, Mitzi," I said, my mouth full.

Nelson sipped his beer. I kept eating. Nelson had yet to take a
bite. It didn't look like Mitzi was going to.

"Ed Sullivan is on tonight," Mitzi said. "That Italian ventriloquist is one of the acts. Señor . . . I forget his name."

"Wences," Nelson said. "Señor Wences. He's South American, I believe. Isn't that correct, Ozzie?"

"The head in the box," I said.

They both looked at me, confused. Their sham conversation

couldn't handle a third party. "You know," I said. "The guy in the little box who says, *'s all right!* and then keeps on talking with a muffled voice even after the door to his box is closed. Señor Wences. What a panic."

They both lifted their beers to their faintly smiling lips, their eyes distant and distracted.

I finished eating, then cut myself a big square of cake and took it outside. It was almost dark. The Packard was a black hulk under the eucalyptus tree. I made my way back to it and climbed inside again.

The wind had quit blowing and a fine mist beaded the windshield.

"Go figure," I said.

But suddenly it didn't need figuring. Mitzi wanted a stable and ordinary life. It was important to her. None of her other men could offer it. Nelson Glasspie was the opposite of a Stupka, a Duchesne, or a Caulkins. Nelson was Mitzi's attempt to force a different direction on her life. She tried to be good to him, and I never heard them fight. I figured there were worse marriages. I also figured that maybe it *was* possible to forcibly change the direction of your life, after all. You just made up your mind, gritted your teeth, and you did it. You didn't have to stay in one rut. Life had thousands of other, more satisfying ruts. It was a nice thought, entertaining as any fairy tale.

6

Colleen called me up with a dinner invitation. She seemed to have put graduation day out of her mind. I tried to remind her. "Sorry about the other day," I said.

"I love you, Ozzie," she said.

An invisible hand grabbed my throat. "I love you too, Colleen," I said, after the hand let go.

"I don't believe you, you rat."

Seconds ticked away. "Well, it's true," I said.

Her voice lowered. "I want you right now, darling."

"I want you, too," I said. That was true enough. I reached into my crowded Levi's.

"Liar, liar, pants on fire," she said.

"Well, it just so happens my pants *are* on fire," I said.

"Ozzie! You're just awful!"

"I'll be right over," I said.

"Not now, silly. Tuesday. Come at six, okay? We'll go to a movie afterwards."

"Be out in front of your house in twenty minutes. We'll take a ride out to Torrey Pines."

"I *can't.* We've got company."

"Then Tuesday it is."

"I love you, honey."

The hand closed around my neck again. "Me too," I said.

"What did you rowdies do in Mexico?" she asked, a sudden edginess in her voice.

"Not much."

"Why don't I believe you?"

On Tuesday I French-cuffed a clean pair of Levi's, shined my penny loafers, put on my blue Billy Eckstein shirt, pomaded my hair back into a carefully sculptured duck's ass, checked my wallet to make sure the rubber was still in it. I'd carried that foil-wrapped Sheik for the last two years of my virginity as a kind of unearned status symbol. It was time now to think of consequences. I regretted not using it our first time on Palomar. Things had happened too fast that night, and with no control. Words flew out of my mouth in brainless swarms. Some words you can't take back. But it wasn't me, it was my gonads. They did all the talking. They would say anything to get their way. I was just their puppet. Hormonal ventriloquism—the most unacknowledged force in the world. It erased conscience and made everyone a hopeless liar, from stock clerks to stockbrokers.

I arrived at the Vogel house at six-thirty. It was a huge three-story house with two separate entrances. I'd been here before but the place still intimidated me. One entrance had a small blue neon sign over the doorway:

VOGEL-DARLING MORTUARY

I knocked at the other door. Mr. Vogel himself opened it. He was a big, slope-shouldered man with a formidable belly. He looked at his watch. "We eat at six," he said. Then he smiled. It was a warm and genuinely friendly smile. He looked as though nothing had ever made him mad. He put his heavy, welcoming hand on my shoulder and brought me into the dining room, as if I were an honored guest.

Mrs. Vogel was another story. She was a frail, gray-haired, severely dignified woman. She didn't look at me as Mr. Vogel led me to the chair next to Colleen's. When I was seated, she picked up a little crystal bell and rang it with delicate ferocity. A servant came in pushing a cart loaded with heavy silver trays.

"I got hung up in traffic," I said. It was a lie, but I had no other excuse. Dinnertime at our house varied a lot. There were no formalities. Mitzi would put it on the table, and we ate when we got there, either together or alone.

Mrs. Vogel, detecting the lie, looked at me with one eyebrow raised. Her thin, ungenerous lips curled down with such finality that I knew there was nothing I could ever do to please her. She looked at my shirt, my pomaded hair, and shuddered visibly. What she was seeing was an interloper from the lower classes.

She was right. I had trouble with the forks and spoons and had to watch Colleen to make sure I used the right ones. The soup was cold and I almost complained to the woman who served it—a stout, red-faced Swede they called Mrs. Sorenson—until I saw everyone else dipping into it without comment. I made a mental note of that: rich people ate cold soup. The salad was full of shellfish and leafy vegetables I didn't recognize. The main dish was rack of lamb with mint sauce and perfect little new potatoes sprigged with parsley. I'd never tasted anything so delicious in my life. I had seconds, then thirds. When I signaled for fourths, Colleen nudged me under the table. I waved off Mrs. Sorenson, acting as though the mistake was hers.

"We're going to see *The Robe*, Mother," Colleen said.

"Another dreary epic," Mrs. Vogel said. Her raised eyebrow was a permanent condition, but it made her seem more world-weary now than skeptical.

"I admire that fine young English actor," Mr. Vogel said enthusiastically, as if making up for his wife's indifference.

"Richard Burton!" Colleen said. "He's too *dreamy* for words!"

"Yes, that's it," said Mr. Vogel. "The young man has style." He looked at his watch. "But it's still early, isn't it? How about a tour of the facilities before you run off, Ozzie?"

"Oh, Daddy!" Colleen said. "He doesn't want to see all that boring stuff!"

Colleen was wearing a pink angora sweater over a silky rose blouse, a creamy pleated skirt, and white saddle shoes. She looked like dessert. She folded her arms across her breasts and stamped her foot. Her cute pout made her father wag his head defensively—an old comic routine of theirs, I figured. I liked it. I liked to think there were families that were close enough to allow such pantomime play. It didn't take a genius to see that she had her old man wrapped around her little finger. I guessed that was why I was getting the red-carpet treatment. Her mother, though, was something else.

"I'll give him the short tour, Collie," Mr. Vogel said. He put his arm around my shoulder and led me down the long dim hallway toward the cold room. He unlocked the heavy door, and the dank air put instant goose bumps on my arms. We went inside. He closed the door, then locked it behind us.

Mr. Vogel lit a cigar. He offered me one; I took it. We stood there for a while, blowing smoke into the morbid chill.

"These folks"—he waved his cigar at half a dozen sheet-covered bodies—"await their final grooming." He glanced at his watch. "I'll get to at least two of them tonight, before Milton Berle comes on. Do your people watch Uncle Milty?"

Before I could answer he said, "I'll give you a shot in the *head*!"

His imitation of Berle was perfect, complete with the sputtering lisp and the effeminate brandishing of his fist. I choked a little on cigar smoke, and we both laughed. He had a fat man's joviality, but his eyes were flat gray, unreadable as stone.

He led me to the large stainless-steel table with gutters running down either side. "This is the embalming table, Ozzie," he said. "These gutters are for waste fluids from the tired old body. We drain them, then send the runoff down the sewer where it belongs. All accomplished by an aspirator—a half-horse electric pump that removes waste from the abdominal cavity and thorax. Very simple, once you get the hang of it.''

He tapped his cigar ashes into one of the gutters. The aspirator along with a collection of other stainless-steel instruments sat on an immaculate white table next to a large porcelain double sink. Red rubber hoses were coiled on the faucets of this sink. I pictured a body quivering helplessly on the table as the roaring half-horse pump sucked it dry of its once hot juices.

I sagged a bit. My dinner sat in my stomach like a bag of stones. I glanced at my watch. "Whoa, look at the time," I said.

"In goes the big needle," he said, ignoring me. He held up something that looked like a polished spike with a clear plastic hose attached. "Ka-whoosh! Ka-whoosh! And out comes the filth!" He chuckled a bit at his own dramatics.

"Ka-whoosh," I said, trying to get into the spirit of the thing.

"Climb up there, Ozzie," he said.

"You're kidding."

He raised his fist. "I'll give you such a shot in the *head*!" he sputtered.

He laughed, and then I did too. He swiped at my face comically with his Milton Berle fist. "Go on, go on. Not to worry! I just want to give you an idea of what we do here, Ozzie. Relax, I promise not to remove your lamb and spuds!"

I wagged my head, mimicking the playful resistance he'd offered Colleen earlier. And then it occurred to me that Colleen was somehow behind this tour, that her objections had been part of an act she and her father had rehearsed. He seemed to sense my suspicion and put his big reassuring hand on my shoulder. He pushed me toward the steel table. It was slanted, the head several inches higher than the foot. I backed against it, eased myself up, then lowered myself gingerly.

The cold pressed into my shirt and then into my skin, and I shuddered. My teeth even chattered. Mr. Vogel didn't seem to notice. He took my hands and folded them over my heart. He poked my quivering arms and legs, testing the flesh.

"No rigor mortis here, by golly," he said. "But if there were, here's what we'd do. We'd massage it out. Like so."

He began to rub my arms and neck expertly, his flat eyes mysterious above his burning cigar.

"You see how easy it is, son?" he said. "There's really not much to it, once you get past the . . . *unique* nature of the work."

"Simple as pie," I said, or tried to, as he seized my jaw muscles and rotated them under his fleshy thumbs.

He turned to his table full of instruments. He selected a tray of small gleaming tools and showed them to me. "The face can sometimes offer problems," he said. "Even if death was peaceful, the face can twist a bit on you. Usually the face, after death, is not pretty to look at, no matter how handsome or lovely in life."

He lifted a slender length of bright steel from the tray. It was about four inches long and looked like a needle, except that it was much thicker and it was curved. Instead of thread it had fine steel wire dangling from it.

"We have to sew the jaws together—on the inside, through the gums and again through the nasal cavity—to keep the mouth closed. Its tendency is to open—just as in life!—but you cannot put an open-mouthed corpse in the slumber room, can you? I should certainly think not. It's aesthetically displeasing and would be disturbing to the family of the deceased.''

His voice had changed. His was talking like an actor playing a lofty role. I thought of Boris Karloff in *The Mummy's Curse*. But his voice was comforting, too. It was smooth and full of certainty.

"Lip drift," he said. "Lip drift is something you have to watch closely. It can happen anytime, behind your back. You think you're finished, then *bingo*, the lips crawl up. A little show of teeth can ruin everything. The unexpected mordant leer, the spurious smile, can seriously degrade the mourning experience." He showed me a handful of ordinary straight pins. "This is how we control lip drift, son. We pin the stubborn little chaps down."

My dinner didn't feel like a dead weight any longer. I even felt drowsy, lying there on his embalming table. I tapped some ash off my cigar and drew on it.

So this was what it was like being a corpse, attended to by a careful mortician. I felt pleasantly alive, just as the dead around me were pleasantly dead. We differed in body heat and mobility. Finished business and unfinished business. As he resumed massaging my legs to get rid of the last bit of rigor mortis, the thought entered my mind that I could probably do this. Maybe not forever, but for a while at least. Then it occurred to me that this was the exact thought he—and Colleen—wanted me to have.

As if to certify this notion, he said, "Colleen has told me that you two are practically engaged." He pushed his thick finger gently into my solar plexus. "In goes Mr. Trocar here," he said abstractly, "and out comes the bloody stew." He tapped my shirt as if warning my innards of their eventual fate. My guts growled. He cocked his ear at my stomach and responded to its liquid complaint by making his *ka-whoosh! ka-whoosh!* sound again, reminding it of the relentless power of his gut-sucking half-horse machine.

"I guess we are," I said lamely. "Sort of."

"Sort of," he mused.

"I mean, we've been kicking around the idea, I guess."

He looked at me peculiarly for a long moment, then went back to his lecture. "And now we reverse the procedure," he said. "We fill up the vacated thoracic cavity with a powerful formalin solution that kills off all the nasty little microbes we all harbor. The chemical is strong enough to literally cook the remaining organs." He patted my stomach affectionately. "You see, Ozzie, we cannot bury unclean bodies. The law forbids it."

He loved his work and he loved his daughter and I was being tested. And I wanted to pass with flying colors. Mainly because I liked him. I had all the usual negative ideas about morticians— ghoulish parasites who lived off the grief of others. But that was wrong. There were morticians who honored the dead and cared for them with respect. Mr. Vogel was one of these. His concern was like that of a good doctor. It was devotion, tenderness, and professional pride that moved him, not vulturous greed. He wanted to produce a presentable body, something the family of the deceased could view and be comforted by. Death was clean and simple, not ugly. It wasn't a punishment. You come into the world out of the dark naked, screaming, and bloody, and you went back to darkness well-dressed, respected, and with a noble expression of calm acceptance on your face. It was proper, and as Art said, somebody's got to do it.

"The eyes," Mr. Vogel murmured, brushing my eyelashes gently. "They also give us a minor problem. They want so pathetically to stay open. It's as if they have not yet had their fill of the brilliant sights of this crazy old world." He closed my eyes and kept his flesh-cushioned fingertips on the lids as he spoke. His voice was sad, almost stricken. "Yet, they must be closed, once and for all. Little plastic cups liberally studded on both sides with short pins are pressed into the eyeballs. The lids then are pulled down over the outer pins. The arrangement holds the lids closed, forever closed."

He paused; his breath shook. I dropped my cigar. I stared straight into a darkness that was far away and close. I pushed his hand off my face.

"Do you understand what I've been saying, Ozzie?" he said.

I picked my cigar out of the gutter. "I think so, sir," I said.

"She's precious to me," he said.

"I know, Mr. Vogel."

I got off the table. We started walking toward the exit. I saw a long yellow toe with a dark untrimmed nail sticking out from a sheet. My legs suddenly felt like bags of sand. He saw me staring at the horrible toe.

"Ah. That's your ex-principal, Ozzie," he said. "Mr. Elwood Flooding. A fine, fine man. So tragic, dying at his age."

The jaundiced toe glowed in the half-light of the cold room. It grew like a toadstool out of a thin gray foot. I staggered against

Mr. Vogel. The hypnotic calm he'd created in me dropped away. He put his heavy arm around my shoulder. We made it to the doorway. It took forever.

Colleen and I drove downtown to the Spreckles Theater in her MG. We got there just in time for the second show. I couldn't concentrate on the movie. Marching legions, racing chariots, tender love scenes, Roman ships on stormy seas—they all blended into each other randomly. A CinemaScope spectacle in Technicolor, crammed with degrees of noise and cornball music, punctuated by visions of the yellow toe of that fine man Elwood Flooding.

At one point I realized that Colleen had been crying. She squeezed my hand hard. Some agony or other was making Richard Burton lose his grip on sanity, but my inattention was too ingrained for me to figure out why. The sweet Christian girl, Jean Simmons, had apparently touched Richard's heart, disturbing his centurion arrogance.

It was all very tragic and would end badly in persecution and wretched death—made amazingly attractive by Hollywood—but even so, I couldn't get interested.

A man sitting in front of us didn't like the movie. He gave a loud running critique of the acting and the plot. "Oh for Chrissakes!" he grumbled. "That lime-sucker thinks he's playing Hamlet!"

Colleen turned her fierce wet face to me, her teeth gritted. "Oooh!" she whispered. "That man is so *horrible*! He makes me so mad! Why doesn't he just *leave* if he hates it so much?"

I got up and went out to the lobby for a Coke. There was a line, so I stepped outside into the night. The crazy idea of just walking away occurred to me. Horton Plaza, across from the Spreckles, was all lit up and filled with people chatting normally about ordinary things.

When I got back to my seat, the man in front of us was laughing nastily at the movie's big love scene, where Richard Burton, arrogant pagan Roman, becomes a humble soft-spoken Christian. His love for Jean Simmons was a spiritual thing, a lofty communion of souls, but the critic guffawed and snorted. Colleen turned her anger at me. Her lips were tight and her eyes were wide with accusation, as if to say, Why don't you *do* something?

So I did.

I poured my Coke down the critic's neck, ice and all. He jumped up roaring. I gave him a little push, and while he was trying to stop himself from falling into the next aisle, I pulled Colleen out of the theater. "We'll come back tomorrow," I said.

Her mouth was wide open with shock, but the laughter didn't come until we got into the car. She screamed, helpless with delight, and couldn't get the key into the ignition. We traded seats and I got the car going. I headed for the Balboa Freeway.

I liked the sound of her screaming laugh. I laughed too. Laughing made the car swerve. The tight steering of the little sports car was new to me. I had driven the Packard and the Nash, and the steering of those cars was about as responsive as a boat tiller. But every nudge of the hardwood steering wheel of the MG made it change direction sharply. I calmed myself down so we wouldn't wreck.

"Oh, Ozzie," she said when she was able to talk. "That was *so* perfect! I can't believe you *did* it!"

"The guy was a drag," I said, congratulating myself more than a little.

We went up El Cajon Boulevard to Oscar's Drive-in, where we had cheeseburgers and shakes. A car club was there taking up most of the spaces. Gleaming chrome engines and metallic paint and the roar of glasspack mufflers—the "North Park Desperadoes" were having a "meet." Some of them—all sideburns and leather jackets—came over to inspect the MG.

"What you got under the hood, man, a sewing-machine motor?" one of them said.

"You got a full-race *Singer* under that hood, man?" another one said.

Whatever heroism I had felt in the movies was gone. I wasn't about to shoot the dozens with the Desperadoes. "Probably," I said. They laughed derisively and moved on.

I drove out to Sunset Cliffs. The moon was nearly full. It laid a path of silver before us, from the whitecaps below to the far horizon.

We kissed in the cramped cockpit of the MG. Under the raging activity of our mouths and tongues, my burning hands worked at the buttons of her cardigan, and then her blouse, and finally at solving the hooks of her brassiere.

Uncovered in moonlight, her breasts were like a dream of breasts. Jean Simmons wasn't in the same league. I imagined Richard Burton thinking what a pathetic set of jugs Jean Simmons had, tender Christian enlightenment aside.

"Kee-rist," I whispered.

I got my hand into her panties.

"The button, Oz," she said, deliberate as a wife. "Touch my little button."

After a minute I found it. Her back arched dramatically. She groaned. I broke a sweat. *This is love, isn't it?* I thought.

The mindless traitor in my crotch got a little ahead of the action, and so I backed off. I lit a cigarette and stared out at the silver ocean toward Korea.

Someone ten thousand miles away was sleeping in his own shit. Others were listening to an opium-crazed North Korean scream insults in bad English over a PA system. What did that have to do with me?

I threw the cigarette away and we started again. We got out of the car and Colleen spread out her beach blanket. We were alone on the cliffs.

Something oceanic pulled us out of ourselves. It was a tidal wave that didn't know or care that we were caught in it. With us or without us it would flood the world with abundance as it always had and always would.

Calling my name again and again, as if calling to a lost swimmer, Colleen pulled my face down to her sweet buoyant breasts.

"I love you, honey," my ventriloquist said.

"Say it again," she gasped.

But my ventriloquist was content. He'd got what he wanted.

"What, don't you believe me?" I said.

7

We went back to see *The Robe* on a weekday afternoon. We were the only ones in the theater. I put my arm around her, but that was all. She put her head on my shoulder and wept happy tragic tears. I couldn't wait for the movie to end. I ran the caustic commentary of the loudmouth critic through my brain for entertainment. *The lime-sucker thinks he's Hamlet. What is this, a movie or a postcard from the Vatican?*

"What's wrong with you, Ozzie?" Colleen said later.

We were in a Kresge's drugstore downtown, having tuna salad sandwiches and chocolate milkshakes at the soda fountain.

"Nothing," I said.

"You're always so moody," she said.

The tuna was old; you could taste the sweet acids of stale fish. I didn't mind. In fact, I kind of liked that taste. Fresh tuna didn't taste right. When Mitzi had a job canning tuna at the Van Camp cannery she brought home a huge chunk of fresh yellowtail. It weighed as much as a tom turkey. She'd slipped it into a shopping bag and walked out of the cannery with it, unnoticed. This was right after she broke up with Wayne Duchesne and she was low on money. She baked it and served it with lemon wedges and scalloped potatoes. It was good, but it didn't taste like tuna. It could have been ostrich, for all I knew.

"Who, me? Moody?" I said.

"You scare me sometimes, you get so quiet."

I didn't answer her. I bit into my sandwich, took a sip of chocolate shake. The girl behind the counter in her starched white uniform crackled as she wiped the gleaming shake mixers, urns, and toasters. She looked distracted. I imagined her thinking about *The Robe*. She'd just seen it last night with her boyfriend and was now seriously considering entering a convent. In fact, she kind of looked like a nun in her starched uniform. So clean, so crisp. What's eating you, honey? her boyfriend asked. Oh, I don't know, Fred, she said. I just can't get those martyrs out of my mind. I wish we were Christian martyrs, too. It's so beautiful and sad. The boyfriend—I pictured a tall thin guy who worked at Convair harnessing bundles of electrical cable together inside a wing section of the B-36—didn't like the movie either. They don't kill Christians anymore, he said. It's the Christians doing all the ass-kicking now, babe. He cut a downward arc in the air with his hand, whistling the ballistic fall of the big bomb, then followed it with the city-vaporizing ka-boom and ker-splat. His girlfriend shuddered. You scare the liver out of me sometimes, Freddie, she said.

"*Scare* you?" I said to Colleen. "Are you kidding?" I picked up her chilly hand and squeezed it. Her fingers were chubby and her bones were soft.

"Well, not exactly *scare*," she said. "But you go so far away, like you're in a trance."

Mitzi said that once: "That damned bebop music puts you in a trance, Ozzie." It was true. I could listen to Ventura, Parker, Mulligan, Jacquet, and disappear. It was like the music crowded out everything else in my head, including me. Maybe it happened to the musicians, too. No musician, no listener, just music. Sometimes I was so far gone I couldn't remember hearing it. So I'd play it again and the same thing would happen. This didn't happen every time, but it happened often enough to make me think about it.

"I guess so," I said. "Sometimes this feeling comes over me, like everything isn't exactly what it is, you know?"

"No, I do not know. That makes no sense at all, Ozzie."

"I mean, I'm like this Martian person who's been dropped into the middle of everything and it's so *weird*, you know?" I put her chubby, boneless hand back on the counter.

"Ozzie, I don't like you to talk like that. It isn't normal."

I looked at her. She was so pretty and strange. Her hair was pulled back into a tight ponytail that seemed to stretch the skin over her high cheekbones so that they looked like polished white stones. She was wearing a forest-green V-neck sweater and a white dickey. My senior ring hung from a thin gold chain around her neck, signifying, for high school kids, engagement. Her little lips formed a pink heart.

"Why not?" I said. "I mean, that's the way I think."

"It sounds crazy, that's why not."

"Maybe it is crazy. Does that make a difference?"

She shrugged, sucked on her straw, creating lovely hollows in her cheeks.

I thought of Mr. Flooding's yellow toe, the ragged nail dark with final grime. Was it crazy to think about that? And if it was, then what was sane?

"Sometimes I think I was born with a section of my brain miswired," I said.

It was a dumb thought, but wasn't it possible? Wasn't anything possible? And if anything was possible, then everything that was in place *now* was on shaky ground. Didn't that make sense?

"Like I can't figure some things out half the time," I said. "I mean the easy things. Things that everyone else figured out long ago. Things people don't even have to think about anymore, they're so goddam figured out."

"Let's talk about something else, honey," she said, patting my hand.

The sharp pats made the girl behind the counter turn around. "Give me a minute, will you, hon?" she said. "Charlie didn't do the dadburned urns, so I'll give you three guesses who's got to do it," she said.

We took a ride up to Lake Murray, a little reservoir nestled in the foothills east of town, and watched old men fish. They fished with cane poles, and now and then pulled planted bass or crappie out of the water. It was a vision of boredom in its most suffocating form. "Jesus Christ," I said, and she didn't ask what was wrong with me *now*, though I could tell she was reaching her limit. Then we went to her house. She asked me in to play double solitaire, but I'd had enough excitement for one day.

"Mitzi—I mean my mother—wants me to mow the lawn," I said. It wasn't a lie. Mitzi had been after me for days to get it mowed.

I knew Mrs. Vogel was spying on us between the living-room drapes—I saw them move—so I gave Colleen a long wet kiss, then kicked the BSA alive and peeled out of the Vogel driveway, marking it with a black stripe.

When I got home, Emile Stupka was there. He and Mitzi were having a fight. It was over Inez Watson, one of his old girlfriends who Mitzi believed still had some kind of hold on him. Mitzi was enraged. She slapped his face, but he only grinned. She slapped him again, and he laughed. Some people would have considered him dashing. It was obvious he was first among those who thought so. The more Mitzi slapped him, the more dashing and amused his smile became. He didn't duck or fight back. You had to give him credit for that. A trickle of blood ran down the cleft of his dashing chin.

I put on some old clothes and went out to mow the lumpy and weed-choked patch of ground that passed for our lawn. Crab-grass and dandelions, edged with ice plant. I got out the lawn mower and pushed it around for a while, not making much progress against the tangle. After a half hour of this, I took a cigarette break. I sat at the curb in the sparse shade of a young banana palm.

Nelson Glasspie, lunch pail in hand, came up the street from the bus stop on El Cajon Boulevard. He was at least an hour early.

"They sent us home," he said. "We had to watch a movie about Communist spies in the defense industry, and when I got back to my section the power was out."

"Sabotage?" I asked.

"Rats. They'd gotten to the insulation in a transformer. Shut down half the plant."

We both heard Mitzi screaming at Emile and Emile's answering bland chuckle.

"Well, I see you've started on the lawn, Oz," Nelson said, ignoring the outburst.

"We ought to dig it up," I said. "That crabgrass wraps around the mower like twine."

"You can't get rid of crabgrass, Oz. We'll just have to live with it."

The way he said that made me cut a quick glance at the house. He took off his jacket, laid it on a clump of ice plant. "Let me have a go at it." He rolled up his sleeves and leaned into the mower.

Emile came out of the house holding a washrag up to his eye. He was still laughing and smiling, but blood was now streaming down his face. Mitzi had hit him with something more than her hand. Probably a beer bottle. I could hear her vocal sobs coming from somewhere in the back of the house.

Emile shrugged when I looked at him. If he wanted some kind of sympathy, he was wasting his time. He even tried the same gesture on Nelson, who barely glanced at him.

"I fell down," Emile said. "It's nothing. Please, don't trouble yourselves."

As if we were.

Emile followed Nelson as Nelson pushed the balky mower through the tough lemon-yellow grass. "You need to water it more often," he said.

Nelson looked up but kept mowing.

Emile was a big, angular man with a square head and clever blue eyes that needled you into thinking he was one step ahead of the crowd. His heavy wrists were knobbed with bohunk bone. He was a boilermaker by trade, but worked only part of the year.

Nelson shrugged as he pushed. "If I watered it more, I'd have to mow it more."

Emile made a show of giving this some thought. "But look there—it is wild, and full of weeds. It is dying of thirst. A man should pay more attention to his lawn."

Nelson stopped mowing and looked straight at Emile. "It's only a lawn," he said, his thick glasses crooked on his nose and fogged with steam. Next to the huge and bloody Emile Stupka, pale Nelson Glasspie looked half real. "And incidentally, it's *my* lawn, not yours. Suppose you worry about your lawn, all right?" He picked up the mower handle and started pushing it again.

Emile chuckled, his dashing smile glistening red. He lifted the washrag and I saw the gash above his left eye. It went to the bone. He followed Nelson around the crisp lawn. It looked now like a chase—Nelson half trotting, Emile dogging his heels. "Still," Emile said, "it is the only lawn you have, is this not correct? You do not strike me as a man who possesses many lawns." He was practically talking into Nelson's shirt collar.

I'd heard enough. I went into my room and played a new record. Flip Phillips had just made an album with Charlie Parker with the Machito Afro-Cuban Band and I couldn't get enough of it. Backed by the clave beat, along with bongos and congas, the two incredible horns burned gaping holes all the way through the dismal shit that passed itself off as the world. You could almost make yourself believe there was a bright place beyond it. A place where musicians thrived and only the hip were allowed. If you couldn't dig bop, you were *out*, you were in nowheresville forever. I turned the volume up full blast.

Mitzi came in and turned it down. "Put your shoes on," she said, a wet cigarette dancing furiously between her lips. She looked scared. "Ozzie, you have to drive the car."

I followed her outside. Emile was sitting on the curb. The back of his shirt was sprinkled with fresh blood. "Shit, what happened now?" I said.

"Daddy hit him with the rake," she said.

At which point, Nelson hit Emile again, the rake bouncing off the big skull, making a musical twang.

"Stop it! Stop it!" Mitzi screamed.

Emile tilted to one side as blood from his head sprinkled the ice plant. Nelson dropped the rake and climbed into the Nash, locking the doors. A few neighbors stood around, at safe distances, watching our little drama.

"I don't want anything more to do with this, do you hear me?" Mitzi said this to me. She said it as if the whole thing had been my idea, from Emile coming over to eat pork chops and drink slivovitz and listen to bohunk music to Nelson's hitting him with the rake.

Emile, leaning precariously, still had his dashing smile in place. He was humming something, a bohunk tune of some kind, as if nothing concerned him. He looked up at me and winked, his eyes leaky and bloodshot. "Your pa gave me a hell of a good lick there!" he said. "You have to hand it to him!"

"Come on," I said. "I'll take you to the hospital."

I stood behind him and caught him under the arms. He was heavy. It was like trying to hoist a sack of cement, even though he'd gotten his legs under him. The metallic stink of blood made me a little queasy.

"Get out of there, Daddy!" Mitzi screamed. She pounded the window of the Nash, but Nelson paid no attention. I guess Nelson was hiding from Emile. He had no permanent violence in him, and was now afraid of what Emile might do. But Emile wasn't in any shape to go after Nelson. I leaned him against the car. His breath was spiced with slivovitz.

Mitzi opened the car door with her key and yanked on Nelson's shirt. Nelson looked up, annoyed, as if she were a stranger taking liberties. Then he got out and walked with exaggerated dignity into the house.

Mitzi and I got Emile into the car. He was still humming and grinning, as if he had been nothing more than an amused observer from the outset.

I got in and started the engine. "Take him straight to the La Mesa hospital," Mitzi said. "It's closest."

I pushed the gear lever into first and let out the clutch. The car lurched ahead and Emile put both hands on the dashboard. The neighbors on their lawns were frozen in their tracks. Our house was a sore spot in their eyes, the one blemish in an otherwise optimistic neighborhood.

By the time I got out on the boulevard, I realized I didn't know where the La Mesa hospital was. I told Emile this.

"To hell with it," he said. "Take me to North Park. I live in North Park. There is a much better hospital there. Eight-nine-two Pearl Harbor Street."

"Is that where the hospital is?"

"I don't need the hospital," he said.

"You have to go to the hospital. Your skull might be cracked."

"My skull is hard as stone," he said. "That is my plus, also it is my minus—a head made of rock." He tapped his forehead with a finger and grinned. "Anyway, at the hospital, they will want to know how this happened. If I tell them, your papa will be in bad trouble. I don't want to make trouble for your papa. He already has enough trouble. You know what I mean by this."

Emile lived in a narrow stucco house in a run-down neighborhood. All the houses here were small and the yards weren't big enough for lawns. His yard was a strip of bare dirt. A ragged old pepper tree gave flimsy shade to the front of the house.

I helped him inside. He put half his weight on my arm as we shuffled up the porch steps. A woman met us at the door. The abundance of blood widened her eyes. "What have you done to him?" she asked me.

She was a pale, lanky woman with exposed bony shoulders. She wore a peasant blouse and a festive Mexican skirt. Her feet were bare. She had shocking hair—pinkish orange. It stood out from her head in a bright rage. It looked like a huge tangle of fine copper wires, kinked and knotted. Her face might have been pretty if it wore a different expression. She looked like she was born pissed off at the world. Her shocked-looking topaz eyes were slightly misaligned. The right one tended to drift.

"He should go to the hospital," I said. Emile shuffled away from me and collapsed on a sofa.

The woman grabbed me by the shirt. "This from his assassin," she hissed.

I wanted to put my hands on her wrists to break her hold, but I didn't have the nerve to touch her.

"It wasn't him," Emile said from the sofa. "Get me a towel and leave him alone."

"Emile's bitch did it, didn't she?" the woman said, shoving me back but not letting go. "This is her brat, isn't it?"

I gripped her wrists and forced her arms down. She didn't let go of my shirt and some buttons flew across the room. Her hands, hooked into claws, came at my face. I ducked away, moved toward the door.

"*Adios,*" I said.

"Get me a towel," Emile said. "Let the boy alone."

The woman closed her eyes tight, gritted her teeth. She held her arms rigid against her sides, her fists clenched, as if fighting back some volatile chemical reaction in her body.

I didn't wait around for the explosion. I went out and got into the Nash. I sat there, my heart hammering. Then she came out of the house. I shoved the key into the ignition. She approached the car and leaned into the open window as the starter motor labored stupidly. She opened the door and climbed in.

"You don't know what I'm up against," she said. The battery was losing cranking power. I shut off the ignition. I smelled raw gas.

"None of my damn business," I said.

"I would prefer it if you did not take that tone with me," she said.

"And I would prefer it if you got the hell out of my car," I said.

She reached for me again and I ducked, banging my head against the doorpost. This made her smile. She tried it again and this time I didn't duck. She caught my ear and gave it a little twist. "I'm sorry," she said. "Of course none of this has anything to do with you. It's Emile's fault, and it's my fault, and it's your mother's fault. You're just a kid, but listen, *kid*, someday it will be your fault, too." Her eyes stabilized for a moment and she winked. "You don't believe that, do you?" she said.

"Believe what?" I said.

She shook her head and laughed bitterly at some private joke.

"Stupka should go to the hospital," I said.

"Fuck Stupka," she said. "I hope the asshole *dies*. Maybe

he'd wise up then. That's the only way you can make a thick-headed son of a bitch like him learn anything. You've got to kill them first. Then maybe you've got a chance.''

Emile came out and sat on his front porch. He held a towel to the back of his head with one hand and a cigarette in the other. His eye was closed and crusted over with blood, but he grinned at us—a dashing bohunk warrior home from curious battle.

I pressed the starter button again. This time the worn-out six started. "I've got to go," I said.

"Take me to the Rexall drugstore first, will you?" she said. "I need to get some gauze and Merthiolate."

There was a Rexall on University Avenue, a short drive from the house. I drove her there and waited while she went in. She came out with a pint of gin and a fifth of slivovitz. No gauze, no Merthiolate. She uncapped the gin.

"I hate slivovitz," she said, taking full swallows of the gin.

She offered the bottle to me. I declined.

"I normally don't take a drink before the sun gets under the telephone wires," she said. "But as you probably already figured out, I've got a long night ahead of me. Turn on the radio, will you?"

I started the car and turned on one of the local stations. They were playing a Russ Morgan number.

"God, I love this song," she said.

It was "So Tired," a melancholy fox-trot that wasn't half bad. *So tired of waiting for you, so tired of dreaming of you, but though I'm tired, I'll wait forever, dear.* She offered me the gin again and this time I took it. It was a cheap brand, Oso Negro, distilled and bottled in Mexico. "Ginebra," the label said. A black bear with mean red eyes peered out of the label.

She took the bottle back and held it to her lips. When I started counting, I got to six. "Watch out for me, kiddo," she said. "I get ripped real fast on this stuff."

She winked her traveling eye, squeezed my hand. I slipped the Nash into gear and headed down the street. By the time we got back to Emile, she was singing the Russ Morgan song and weeping.

I took the long way home, through Balboa Park, with all the windows open, listening to the radio. The radio in the Nash wasn't strong enough to pick up the L.A. rhythm-and-blues stations, so I had to listen to the local deejays, who played music that wouldn't offend the retired admirals who lived in rows of mansions out on Point Loma and in Coronado and other posh neighborhoods. Now and then the local deejays would go out on a limb and play an Earl Bostick number—usually "Flamingo" or "Ebb Tide"—and that was tolerable, but never enough. I wanted the destructive sax of Ventura, or the very talky but just as interesting horn of Jimmy Guiffre. The sax was meant to shake you up, not mellow you out. It was an outlaw instrument, not a good-citizen instrument. Everyone under the age of twenty with pubic hair knew that.

I drove up into Mission Hills and stopped. I pulled out the antenna all the way and managed to pick up Los Angeles, a hundred miles north. I dug Lloyd Price out of the static. It was "Lawdie Miss Claudie."

The slow blues walked into my head. The weep-and-shout style of Lloyd Price got to me. I turned up the volume one notch short of ripping the speaker. Still feeling the heat of Oso Negro, I yelled along with Lloyd.

We are in the Mojave Desert, just south of Death Valley, and I am driving. The Packard is running like a Swiss watch and I tie this to the fact that Wes Caulkins is no longer with us. Maybe it was his presence that made the straight six falter. Maybe he was like that character in "Li'l Abner" who was followed by a black cloud no matter where he went. Maybe we've shaken the cloud of bad luck and unneeded grief. Maybe we've outrun it at last.

Mitzi is dozing and I have my window down and the radio turned up. The Packard seems to be sucking the highway into it, like a vacuum cleaner. The radio station is in Barstow, California, and they are playing a Bob Wills record.

> I hear you knockin
> but you cant come in
> I hear you knockin
> but you cant come in

It's a jumpy tune and it has me stomping on the gas pedal. The gas is flowing steadily into the carburetor now, no more vapor locks, and the Packard's engine is throbbing with willing power. The speedometer is dancing on seventy. The song makes me feel good in a way I can't remember ever feeling. I'm flying high. Mitzi sometimes says that when she's feeling good about something.

Kinda busy so you cant come in
Kinda busy so you cant come in
I guess you better let me be

It's an hour past sundown and the sky is as purple as the mountains ahead of us. Somewhere on the other side of those mountains is home. A place Mitzi has promised we would never move from. A place by the ocean, where palm trees sway and clatter in the warm breeze. I can almost picture our new home, a white frame house with a red tile roof. Maybe it's on a cliff overlooking the blue Pacific, or maybe it's down on the white sand beach and you can hear the steady thump and hiss of the waves as they roll right up to your door.

I know you been drinking gin
running round with other men
I hear you knockin but you cant come in
I guess you better let me be

A strange moan in the background behind the singer makes my skin tingle, a second voice running alongside the vocal but undercutting it too, as if it has so much more to say than the singer can put into words. It is a voice without words, full and generous and sympathetic. Years later I will identify that tenor sax, but my opinion of what it could do wouldn't change.

Shake my doorknob but you cant come in
Shake my doorknob but you cant come in
I guess you better let me be

*The speedometer touches eighty and Mitzi wakes up
yelling at me. Are you crazy, Ozzie? Have you lost your
mind? Slow this thing down!*

*The wheel is vibrating in my hands as if the front tires
are trying to come off their rims. The engine is howling.
Puffs of steam shoot up from under the hood and the
temperature gauge reads 212, the needle in the red zone.*

*Goddammit, Ozzie, stop this car! Stop this goddam car
right now! You're going to wreck it! We still have a
hundred miles to go! Are you crazy?*

*Am I crazy? If I am, then crazy feels good. Speed feels
good. Music feels good. It is as though I have found the one
worthwhile thing in my life. But the engine is steaming, and
now, as I slow down, I can hear a chorus of doubts
whistling and grumbling through the firewall.*

8

Max Tbolt roared doggerel through the warehouse while the overhead crane lowered an H-beam for me and my partner to stack. I would take one end of the beam, clumsy Bernard Issel the other.

"Watch those fingers—watch that thumb—that's a ton of steel, boys—don't be dumb!" Tbolt bellowed.

Max was the foreman, a clown with a genius IQ. He was big and soft-looking but he had small feet and was agile as a dancer. Even though he was big, his bald head seemed *too* big. You could spot the shiny, brain-packed dome across the parking lot reflecting sky, or in the warehouse glowing white-blue from the overhead arc lamps. He had a degree from State College, and was working on his master's at night.

Max was in love with Elizabeth Urquiza, the secretary. But then, everybody was "in love" with the beautiful Elizabeth, even buck-toothed Bernard Issel, my stacking partner. The only trouble was that Elizabeth was married to the company senior vice president in charge of sales, Norbert Urquiza.

Max dreamed big, but it was only dreaming. He recited, in gravelly, singsong, blues-style rhymes, what he and Elizabeth would do for each other in bed—when Elizabeth wasn't within earshot, of course.

> Take your hand, baby, put it right down there
> Take your hand, baby, put it right down there
> When you do me like that, baby,
> I love it more than one man can bear.

After reciting, he'd do a snappy little dance step, then undulate his big stomach in a clown's parody of sex. He'd roll up the whites of his eyes as if sick with lust. Max was pretty safe, since Norbert Urquiza was never around. Norbert had an office in the building, but he spent almost all his time entertaining big-money customers—the shipbuilders, the defense plant managers, the Navy admirals in charge of procurement.

After stacking H-beams, I-beams, sheet steel, and sheet aluminum all morning with Bernard Issel, I'd spend the afternoons alone in the Bins, cleaning chain, stove bolts, shoulder bolts, U-bolts, hooks and swivels and pulleys, and whatever else needed treatment. Iron rusted quickly in the damp seaside air. So I had to rub the stock down with some foul-smelling acid-based goo that removed and prevented rust. Sometimes Elizabeth herself would come back to the Bins to check on an item for a customer.

I was in love with Elizabeth too. It was impossible not to be. If you were breathing and even marginally male you had no choice. She wore thigh-hugging sheath skirts with long splits, low-cut blouses, and velvet pumps with spiked heels. She smelled like a garden full of flowers. A few years earlier she'd placed second in a Miss San Diego contest, and everyone knew she'd been robbed by a judge who was related to the winner.

When she'd come back to the Bins, an explosive rush of hormones left me tongue-tied and unbalanced. We were together and alone in dark seclusion. Reaching out and touching her seemed completely reasonable, but I had to pretend that rubbing goo on rusty chain was more interesting to me. She was friendly and totally indifferent to the effect she had on men, even though a single careless glance from her welcoming brown eyes would haunt your waking dreams for days.

"Gee, how can you work in this dark stinky place, Ozzie?" she once said, nearly stopping my heart. "I can barely see you, hon."

That was probably a good thing. I was a slack-jawed idiot sucking drool.

"You get used to it, Liz," I mumbled, outwardly stoic but spasming with checked impulse.

Ducrouler Finished Metal Products was a good place to work. I saw the job in the want ads of the *San Diego Union* and got it. Everyone here was on a first-name basis, and Elizabeth, even though she was only in her mid-twenties, took a maternal attitude toward the hired hands. Her husband, Norbert, had been a linebacker for the Cleveland Rams before the franchise moved to

L.A. He had a smashed nose, boxer's scars in his eyebrows. With his padded-shoulder suit jacket on he had to turn sideways to pass through ordinary doors. He had a reputation as a brawler, someone who loved a good fight now and then just to clear the sludge out of his veins. Anyone who got fresh with Elizabeth would have to have a suicidal streak in him.

After she came in second in the Miss San Diego contest, Elizabeth worked at the Hollywood Theater, a burlesque house downtown, using the stage name Eloise Deer. In masturbatory dreams I thought of her as Eloise—in sequined G-string with tassels twirling on her breasts. She was tall, with steep curves, and her black hair was pulled back into a silky French braid. She stirred men down to the disorderly roots of their ordered lives. Even the old dry-as-dust accountants who punched numbers into their ratcheting calculators all day long would look up from their labors when she swayed past their desks. They would sigh inaudibly, their faces pinched into wistful smiles.

Bernard and I stacked a few dozen H-beams and about a hundred flats of sheet aluminum onto double-decked pallets, then took our first break. Max and I carried our coffee out into the yard and sat on spools of copper wire. Bernard usually took his break with us, but he'd cut himself on the last flat of aluminum and had gone home for the day. When the crane operator dropped the flat onto the stack, Bernard hadn't stepped back fast enough and a corner of the sheet aluminum had sliced through his Levi's from mid-thigh to knee, drawing blood. It wasn't serious, but it was more than a scratch. Issel tended to be accident-prone. Max wanted to fire him for his own sake, but Issel had a wife and three kids. "The guy should be selling slippers to old ladies," Max said. "Although he'd probably get a toe in his eye and go blind."

I liked Max. He was a jazz fan too but was far more knowledgeable about it than I was. His appreciation of it was intellectual, where mine was purely emotional. He lived with his crippled mother in an apartment house a few blocks from Ducrouler's.

I went over there after work for a beer and to listen to his records. He had records that went back to the origins of jazz—old 78s that had been mechanically recorded—King Oliver, Blind Lemon Jefferson, Freddy Keppard and the Original Creoles, Luckey Roberts, Willie "The Lion" Smith, James P. Johnson— names I'd never heard of. We'd listen to a few bars of a song, and then he'd pick up the tone arm to tell me something about what I'd just heard. "You hip to that sound, man?" he said. "That blue tone is from Dahomey in West Africa. You dig the blue note, man, the flatted fifth? Pure *vodun*—voodoo to you. That old East Coast cat, Rudy Vallee, blew it twenty years ago by *accident* on his tenor and the college kids went crazy. You know what Vallee said? This fractures me—he said, 'I have played a certain note barbaric in quality upon my saxophone and observed the livening up of young legs and feet.' Doesn't that just break you *up*, man?" When Max finally saw my blank look, he said, "Okay, so it was before your time. But listen, they should be teaching kids this stuff in school. You can't know squat about this country unless you are hip to its original music, 'cause that's its wild-ass *soul.*"

Max was about thirty-five years old and had been in the Navy during the war. His ship, a freighter, had been torpedoed and he'd floated for a month in a life raft before he was rescued. He said jazz helped him survive. He and a couple of others on the raft improvised a little jazz band, making instruments out of empty water cans and wires from a dead emergency radio. "The Rubber Boat Blues Band," they called themselves.

He'd been married but it lasted only a year. "She wanted a Home and Garden type of life, man," he said. "All I wanted was music and a free mind."

When I told him I was probably going to get married, he shook his head sadly. "You don't know what you're buying into, Oz," he said. "And the worst part is that you won't know what you've bought into even after you've paid the bill."

"I think I'm in love," I said.

His jaw dropped and he roared. Usually his rich, deep-lunged laugh was infectious, but now it only pissed me off. His bald dome got red and tears streamed down his cheeks. "Sorry, man," he said when he calmed down. "It's just the expression on your face when you said that. Like you just remembered you couldn't eat chile peppers after ordering a plateful of green tamales. You're too young to get domesticated, laddybuck. So am I. Long may we wave."

Colleen had been pressing me to set a date for our marriage. When I took the job at Ducrouler's she was disappointed. I told her I didn't want to get married dead broke. She said I could go to work for her father right away. Why work as a stock boy in a dumb warehouse down in National City when I could be learning a real trade? A shrug wasn't the best of answers, but that's all I had to offer.

"So, you're going to put your young butt into harness," Max said.

"That's one way of looking at it, Max," I said, finishing my beer.

"Hey, don't go away mad, kid," he said.

"What's so terrible about marriage?" I said. I had my own ideas about that, but wanted the benefit of his experience.

He shrugged, not looking for a debate. He opened another beer for me. "It's like this, man. It'll be great for a while. Then, not so great. I mean, you'll suddenly be getting a lot of sexual *intercourse* but practically no fucking, if you get what I mean. It's just like everything else, Oz. After a while the shine comes off."

"Tell me something I don't know, man," I said. I could act sophisticated, too.

He put on a new record, a recent Kid Ory release. He had a great hi-fi system—Swedish turntable with balancing weights on the tone arm, and a mahogany loudspeaker cabinet big as a refrigerator. The walls of the apartment shook, and his mother, a small white-haired woman with rheumy eyes and the telltale herky-jerky of Parkinson's disease, came wobbling out of her bedroom knocking the floor in enfeebled fury with a thick black cane. "Where is my *supper*, Maximilian?" she screeched. Max turned down the volume and steered his mother back into her bedroom. He went into the kitchen and started rummaging through the pots and pans.

He took some ground beef from the fridge and shaped it into hamburger steaks. He melted Crisco in a skillet and when it got hot, he laid the meat in. He peeled a few potatoes and ran them through a dicer to make hash browns. Then he put a pan of water on the stove and when it boiled he dumped in a can of peas. He filled a teakettle from the tap and set it on a burner. Then he set the table for two.

"There are *all* kinds of harness," I said, with too much significance.

He ignored the remark as he washed lettuce and tomatoes for salad.

"See you tomorrow, Max," I said, heading for the door.

He waved his spatula, sipped his beer.

Bernard Issel lost his thumb while watching Elizabeth Urquiza climb the stairs from the warehouse to the dais where the business offices were. We were stacking H-beams and he glanced up just as the crane operator turned the grapple loose. Bernard had his thumb between the beams and it was guillotined neatly, glove and all. I studied Elizabeth too but had waited until the crane operator had dropped the beam. Her fine Hollywood Theater haunches rocked hypnotically as she climbed the stairs. The split in her tight skirt parted and closed with each step, yielding snapshot glimpses of the back of a knee or the beginning of a thigh. Bernard's lengthy, high-pitched scream broke the spell.

I reset the grapple and the crane operator hoisted the beam a dozen feet, but Bernard's severed thumb had dropped between the cracks of the stack. All the beams had to be picked up and temporarily restacked elsewhere. It took time. While we—Max, Elizabeth, the forklift operator, and I—hunted for the lost thumb, Bernard sat leaning against a wall of the warehouse, in shock and blubbering, his buckteeth hanging out in a terrible white grimace.

Max found it—still in the ripped-off thumb of Bernard's glove—and drove Bernard to the hospital, his severed thumb packed in ice. Some fussy guy in a suit came out of an office and told us to restack the H-beams, but I'd had it for the day. My lunch was in my throat. The time clock was next to Elizabeth's desk. I punched out.

"Did you get permission to leave, Ozzie?" she said.

"I think I'm sick," I said.

"I'll tell Mr. Merrick," she said. "I don't feel so great either."

I leaned on her desk with both hands, suddenly woozy. She put her hand on mine, squeezed. "I'll clear it for you, hon," she said. Her warm breath touched my face and the sweet perfumes rising from her cleavage went straight to my brain.

I went into the bathroom and sat down in a stall. I had my inhaler with me. I sniffed Benzedrine for a while. But that only intensified my problem. I had to have immediate relief before I did something stupid and unretractable. I unbuttoned my Levi's. I closed my eyes and saw her onstage, tassels spinning, my name on her lips. Where have you been all my life, Ozzie? Don't you know how much I need you, don't you know how much I care? I've got the fever, Ozzie, the fever.

Happiness was a good strong thumb. She reached behind her back and untied her G-string. Come to me, baby, come to me, baby.

I'm coming, I'm coming.

9

I took Colleen to a Big Jay McNeeley concert in Logan Heights, the black section of town. She didn't want to go. "People like us aren't supposed to go over there," she said.

"People like *who*?" I said. I guess she had a stronger sense of who she was than I did of who I was.

"Don't be a smarty-pants," she said. "You know exactly what I mean."

I would have gone without her if she refused. I wasn't about to miss a Big Jay performance. She gave in, but only if I promised that we'd leave early.

The concert was held in a school gym just off Imperial Avenue, not far from Ducrouler's. Houses in this neighborhood were small and huddled together. About five hundred people showed up, mostly black. At least a dozen uniformed cops were there. But Colleen couldn't get the fright off her face. Her eyes were big and she hung on my arm. I could feel quick shudders travel through her body.

"Come on, Colleen," I whispered. "These people are just out to have a good time. They're not interested in us."

"I feel like Snow White in Africa," she said. She'd tried to whisper, but the small fearful convulsions of her body made her blurt it out loud. "I feel kind of *surrounded*."

Several people looked at her, then at me.

"You're going to get us *both* surrounded if you don't shut your mouth," I said.

But the people looking at us seemed more amused than pissed off.

"How can you talk to me that way?" she said.

It was a good question. I'd surprised myself too. "I'm sorry, Colleen," I said.

"Sometimes I think I don't know you, Ozzie," she said. Tears welled in her eyes but did not fall.

"Join the club," I said.

She started to say something else, but Big Jay's bass sax man rolled his huge instrument out onto the stage and the crowd screamed in delight. The bass sax actually had wheels attached to it. They billed it as "the biggest reed in the world." The brass tower was a head taller than the little musician who had to play it. It didn't seem possible. How could he reach the keys? Then Big Jay himself came on and the roar increased. The drummer and the bass fiddle player were already onstage, laying down a rhythm, along with the piano, that the sax men would jump into any second, and the crowd clapped along with the beat.

The band started with its theme song, "The Big Jay Shuffle," a slow number that began with the two saxes blowing a harmonious duet that eventually broke up into unspectacular solos. It was like bait, pulling you in, aggravating in its unhurried so-what tone. The bass horn added to this indifference with fatigued blasts that seemed to sink of their own weight. Big Jay on tenor answered the drugged call of the bass with a slightly more energetic pursuit of the melody. Then they harmonized again, back where they started, and blew the long final note. It was short and sweet, and the crowd cheered because they knew it was just the band's way of saying "Hello, everybody, glad you came," Texas-style—slow and loose, but definitely not cool or mellow. This band was white-hot and frantic, never mellow, never cool.

Then things got crazy. They started off with "Texas Turkey," a honk-and-screech number played at lightning speed. It had been billed as a concert, but it was really a dance. Most of the white kids came to hear the music. They crowded up to the stage, getting close to the fire.

Big Jay pulled off his jacket and got on his back, honking and moaning, the sax becoming his true voice—the voice that stripped off veneer, exposed lies, cremated fraud. The sax told the story of the man. Only his shoulders and feet touched the floor, his back arching with each detonation of sound, and the white girls went wild. Some climbed onto the stage and kissed the bell of the sax, others looked like they'd gone into convulsions. Meanwhile, the blacks danced. Shimmying, spinning, jumping, twisting—dancing that made every bone in the body work. No white couple dared to compete. But then Colleen surprised me.

"Let's dance," she said.

"I don't think so," I said.

"We can do that," she said.

"Colleen, I couldn't do that in my dreams." Her eyes looked a little glazed and her upper lip was beaded with sweat.

I watched a short muscular man limbo between the legs of a tall woman. He scooted along, his back dropping low, until he was under her. A crowd gathered around, clapping fast and shouting. The woman tossed her head back and laughed as the man limboed through her pulled-up skirts.

"You take me to a dance and you won't dance," Colleen said.

"We came for the *music*, Colleen," I said.

I put my arm around her, but she broke away from me. She made her way to the stage. The bass fiddle player was spinning out of control. He staggered and fell into the piano. It became part of the performance—control was not a virtue here—and the band played on. He righted himself, his expression unchanged, and slapped his strings. Colleen pushed herself against the stage, along with the other white girls. Spasms of music rocked her bones, and she was screaming along with everyone else, hair flying. I lit a cigarette. A cop strolled up to me and told me to put it out or take it outside. I put it out. His face was stone against the voodoo of the music.

Later, on the way home, I said, "So, did you have a good time?"

"It was all right," she said.

"You got kind of wild," I suggested.

"I did *not*. I was just enjoying myself, since you wouldn't dance. Did *you* have a good time?"

"Sure," I said.

"Just standing there like a stick?"

"I went to hear the music," I said.

"It was a *dance*."

"Can't dance," I said lamely.

The streets were dark and empty. I pushed the little MG hard, taking corners without braking, shifting gears with vengeance.

"If you can't dance why didn't you just say so?" she said.

"Well, I can't dance," I said. "Not like that, anyway."

"I *told* you we didn't belong there, Ozzie."

I guess I had been testing her, by taking her to the McNeeley concert, and she had turned the tables on me. But I didn't see it that way at the time. I was just mad at her, and she was mad at me. I headed for the funeral home, not bothering to stop at Oscar's for our usual cheeseburgers and shakes.

She mellowed in the driveway while the MG's overworked engine cooled. "What's the matter, honey?" she said.

I shrugged. We kissed. Tepid. Sparing use of tongues. "Don't know," I said, coming up early for air.

"You're so moody."

"I guess."

"Don't be. I want us to be happy all the time. Is that too much to ask?"

I looked at her. She was serious. She was also beautiful. A sensible American beauty under the crisp streetlights. I touched her breasts under her sweater. She gave this to me now, an earned right. Just as she had a right to happiness.

"You think I'm being silly," she said.

"No."

We kissed again, longer, harder, testing our endurance.

"We will be," she gasped. "I promise."

"Will be what?"

"Happy, darling. Happy all the time."

It was just eleven o'clock, so I rode my bike to Art's house. All the lights were on. When I shut off the BSA's engine I heard the commotion. Voices, guitars, mandolins, a clarinet, an accordion—not making music, but winding down, as if they had just finished playing some energetic piece. A drab Chevy with a whip antenna attached to its bumper was parked across the street. The man slouched behind the wheel sipped from a thermos cup. He was wearing a hat. FBI. Benedetto and his Communist friends were having a "meeting," it seemed, and the Feds were keeping tabs on it.

The front door was open. I went in. Art and his girlfriend, Denise Linstead, were sitting on the couch watching wrestling on TV from the Olympic auditorium in L.A. Sandor Szabo against Gino Garibaldi.

"What's happening, gang?" I said.

"Usual shit," Art said. He was wearing a T-shirt with the sleeves rolled up. His veined biceps twitched nervously as the wrestlers grappled for advantage.

"We've set the date," Denise said. She grabbed Art's arm to

stop the twitch. Denise was pretty—fine-boned, almost fragile.
She'd done her wavy blond hair in fat corkscrew curls. The effect
was wrong—it made her seem top-heavy. Her long, thin neck now
had too much weight to bear. She usually wore her hair in a page-
boy, which seemed proper.

"Congratulations," I said.

"August sixth," Denise said.

"The famous day," I said.

Denise looked at me, suspecting a joke. "I don't get it," she
said. "What's so famous about it?"

"Hiroshima," I said. "They dropped the bomb on Hiroshima,
August sixth, 1945."

Denise studied me for a few moments. "Are you serious? Then
we'll have to move it up a week. What do you think, honey?"

Art stood up, flexed. "Hey, I'm not a Communist. The Communists are out in the backyard, having a blast. August sixth is
fine by me. We should of blown up Russia, August seventh."

As if responding to Art, the musicians in the backyard struck
up a furious Italian tune, a pungent folk dance. You could almost
smell the spices. I went to the kitchen window and peeked outside. Men in their shirt sleeves sat in a circle on folding chairs.
Mrs. di Coca hovered nearby. Jars of wine teetered on a card
table as the men stomped the deck in time to the manic tarantella.

"Let's go downstairs," Art said. "Too much noise up here."

We went down into the basement. Benedetto made wine every
fall and kept it in barrels. Art found three mason jars. He blew
the dust out of them, then filled each one halfway from a spigoted
barrel with the almost black dago red. We sat on a couple of army

cots that had been pushed up against two walls and sipped our wine. This was a true wine cellar, lit by a single bulb hanging from the ceiling. The walls were solid concrete, but even so, we could still hear faint music and the echoing stomp of leather heels on wood.

"Shit, man," Art said, glancing up. "That scene is going to track me through life."

"He's worried," Denise said, "about Convair turning him down."

"But your old man's scene isn't your scene, man," I said.

"There's an old saying," Art said. "About the sins of the father coming back to shaft the son."

We sat there on the army cots thinking about this.

"But this is America, Art," I offered.

"No shit," he said.

The summer I worked for Benedetto, he brought lunch for both of us every day. He couldn't stand to see me eat peanut butter and jelly sandwiches. "That junk rot you guts," he said. "You work for me, you *eat.*" So we ate sausages and hard sourdough bread and cups of hot *zuppa*—*zuppa* with vegetables, *zuppa* with prosciutto, *zuppa* with ravioli. And always, a jar of black dago red. I gained ten pounds that summer, none of it fat.

The neighbors both loved and resented Benedetto. When the trucks rolled in every September loaded with dark Concords from up north, they resented him. The yard would reek of crushed grapes, and swarms of bees and wasps hectored the neighborhood for days. Benedetto had built his own winepress, and he worked efficiently. And when a batch was ready he gave

away gallons of the stuff to his neighbors, as a kind of atonement.
He also did a lot of work for them, gratis—repairing stone walls,
patching driveways and chimneys, putting in brick or flagstone
planter boxes, giving masonry advice. He was tireless and good-
hearted, and this outweighed whatever nuisances he created.
Once in a while, though, someone could call the cops when Benedetto and his Communist friends got drunk and played Italian
music into the wee hours. Sometimes they'd go until one or
two a.m.

Benedetto wasn't a theoretical Communist—he practiced what
he preached, though he never exactly preached. He would curse
the priests and the Fascists now and then, but that was the extent
of his political talk. The cots we sat on in the wine cellar were for
Mexicans, *mojados*, that he would house, in violation of the im-
migration laws. He would house and feed them for days, and Mrs.
di Coca would find decent used clothes for them. Then Benedetto
found them jobs on outlying farms or in small businesses around
town that weren't so law-abiding that they would turn down
cheap, dependable labor.

"So, what about you and Colleen?" Denise said. "Are you getting married or what?"

I shrugged.

"He wants to go to Korea," Art said. "He likes the idea of
crawling around in the mud with a great big gun."

"Getting married won't exempt you," I said.

"Getting married and having a baby *will*," Art said.

I looked at Denise. She turned red and grinned. Art patted her
belly.

"Come *down*, man!" I said. "You're putting me on!"

"Being a daddy *and* working for Convair will guarantee a deferment," Art said.

"And it's what we *want*, Ozzie," Denise said. "And I know it's what Colleen wants. I mean, what's so terrible about it, anyway? The sooner you get started the better."

"Get started?" I said. I knew what she meant, but put in those terms turned it into a mystery. I felt like an outsider, missing some privileged information. Everything suddenly seemed more than strange, strange beyond belief. I felt my scalp tighten, my hair get stiff. I didn't know who these people were—did not understand them.

"He's playing dumb," Art said. "Which in his case doesn't take a lot of work."

"Thanks, buddy," I said.

They started making out. I finished my wine and left.

It didn't make any sense at all to me when Norbert Urquiza left Elizabeth for another woman. He also left Ducrouler for another job—in Pittsburgh! San Diego was God's country, everyone knew that, and his choosing to live in the smoke and soot and cold of Pittsburgh when he could just as easily live in San Diego made no sense either.

I connected the other woman and the city of Pittsburgh: Compared to Elizabeth she must have looked like Pittsburgh, or worse. Norbert obviously had lost any good sense he might have once had. Maybe too many knocks on the head backing the line of the Cleveland Rams had bruised the brain cells responsible for making commonsense choices.

Not that I cared. I was overjoyed. So was everyone else in the warehouse, especially Max Tbolt. He was promoted from fore-man to assistant manager of sales. Not as high a rank as Norbert had, but definitely front-office. We no longer heard his crude doggerel echoing around the stacks of steel and aluminum. He came to work wearing a suit and tie, and, I swear, a *corset.* Where else did his belly go?

He was flat as a board. Tight. In his shoulder-padded suit he looked formidable. From his small feet to his big head he was a human V. The effect was comical to me, but I could see that to others he must have looked imposing. This was all for Elizabeth, of course, though he knew better than to press her too hard while she was grieving over Norbert's betrayal and desertion. Around her, he was like a sympathetic uncle, but the top of his big head gave him away: It lit up in rosy incandescence.

"He's making a fool out of himself," I said to Bernard Issel, who had returned to work. The doctor had stitched his thumb back on. It was heavily bandaged, with metal splints over the gauze. He had cut the right thumb out of his new glove so that he could pull it on, over the bandage and splints.

"Who is?" Issel asked.

I nodded toward the dais. Max was leaning importantly on Elizabeth's desk, showing her a clipboard full of memos. He was tight-lipped, all business; no hint of his true intentions leaked through his frown. Elizabeth was frowning, too, as she tried to follow whatever made-up nonsense Max was pretending to explain.

"I don't get you," Issel said.

"Shit, use your eyes, man. Max is trying to nail Elizabeth, fat old Max in his hundred-dollar suit and Sears and Roebuck corset. It'd be funny if it wasn't so pathetic."

We guided the last H-beam into place, then took our break.
"You sure you're not just jealous?" Issel said, knowingly. His
lips slid up his protruding teeth in a sticky smile.

"Me? Jealous? Hell, I'm just about engaged, Bernard."

"That doesn't mean shit. *I'm* jealous, and I've been married
for ten years. Hell, Oz, I've got three kids, but I still think a lot
about Liz's fine knockers. Even when I'm throwing the bone to
the old lady I see those rose-tipped headlights. Hey, *especially*
when I'm throwing her the bone." He laughed, a hee-haw
horselaugh, all teeth and slobber.

I didn't like Bernard talking about Elizabeth like that. Who
did he think he was, imagining her breasts while screwing his own
wife?

"You're a creep, Issel," I said.

"And you're the fool, if you want my honest opinion," he said.
"Not Max. At least Max knows what he's doing."

"What's that supposed to mean?"

"I mean what I mean. Max is cool. Max is in control."

"And I'm not?"

"You'd go down on her during the Second Coming if she gave
you half a chance."

"You're disgusting, Issel."

"And you're a sweet, All-American kid, right?"

I tried to grow a mustache. After a week of not shaving a smudge
of stubble shadowed my upper lip. Every morning before leaving
for work, I splashed some of Nelson's bay rum on my face. And
when I punched in at work, I lingered at Elizabeth's desk for a

minute or two, trying to make small talk, hoping that she would see a more grown-up version of me.

But she didn't seem to see me at all. She was subdued, less outgoing. Norbert's desertion had demoralized her. Where once she had been perky and cheerful, she was now lost in gloom. A disheartened pout pulled the corners of her full lips down. Her eyes had darkened, and the invisible weight of sadness made her shoulders slump. These were the telltale signs of her new vulnerability. It made her even more beautiful to me. The tragic side of her personality was now exposed. As Eloise Deer, the stripper whose bump-and-grind gave a rhythm to my masturbatory daydreams, there was a shallow quality to her beauty. Now her beauty was crossed with suffering. I wanted to hold her in my mending arms, I wanted to absorb her tears, I wanted her to tell me over and over how life had become meaningless for her, and I wanted to tell her how I could make it become meaningful again.

I love you, Liz, I said.

Oh God, Oz, I'm not worth it.

Don't say that, darling.

You're sweet, hon.

Variations of this conversation played themselves in my brain on my way to work every morning, but when I arrived, all I could actually say to her was, "Hi there, Liz, how's it going?"

"It's going," she'd say, not looking up at me.

I'd take my time punching in, but I had nothing more to say. My mind was a cheerless blank divot in my thick skull. I needed Max's clipboard and fake importance. All I had was love without props.

I love you, Liz, I said.

Oh God, I'm not worth it.

Don't you ever say that, darling. It makes me angry. (Maybe a sterner approach was called for.)

What about your fiancée, Colleen? (Jealousy? Did I see a flash of jealousy ignite those dark dark eyes?)

I dropped the BSA into second and roared past an old couple driving a Hudson.

Cat got your tongue, lover boy? she said.

Sometimes these road conversations got out of hand.

But this is different, isn't it, Liz? Can't there be two kinds of love?

Maybe you think you know what you're talking about, hon, but I doubt it.

"Bebop, it's only as good as the musicians who play it," Max said. We were in his apartment drinking beer and listening to records. I had brought my Charlie Ventura record, but he wouldn't let me put it on. "Ventura is all right, but he's more showman than musician."

"Both *Metronome* and *Downbeat* said his was the best bebop band of the year," I said.

"Like I said, Oz. Show biz."

"I think he's great. And his baritone sax man, Boots Mussilli, he's fantastic."

"Well, you gotta like what you gotta like," Max said, pouring himself another beer.

"Play it, you'll see."

"In a minute. I want you to hear this one first." He put on another one of his ancient platters, some soprano sax with enough vibrato to curdle milk.

"Ventura's fine, man," he said, seeing that I was getting pissed off. "He's gutsy, in a way. It's just that he's *unsubtle*, if you get what I mean."

"But this guy you're playing is *subtle*?"

"This guy recorded thirty years ago, Oz. Things have changed a bit."

"How about Big Jay McNeeley?" I said. "You like him?"

"Oh, *please*, Oz, give me a break. That's not music, that's teenage junk. Subtlety is a disease to those guys."

We stopped talking. We sat and drank and listened to rare recordings. His uncorseted gut spilled out over his belt. Eventually, his mother came out of her bedroom pounding the floor for food.

"Stay and eat with us, Oz," Max said.

I was drunk enough to say yes.

Max fixed pork chops and fried potatoes and boiled carrots. His mother was too crippled up to feed herself. He cut her meat and potatoes and carrots into tiny cubes and fed them to her. She stared at each morsel doubtfully before accepting it. Her old jaws worked slowly, as if each chew would be her last. Max wiped her chin when she drooled, gave her sips of water when she turned her nodding head toward her water glass, helped her burp when she screwed up her face in gastric distress. When she finished, Max walked her back to her room, listening sympathetically to her garbled complaints. Then he sat down to eat his cold dinner.

I was on my fourth beer. Sentiment clogged my throat. Max

was a good person, a fine person, a self-sacrificing hero. I wanted to say so. He sat down and started to eat. He'd put a Miles Davis record on. I didn't understand Miles Davis. He was too cool for my tastes. He was beyond cool. He was ice. I lost track of the sentiment that made me want to compliment Max.

"Now, *this* is a musician," Max said, chewing vigorously. "Listen to those delicate modulations, those cleverly retooled riffs."

I listened. But I didn't know what I was listening to.

"You're looking for melody, the usual harmonies, right?" he said. "But you've got to find another framework, Oz. Melody, for these guys, is what *was.*"

He smiled. I guess I looked puzzled.

"Times change, Oz. You've got to make the jumps, or you'll be left whistling 'Dixie.' "

"Some things don't change," I said. I wasn't thinking about music. He seemed to sense this.

"People, you mean."

"Men, women."

"Hormones, Mister In-Between, the mating dance, stand up and shout for the old in and out—that sort of thing?"

"Right, and a lot more."

"No argument there, Oz. But we're talking about the mind, the intellect, the way you sort out what all the other shit means and how you got neck deep in it in the first place when you thought you were so cool."

"I'd better go home, Max. You're beginning to make sense."

But I didn't go home. I opened another beer. He finally let me put my Ventura record on. It was my chance to show him what hot bop was, how it could rip down walls of crap, how it didn't have to be subtle because there was still room in the world for big bad loud fuck-you jazz.

But he only listened politely, sipping his beer, shrugging now and then or raising an eyebrow, even though on his hi-fi system it sounded ten times better than on mine.

"Great, huh?" I said when the tone arm lifted and recradled itself.

"Well . . . it's catchy, at times. 'Great' is a word I use carefully, Oz. No, he's not great. Bird is great. Lester Young is great. This man of yours is very good—ballsy, tough—but like I said, he goes for the obvious. He's like a pitcher who can only throw the sinker, or like a boxer whose got nothing but a left hook."

I didn't think I'd ever be able to listen to my Charlie Ventura record again. I was pissed off and depressed. I wanted to return the favor, take him down a peg or two.

"So, Max—Elizabeth given you the time of day yet?" I said, casually changing the subject.

He sat up straight, as if I'd kicked him in the shins. "That's a little personal, isn't it, Oz?" he said.

"Just wondering," I said. "I mean, I see you feeding her a line almost every day. She falling for it? I mean, the corset thing. You sure that doesn't make her laugh? Behind your back, I mean."

His face went sad. I was sorry I'd shot my mouth off. But it was too late to do anything but ride it out. "You still making up those poems about her, Max?" I said, trying to lighten things up. "They used to crack me up. What was that one—'Put your hand on my thing, baby. Ding-a-ling-ling, baby.' "

He stared at me for a long time, then said, "Well, Oz, as a matter of fact, Elizabeth and I are seeing each other."

"Never happen, Max," I said. I poured myself another beer. "I mean, seeing her my *ass*. Who you trying to kid, Max?" I lit a cigarette. "You're too much, Max, you know that?" I choked a little on smoke, laughing. "No shit, Max, you kill me. 'Elizabeth and I are seeing each other.' Jesus, you ought to go into comedy or something with that straight face. Oh man, I'm pissing my pants!"

I got up and ran into the bathroom. I pissed for what seemed a half hour. When I came out, Max was cleaning up the dinner dishes.

"Hey, I got to split, Max. Thanks for dinner. Give Liz a big kiss for me, okay?"

He waved an empty beer bottle, the good-natured guy.

I went outside to my bike. I strapped my record on the back of the seat, then kicked the engine over. It muttered a couple of times, then roared. I sat there twisting the throttle, still laughing to myself at crazy Max. He was one of those guys who could say anything, no matter how ridiculous, and keep a perfectly straight face.

A car pulled up at the curb ahead of me. A woman got out. She headed for the apartment building. I popped the clutch accidentally, killing the engine.

"Elizabeth?" I said, my voice cracking.

"Ozzie? Is that you, hon?"

"What are you doing here?"

"What are *you* doing here? Max and I are going to see *Othello* at the Ken Theater. Orson Welles is in it."

The world was conspiring to make a fool out of me.

"That's cool," I said. I felt an ice floe slide through my veins. "I hope you dig that brainy stuff."

I kicked the engine over, gunned it, stood the bike on its rear wheel for a full block. Then dumped it in a patch of loose gravel. But she was already inside, and I was thankful for that. The Ventura record lay smashed under the rear hub.

11

The fires in the east hills began in early August. It was over a hundred degrees inland and even the beaches were in the nineties. Colleen and I, along with Art, Denise, and Crutchfield, went to La Jolla Shores for a cookout. We swam all afternoon—everyone but Art. He stripped to the waist to show his muscular torso, but would not expose his skinny legs.

We played Horses in chest-deep water. Colleen got on my shoulders, Denise on Crutchfield's. The game was grade-school simple: One rider and horse would try to tip over the other. Colleen pulled Denise off balance. Crutchfield started reeling. Denise's legs were tight around his neck, her feet pressing his waist. They flopped down together and came up gasping for air. Then we switched. Denise got on my shoulders, Colleen on Crutchfield's. The horses charged each other and the riders sparred.

At one point Crutchfield and I were face to face while the

screaming girls grappled above us for advantage. The beating he'd taken from the Marines had left him with a slightly bent and thickened nose. It gave him a mean look. He grinned at me with his new front teeth. It was the grin of friendly combatants, but I didn't like it. Colleen's glistening white thighs flexed on his tanned neck. He fought gamely to stay upright, but there was something shifty in his eyes that had nothing to do with the struggle. "Nice snatch scratcher," he said, meaning my mustache. Then he winked at me and licked his lips obscenely. I raised my right foot and tried to kick his legs out from under him but only threw myself off balance. Denise screamed and her thighs surged against my neck. Her feet dug into my kidneys. I staggered and went down, Denise on top of me, her thighs still clamped on my neck. I tried to free myself but she fought against it, and I scraped along on the ocean floor, her screams of laughter tinkling above me through the saltwater barrier.

When the sun settled in the western haze, we built a fire in a concrete fire ring. This was kind of an occasion. Art had gotten the job at Convair. He was going to train as an apprentice welder, $1.48 an hour. After his six-week apprenticeship was over, he'd jump to $1.67.

The brushfires swept through the east foothills and arroyos, sending up thick veils of smoke. Ash fell on the city like feathers of gray snow. Even at the beach you could see ash collecting on rooftops and lawns. A dozen houses had been burned down to their foundations. One old man had died in a trailer when his propane tanks blew. These fires were seasonal, expected. They came with the hot dry Santa Ana winds and they left when cool damp air from the ocean found its way inland again. Right now, though, the Santa Ana dominated. It snaked over the eastern mountains from the desert and pushed the cool ocean air far off-shore. Crutchfield was a great fan of the Santa Ana winds. For him, fire season in southern California was second only to earth-quakes.

There were local folk myths about Santa Ana weather. Some people went off the deep end. The hot dry winds brought out things in them they didn't know were there. A good, reasonable, well-liked man might take an ax to his family, for instance. No one could explain such a horrendous twist in behavior—except those who believed the "red wind" was to blame. The police be-lieved this folk myth more than anyone. Their records proved that crime, and weird behavior in general, skyrocketed when the desert air traveled westward over the peaks and down the can-yons and washes of the Cuyamaca Mountains. The legends of local Indian tribes were filled with strange events attributed to this red wind that sucked moisture from the earth and parched the grasses and trees tinder-dry. Doors warped and demons slipped into the blood to press vile arguments on the bewildered mind. The Indians threw themselves into the sea to shake off the wind-borne demons.

The sky was tangerine and there was no surf. Tepid waves slumped into the sand. The sea was glassy as oil as far as you could see. The calm water invited poor swimmers to outswim their abilities. They might wade until they were neck-deep, and then swim even farther, only to find themselves tangled in the kelp beds. Or they might be dragged swiftly out to sea by stealthy riptides that would strand them miles from shore where panic would paralyze their arms and legs.

"Great day, isn't it?" Crutchfield said. He locked arms with Denise and Colleen and watched Art and me skewer hot dogs.

"Don't put mine on the end," he said. "I don't want a black crust on mine, okay?"

"Brian, you're so picky," Denise said.

"That's why he doesn't have a girl," Art said.

"Is that why, Brian?" Colleen said coyly.

"That's right," Crutchfield said, pulling both Colleen and Denise hard against him. "The two best ones are taken."

"Come off it, Brian!" Colleen said. "You're such a liar."

"I mean it," he said. "I mean it sincerely. Not that I understand it. I mean, what do you two gorgeous creatures see in these retarded Neanderthals, anyway? Have you seriously considered what your lives are going to be like ten years from now with these two clowns?"

Art glanced up from the hissing hot dogs, his eyes hooded under a shelf of bone. Hunkered down next to the flames, his biceps spread on his knees, the knotted and veined muscles exaggerated in the red firelight, he looked primitive and futureless. I had to grin a little.

"Oh well," Denise said. "We'll just have to take our chances, won't we, Colleen?"

This embarrassed Colleen. We hadn't set a date, hadn't discussed marriage for some time now. In fact, I'd been thinking about enrolling at State College as a provisional student. Nelson said he'd pay my way. My only problem was that I had no idea what to study.

"Cat got your tongue, Colleen?" Crutchfield said.

Colleen pulled free of him, knelt in the sand. "Don't hold your skewer so close to the fire," she said to me. "I don't like a black crust on mine, either."

We ate hot dogs and drank beer until the sky got black. Crutchfield went to his car and brought back a portable radio, a powerful Zenith TransOceanic. It picked up L.A. stations easily, without static. Denise and Art curled up in a blanket and Colleen and I held each other and swayed to rhythm and blues while Crutchfield sat cross-legged by the fire drinking beer and watching us. I glanced at him from time to time and once caught him with his guard down. He was studying Colleen with childlike eyes. I realized what a fraud his sophistication was, how isolated he was. I pulled Colleen away from the firelight until we were hidden in darkness. Ivory Joe Hunter was singing "I Almost Lost My Mind." We lay down in the cool sand and kissed.

"Do you love me even a little, Ozzie?" she said.

"You know I do," I said. "You know I love you a lot, Colleen."

We kissed again, harder this time, but she broke off early for air. "No, I don't know that, honey. I mean, how can I be sure of you?"

I lifted the tight nylon of her suit and touched her pubic hair.

"Not here!" she hissed, but did not push my hand away.

Her hand went into my trunks. She hadn't been this bold before. We kissed, hands busy, the sweetness of the moment rising fast until neither one of us could stand it, and at that point she took her hand away and repeated, her voice dark and trembly, "How *can* I be sure of you, honey?"

For which there was no answer other than the one I almost believed at times: "I love you, Colleen, you have to trust me. I love you."

Heat made it true. The accumulating sweet moments, moments like this, made it true. Whose fault was that?

We got up and walked farther away from the fire and made a nest in the warm sand. *When I lost my baby, I almost lost my mind*, Ivory Joe crooned.

"He's got eyes for you," I said.

"Who does?"

"Crutchfield. He was looking at you like a lost puppy."

"That's the most ridiculous thing I've ever heard," she said. "Most of the girls at school thought he was—you know—kind of . . . *funny*. And I don't mean funny ha ha. I mean, do you know any girl who ever went out with him?"

"He's weird, but he isn't *funny*."

"It's still ridiculous. Don't you think?"

"I think it's hilarious. Mr. I've-Seen-It-All getting misty over a hometown girl."

"Really? Ozzie . . ." I clamped my mouth on the rest of what she had to say, the spiky bristles of my mustache rashing her upper lip.

After the beach party we all went up to Crutchfield's house on Mount Helix. It was a huge flat-roofed house with redwood decks surrounding it. It had the vague shape of a boat. There was even a bowsprit at one end of the deck, salvaged from some old sailing ship. The bowsprit had the shape of a mermaid with wild hair and the shocking eyes of a goddess. The hardwood burls that formed her breasts hovered nippleless over a grove of pomegranate trees and Indian fig. I'd been to this house many times before, but I never got used to it. It had the shape and feel of people who believed their daily lives were artistic events.

We sat in wicker chairs out on the west deck, where the view of the city was spectacular. Beyond the city, the blacker-than-black ocean spread out to the starry horizon. Crutchfield made up a tray full of expensive cuts of sandwich meat, wedges of cheese, kaiser buns, and gourmet mustards. Then he went back inside and returned with a bottle of French champagne. He popped the cork and the white foam erupted from the bottle, dousing Colleen. Her laughing screams set neighborhood dogs barking. Then we all drank toasts to Art and his job, and then to Denise and Art and their upcoming marriage. Crutchfield refilled the glasses and raised his tentatively. He looked at Colleen and me, and said, "Well, how about it, you two? Are you going to announce, so that we can finish the bottle in style?" I had just fixed myself a sandwich and was about to lay into it. Colleen grabbed my wrist, stopping me. She applied significant pressure. *You troublemaking son of a bitch*, I thought.

"Not yet," I said.

"But soon," Colleen said. "Right, honey?"

"Soon," I said.

"Well, here's to soon," Crutchfield said, raising his glass. "Soon is better than late, and late is better than never."

We drank the rest of the champagne. From somewhere in the huge house, someone started playing a cello.

"That's my old man," Crutchfield said. "That's how he unwinds after a day of looking into the business ends of the local hausfraus with flashlight and tongs. You wonder how the old boy can get interested in it for strictly entertainment purposes after slopping around in those things all day long. Maybe he imagines—"

"Crutchfield," Art said. "Shut up."

Crutchfield laughed. "I forgot," he said. "Art the prude. Hey, Art, join the twentieth century. No one's offended, right, ladies?"

"Where's the little girls' room?" Colleen said, breaking the tension.

"Come on, I'll show you," Crutchfield said.

When they were gone, Denise said, "He's such a crazy guy."

"He's sick," Art said.

The cello scraped against a sour chord and a man cursed.

I visited State College with Crutchfield. He had already enrolled and had chosen physics as his major. We walked around the Spanish-style buildings, through the courtyards they enclosed, and then had Cokes at the Student Union. It was Saturday morning, and summer school was still in session. It was a no-classes

day, and a few students sat together at round tables talking ener-
getically. I had a good feeling about the place, a feeling I never
had at Melville High. Crutchfield was enthusiastic. "Man, I love
this scene. You get the feeling that you could actually learn something here."

Maybe getting kicked around by those Marines had done him
some good. This sort of positive attitude was a little hard to swallow. I didn't trust it. But the sincerity in his eyes seemed honest
enough.

"I'm going to get my degree in physics here," he said, "and
then I'll go to Cal Tech for my doctorate."

"So you can make H-bombs?" I said, teasing him a little.

"Fuckin' A, Oz. They say there's no top limit to the power of
those bombs. You can make a hundred- or even a thousand-
megaton bomb. You know what that means? A hundred-megaton
bomb would take out the L.A. Basin, right up to the San Gabriel
Mountains. Clean the fucking place out, man. Fuse the rubble
into clean green glass, wall to wall."

This was almost a relief. Same old Monster. He was just convinced now that his dreams of working in atomic energy would
come true. And this eliminated the need to posture. He was full of
innocent enthusiasm. Which was, in a way, worse than bragging.

"You'd better sign up too, Oz," he said. "We could have a
ball."

"I wouldn't know what to sign up for," I said.

"Don't put yourself down, man. You could do anything you
wanted to do."

"That's just it," I said. "I don't want to do anything."

"That's stupid, Oz. Everyone wants to do something. Christ, a fucking *ant* wants to do something."

"Well, I should have been an ant. But I can't think of a single damn thing I want to spend my life doing."

We sat for a while, drinking our Cokes, listening to the chatter of college students.

"I know what your trouble is," Crutchfield said. "You're bored out of your mind."

"Brilliant," I said.

We got up and headed for the parking lot. "I'm serious," he said. "You're bored. And don't flatter yourself, I don't mean you're bored because the world can't live up to your high standards. You're bored because you won't take risks. You'd rather sit on your ass playing pocket pool and listening to that crappy bop. You're kind of fucked up, Oz."

"Send me your bill, Dr. Freud."

"No charge, Oz."

A big Buick Roadmaster was parked next to his tiny Hillman, so close that he couldn't open the driver's-side door. "Son of a bitch," he said. "Some people have no concept of how to fucking park." He rummaged around in the trunk of his car for a few seconds, then pulled out an ice pick. He knelt down next to the Buick and punctured the right rear tire. Then he did the same to the front right. He fished a jack handle out of the Hillman's trunk and swung it into the Buick's windshield. The windshield burst into a million spiderweb fractures.

I knew this was partly for my benefit. He wanted to show me

how a real risk-taker lives. But I didn't give him the satisfaction of letting myself get unglued over his vandalism. I sat in the car while he took his risk-taking time putting away his tools.

"You're the one who's fucked up, Crutchfield," I said. I got out and he crawled into the driver's seat.

"The only people who count these days are," he said.

12

Art and Denise got married the weekend after I registered for fall classes as a provisional student at State College. I was best man, Colleen was maid of honor. It was a church wedding, but Benedetto and Mrs. di Coca attended, because it was a Presbyterian church, not Catholic. Not that Benedetto approved of the Presbyterians. As far as he was concerned, religion existed for one reason only, and that was to pacify and control the workingman. "You make him believe in hell, then you tell him that's where he go if he no work for you for nothing," he once said.

He sat in the back of the church, even though the minister tried to get him into the front row. The minister, a rosy-complected, fleshy man with thick glasses, tugged good-naturedly on Benedetto's wiry arm. "Be a good sport, Mr. di Cola," he said. Benedetto took the minister's soft hand in his own big-knuckled, callused hand, and, blowing a garlic-and-dago-red steam into the minister's Protestant smile, said, "No, *grazie*, I do not think so, padre." The minister opened and closed his hand several times, after Benedetto let it go, to see if it still worked.

After the brief ceremony we all went to the di Coca house for the reception. Colleen was with me, but she was not happy. She thought my registration at State was just one more scheme to put off our wedding. I couldn't convince her otherwise, mostly because she was right. It wasn't that I didn't love her—not that I was sure I did—it was just that my notion that I should avoid all future-determining traps had gotten stronger. College seemed like the least confining of all possible traps. I had listed my major as "Psychology," but only because of a formal requirement to put down something as my academic goal. My adviser enrolled me in five courses of study: college algebra, English, astronomy, Introduction to Human Behavior—I loved that title!—and Air Force ROTC. Being in ROTC automatically gave me a 2-S selective service classification, which protected me from the draft. School didn't start for another month and a half, so there was time to duck out of this future complication, too.

I noticed the drab cars parked across the street from the di Coca house when we arrived, but didn't think much of it. I'd seen FBI cars there many times before. The men inside the cars were smart enough to know that Benedetto and his friends were no threat to the national security. They read newspapers or ate bologna sandwiches, bored with pointless surveillance.

Benedetto's Communist buddies were in the house, providing the music, a hot Italian band blasting out tarantellas and political anthems, while Benedetto poured the wine. It was a good party and everyone got loose with one sentiment or other.

Art was heroic in his rented tux, tall and broad-shouldered, with a tight grin locked in his tanned face. Denise in her brocaded white gown looked like a stung angel, her eyes red and leaky, her smeared lips swollen from the bout of passion in the back of the limousine that had carried them here from the church. All the women had red and leaky eyes, except for Colleen, who was feeling left out, let down, and blue, even though she had caught the bride's bouquet and I had caught her garter.

"All this means nothing to you," she said.

"Here we go again," I said.

She bit her lip. "God, I just hate you sometimes. Why can't you be like other people?"

"Like Art, you mean."

"What's wrong with that?"

"Nothing. It's just that . . ."

"What? What?"

"I'm not Art."

Someone carrying a tray of water glasses that had been filled to their brims with dago red passed by. I took two glasses, gave one to Colleen.

"Let's talk about something else," Colleen said.

"Good idea."

But we sipped wine in silence as the musicians started to play something wild. A few people began to stomp the floors and sing defiantly.

Crutchfield shouldered his way toward us. "The 'Internationale,' " he said. "The Commie theme song."

"Why are they playing it now?" I said.

"They want the Feds outside to hear it."

"Waving the Red flag in front of the bulls," I said.

"Hey, that's good," Crutchfield said. "And you're right. But it's pretty damn stupid. The Reds are basically out of their tree, don't you think so, Colleen?"

Colleen sighed. "I don't care about politics," she said.

"I'm with you, Colleen," he said. "Personally, Communism, capitalism, Fascism—the whole ball of wax bores the mud out of me."

Crutchfield was a little drunk. He threw his arms around Colleen. "Me and Colleen here, we think the same," he said.

"I don't think so, Brian," Colleen said, giggling nervously.

"Oh yes we do. We know a phony baloney when we see one."

"Are you trying to make a point, Crutchfield?" I said.

"I just did, Oz. Weren't you listening?"

"Fuck off."

"Ozzie! I do not like that awful word! You know that!" Colleen said.

"Now you've made your fiancée angry, you foulmouthed beast," Crutchfield said.

I pushed through the crowd before I said something else to him. I found Art and a few high school friends out in the kitchen. They were passing a pint of Four Roses around.

"Old Donny brought this by," Art said.

Donny Luburich, the tallest kid in high school who didn't play basketball, grinned ear to ear. He had shot up to about six feet seven in a couple of years and looked like he still might be growing. He came from a religious family that had never been able to control him. By the time he was a senior, Donny was a committed alcoholic. He was also one of the nicest guys in school, and one of the strongest. We had been friends up to about our junior year, then went our own ways.

"Long time no see, Donny," I said.

"Hey, Oz," he said. "What's the skinny, man?"

Donny looked good in his rented blue suit, sharp and not at all ungainly, but his eyes looked about as conscious as nail heads in his red-splotched face.

The bottle came to me and I lowered it an inch.

"Man, that music is driving me nuts," Art said.

"Why don't you take Denise and haul ass?" Donny said. "You don't have to stick around. You got a hard night's work ahead of you, man."

Everyone laughed, except for Art, who took what Donny said to heart. Denise was in the dining room, surrounded by older women. "How am I going to shake her loose?" he said.

Donny put his fingers in his mouth and blasted a shrill whistle that made my ears ring. I hadn't heard that whistle for years. When he used to come by my house, he'd call me out by whistling like that, a piercing blade of sound that used to drive Mitzi up the wall.

Heads turned our way, but then turned back. Donny decided we needed to know about his future plans. He was going "into wallpaper." His father owned a shoe repair shop and had wanted him to learn the trade, but Donny was adamant about the future of wallpaper. "Seventy percent of all Americans hang their own wallpaper," he said. "And I . . . li'l old Donny Luburich . . . am gonna change all that." He went on and on, about the money to be made hanging wallpaper, but no one listened.

Art pulled me into the hallway between the kitchen and front room. "Colleen is about fed up with you, man," he said.

"No she isn't," I said.

"I wouldn't be so cocky if I were you, Oz."

"Guess I'll have to take my chances," I said.

"She's in the bedroom crying. Guess who's in there with her, offering a sympathetic shoulder."

I shrugged. "Let's get another drink," I said.

Back in the kitchen Donny was still talking to himself about wallpaper and sipping from his pint. When he saw me he interrupted his glassy-eyed monologue on the future of wallpaper and handed over the bottle. I took it down another inch.

"Gon' ta be reech," he said. "Gon' ta be one reech mother-fuckeen somebeech, *muchachos,*" he said. He started leaning toward me. I pushed him upright. He giggled and threw his big arm around my neck. "'member how we used to rassle, Ozzie?" he said. I remembered. Back in our sophomore year, when he was a foot shorter and a hundred pounds lighter, we used to play catch-as-catch-can wrestlers, imitating the TV wrestlers of the time, Lord Blears, Wild Red Berry, Gorgeous George, Baron Leone, Antonino Rocca. We would spit insults, strut and brag, then start grappling in that stagy TV way, looking for advantage. Sometimes we'd forget the act and really try to pin each other or make each other "submit" to escape the pain of a hammerlock or a step-over toehold or a "Boston Crab," and wound up grass-stained and sometimes bloody, but still friends.

As if gripped by nostalgia, he threw a crushing headlock on me, making my ears ring. He was too big to resist, but when he wouldn't let go I kicked his foot. But he acted as if he had drifted off into another stupor and had forgotten me, and I reached out blindly and my hand found a beer bottle and I cracked it on his knee. He let go then and I tripped sideways a few feet with vertigo, while he roared in pain. He looked at me, an ugly twist on his mouth. We were strangers, no longer old schoolmates. He took an uneven step sideways, then came at me, and I ducked under his slow, unaimed punch and rammed my fist into his face. My hand vibrated with pain. Donny sat down, grabbing at a tablecloth, and a tray of snacks crashed to the floor. Runnels of blood fell into his lap. My own nose was bleeding somehow, for old times' sake I guessed, and blood splattered my rented tux and pearl-studded shirt. This made me mad, since it was going to cost me a stiff cleaning bill. I jumped on him and pounded him with my un-hurt fist until Art dragged me off and threw me out the back door of the house.

"You stupid jerk-off," he said, not exactly mad but fed up with me and with the party, which had become more of an excuse for Benedetto and his friends to have a Commie wingding than a reception. I didn't blame him.

"Sorry, Art," I said. "You and Denise have a great life, okay, man?"

"That's the idea, asshole."

I walked around the side of the house to the front and headed home. Colleen was in the doorway, looking at me coldly. There was too much indifference in her eyes. Too much to believe. Crutchfield stood behind her, his hands resting on her shoulders somewhat possessively. He grinned a little. I grinned back in the same spirit. And that seemed to be that. I walked home.

13

A rail spur ran through the back lot of Ducrouler's. A flatcar sat out there in the late-morning sun. It was stacked tall with sheet steel on pallets that needed unloading. The forklift man was down with the flu. "You do it, Santee," said the new foreman, a sour-looking man who haunted the warehouse with clipboard and stopwatch, timing our work, making notes. He was a far cry from the easygoing, doggerel-spouting Max Tbolt. We were instructed to call him Mister. Mr. Stillwater.

Mr. Ennis Stillwater, tall and blade-shouldered in starched khakis and brown felt hat, did not like me. I wasn't about to tell him I'd never operated the forklift. He'd look at me, make a note on his clipboard, then find someone else. And I'd be on his shit-list. Besides, it couldn't be all that hard. A forklift was a simple machine—a couple of levers and a steering wheel.

I climbed up into the seat and studied the controls for a few minutes. It started easily and I ran the forks up and down several times for practice, then shifted the friction-clutch transmission into forward. It took a few tries to line the forks up so that they passed under a pallet, but once they were in place the rest seemed a cinch. I pulled back the lever that raised the forks. The forklift started to tip forward in spite of its heavy counterweights. This was puzzling. I lowered the forks, tried again. The same thing happened, only this time the engine made a ratcheting noise and smoke billowed from the louvers on the side panels next to my seat. I lowered the forks and shut the machine off.

Mr. Stillwater was standing behind me with his clipboard and stopwatch. "You might try taking off those ties," he said, nodding at the flatcar. I looked at the pallets again and saw what he was talking about. They were secured to the flatcar with narrow cables. I hadn't seen them.

I climbed up on the stacked pallets and released all the cables, but when I climbed down to finish unloading pallets, Mr. Stillwater had already started the forklift himself. He raised the forks and positioned them expertly and carried a pallet of steel into the warehouse. He controlled the forklift with abrupt efficiency, demonstrating his superior ability. I followed along on foot, watched him drop the pallet in perfect position for the crane operator who would later haul the pallets to locations within the warehouse that were inaccessible by forklift. Then Mr. Stillwater switched off the engine, stepped down from the machine, and walked away without a glance in my direction.

I finished the job, calling him every foul and scummy thing I could think of under the roar of the motor. I imagined chasing him down with the forklift, spearing him through the back of his crisp shirt, riding his bloody corpse through the streets of National City.

"What's eating on you *now*?" Bernard Issel said during our lunch break. "Seems like you've been on the rag for a month, Zee." Bernard, peevish, sucked noisily on his big square teeth.

He had started calling me Zee. This was one of the things that had been eating on me. He didn't mean it in a friendly way, the usual spirit in which nicknames were given. Unlike "Gash Hound," "Muff Diver," or "Ace," "Zee" had no heroic or even mock-heroic overtones. Zee was the last of everything, the uncontested dead end of all. And it had caught on. Even Elizabeth called me Zee, though she didn't mean it as a put-down. But coming from her it had impact.

I began to *feel* like Zee. In bad moments I saw myself at sixty, stooped and gray, moving from crappy job to crappy job, eating badly, health failing, chest cramped from the lack of oxygen, teeth in rampant decay, breath like sewer gas: Zee.

Hey Zee, get your funky old ass over here and clean this toilet. Hey Zee, you getting any stink-finger from Mrs. Zee? And Zee—his shit-eating grin accommodating their jive—mops the pissy tile floors while younger Zees shred what tatters are left of his dignity to slow their own free-fall into uselessness.

Zee, feeble and wanting to die but afraid. Zee, passed over by good luck and ordinary love. Zee, the stale turd on the sparkling lawn of the prosperous nation. Zee, the man who never should have been.

"I can't work for that prick," I said.

"Mr. Stillwater?" Issel said.

"No, the king of Lower fucking Slobovia."

"Hey, Zee. Stillwater's okay. He knows the business."

"Jesus, Issel, I know you're working at full mental capacity, but this isn't exactly the R&D lab at Convair. What does it take to run a warehouse? Max did it standing on his head. He didn't take it all that seriously, you know?"

Issel had started smoking a pipe. Screwing around with it gave him time to think. He filled it with Prince Albert, tamped it down, took his sweet time lighting it. You could hear the wheels in his odd head creaking as he sucked flame into the bowl. "You're not as smart as you think, Zee," he said, pipe stem clamped in the protruding rack of his bright and sturdy teeth.

We were out at the rail spur, sitting in the opened doors of an SP boxcar. It was hotter than ever, though the fires in the hills had died out. "What are you going to be doing ten years from now, Issel?" I said, half interested.

"This right here," he said, gazing at the big square warehouse affectionately. He sucked on his pipe, eyes narrowed and dreamy, the eyes of a visionary idiot.

"I actually believe you, Bernard," I said.

He made a suddenly bitter face and tapped burning tobacco from his pipe. "Shit, Zee! You made me forget my dessert!"

He opened a half-pint carton of chocolate milk and chugged it. Then he rooted around in his lunch pail and came up with a pink Dolly Madison snowball. He ate the spongy treat lovingly, his long jaws grinding like a cud-happy cow's. I tried to imagine his wife, what she must look like, how she must feel when Bernard rolled over on top of her at night to throw her the bone. Did Bernard have this same Dolly Madison look on his face then? This self-satisfied look of intestinal ecstasy?

No doubt. What Issel expected and what he got were pretty much the same thing. True, the H-beam sheared off his thumb, but he got it back. Bad days came, but they would be followed by good ones. The obedient and procreative Bernard Issels, the uncomplaining brawn and backbone of the nation, pursuing happiness, finding it, believing it was a natural birthright, lording it over the unconvinced and disoriented Zees. Happy all the time, Colleen had said. How could anyone in his right mind *argue* with this? Who was wrong here?

After lunch I went to work in the Bins, cleaning chain. It was an easy but nasty job, brushing big iron links with acid. I hated the smell. It stung my eyes and burned my hands. I'd been given gloves to wear, and I did for a while, but gloves got in the way. Before Mr. Stillwater came, I took my time and did a half-assed job. But unlike Max, Stillwater hectored the warehouse crew with his stopwatch and busybody ways.

He came by to inspect my work. He timed me. "Twelve seconds per link," he said, holding his stopwatch in front of his face. "That's too long. You can get that down to five seconds. That saves the company over half your time. I expect your productivity to double, Santee." He'd been a time-and-motion man at Ryan Aircraft before Ducrouler lured him away. I imagined the party the factory workers at Ryan must have thrown when Still-

water left. Dancing and singing, people linking arms, marching
through the plant as if a war had ended and the boys were coming
home.

I started working faster, but when he disappeared around the
end of the row I went back to normal speed. I stayed with chain
for another hour, then switched to well hooks.

Elizabeth Urquiza came by. "Where are the shoulder bolts,
Zee?" she asked. "God, how can you find anything back here?"

I was on all fours, brushing acid into the heavy black hooks.
Each hook must have weighed ten pounds. I looked back, dog-
like, over my shoulder. She was a bright pink cloud lighting the
dark. I stood up, wiped my hands on my Levi's, tried to talk, my
unmanageable face working in spasms. But she was used to my
goony ways. She smiled. She was wearing her tight angora pull-
over, bright pink. It had a sweetheart neckline that exposed
cleavage and the upper slopes of her breasts. A perfectly placed
mole the size of a pinhead stared at me from the top of her right
breast.

"Shoulder bolts, Zee," she said. "Where are they?"

"This way," I said. I led her deep into the Bins, a dark recess
where mice thrived and proliferated in the constant night.

"Bins fifty-six through eighty," I said. "All sizes."

She rose up on her toes and looked into one of the bins, breasts
thrusting against their flimsy restraints. The bins were like small
steel coffins in funeral vaults. They were on ball-bearing runners
and could be pulled out. I slid out the one she was trying to look
into. Crazy impulses ran berserk in my brain, all of which seemed

reasonable. I wanted to take her in my arms right now. Imagining it made my hands twitch. I broke a sweat. She sensed this, turned quickly around to face me.

"How many seven-eighths-inch shoulder bolts do we have, Zee?" she said. Her face was gone in the dim air. All I saw was the distant blue light that caught her hair like northern auroras.

"I don't know," I said.

"Mr. Stillwater wants a total, right now."

"Fuck him," my stupid mouth blurted. "Excuse my French, Elizabeth," I added quickly.

She took a step backward. "It's okay," she said. "It's pretty icky back in here. I wouldn't want to do inventory either." She touched my arm, then my cheek. Electric chills traveled from her fingertips to my brain, which routed them directly to my crotch. I reached for her and caught her hand. Like a fool I shook it.

"Thanks, Elizabeth," I said. But my hand was sweaty and my grip was hard and too full of meaning. She pulled back and walked briskly away without another word.

I headed for the men's room. There was no choice.

I saw her onstage again, in G-string and tassels. And then with no G-string and no tassels. And then on no stage, but in my bedroom, under me, her long legs over my shoulders, her arms pulling me in, her wide-open mouth whispering hoarse screams of joy.

Spent and sane again, I opened the stall door. Mr. Stillwater was leaning against a sink, holding his stopwatch. "Four minutes twenty-eight seconds, Santee," he said. "Back at Ryan, the average whack-off artist took only three and a half minutes. You can't even pound your pud efficiently.''

I saw two clear choices: hit him or ignore him. I washed my hands, dried them, and headed for the door.

"Oh, by the way, Santee," he said. "You're fired."

14

Art and Denise had rented a small apartment a half mile from Balboa Park, a one-bedroom flat with a kitchenette. After my first week of classes at State College, I stopped by their place. It was Friday evening and Art had just gotten home from work. The apartment had a tiny porch that looked out on Myrtle Street. Art and I went out to the porch and sat in lawn chairs. You could see the swaying tops of the tall eucalyptus trees in Balboa Park from there. We drank beer and watched traffic while Denise made supper. I'd wanted to tell him about my classes, the hotshots, deadheads, and screwballs teaching them, but something was bothering him.

"Fucking FBI pulled me off the job today, asking questions about my old man," he said.

"You got canned?"

"No, but it didn't do me any good."

"What did they ask you about?"

Art drained his beer and crushed the can. "Shit like did I hear him and his friends talk about underground activity. They wanted to know who came to his fucking secret *cell* meetings."

"What did you say?"

"I told them the truth. My old man doesn't have secret cell meetings. Everyone in the neighborhood knows when him and his cronies get together. You can hear them for miles. I also told them I didn't know jack shit about what they talked about because political crap bores the hell out of me."

"They buy it?"

"I don't know and I couldn't care less," he said, punching holes into another can of beer.

But he did care, because his job was at risk. He said he was learning how to use an arc welder. He was excited about it. He described his welding helmet, the bright and dangerous arc from the electrodes, the fine bead he was already able to make and how his supervisor had congratulated him for learning so fast.

I didn't tell him I'd been fired at Ducrouler's. I said I'd quit. I would have quit anyway, since school was about to start. One week into classes, though, and I was ready to drop out. One professor had a speech impediment that made him impossible to understand. He couldn't make certain ordinary sounds, and when he tried too hard he brayed like a donkey. When I first heard him do this I started laughing, because I thought he was putting us on. But everyone around me scowled with disapproval, as though I'd farted in church.

Another professor bird-dogged the good-looking girls in the

class. He had them sit in the front row. "Ladies, would you kindly cross your legs, please?" he said. The blushing girls looked at each other, wondering what *this* was all about, but they obediently crossed their legs. "Thank you," said the professor. "Now that the gates of hell are closed, we may proceed." Everyone laughed, even the blushing girls. It might have been funny, except the professor looked a little too serious. His tall forehead was beaded with sweat and he licked his lips a little too hungrily. The gates of hell were obviously scorching his overactive mind.

I liked my English teacher best, a casual man who looked a little lost. He confessed that he was new on the job and didn't know the first thing about teaching people how to write compositions. His name was Clive Carrington, originally from England, but "at large in the States for the past five years," he said. He had a wooden leg and a glass eye, and he lived on a boat, a converted minesweeper that was anchored in San Diego Bay. He was a full-time writer and a part-time teacher and had been a Hurricane pilot during the Battle of Britain.

"You picked a fine night to drop by," Art said.

"What do you mean?"

"I hate to be the one to tell you this, Oz, but Crutchfield and Colleen have been going out. They're coming over tonight for spaghetti."

I took a sip of beer. It tasted like bile. "That's cool, man," I said. "Doesn't bother me a bit."

He glanced at me, black beady eyes suspicious. "I don't think she really likes him," he said.

"Too bad," I said. "But it's no skin off my ass either way."

"I think you're fucking up, Oz."

"And she's not?"

"Maybe both of you are," he said.

I shrugged. My stomach was suddenly full of broken glass. Which surprised me. I felt a little amazed at myself. On the one hand, I didn't care that she was seeing Crutchfield. In fact, it was good news in a way—I was fired from another job, a job I'd never been sure I wanted to make a career of. And yet I felt this sharp physical pain. The pain climbed up from my stomach and lodged in my throat. I saw her clearly in my mind, up on Mount Palomar, under the gibbous moon, crying my name. I saw her at Sunset Cliffs, both of us on the western edge of the country, acting out what felt like history's ultimate love scene, as if nothing meaningful could ever happen between two lovers after that night. This eruption of memories cooled into jagged shards of glass in my gut and throat. I poured beer on top of them, but the pain only increased.

"If that's the way you feel, Oz, why don't you stay for dinner too?"

"Denise didn't plan for me, man," I said.

"Shit, it's only spaghetti. I'll tell her to boil up a little extra."

I took a long pull of beer, each swallow lacerating my guts. "Okay, that's cool. I could go for that. Denise cook it as good as your mom?"

"Close," he said.

"Close is good enough," I said.

Midway through our next beer, Crutchfield's Hillman pulled

up in front of the apartment building. He climbed out, then went around to open Colleen's door. He was doing things by the book. He helped Colleen out, and they came to the porch, holding hands.

Colleen never looked better. She was wearing her pink cardigan and more makeup than usual. She looked ten years older. I stood up. "Hi," I said.

If she was surprised to see me, she did a good job of keeping it to herself. "Hi, Ozzie," she said, her eyes not quite meeting mine. "How's college?"

I shrugged. I held my hand out and turned it this way and that. *"Comme ci, comme ça,"* I said, borrowing a phrase from my psychology professor. He sprinkled his lectures with foreign words and phrases, showing off his worldliness. Now I needed to show off mine.

"He's the star of Geopolitics 101," Crutchfield said. "No one in the class knew exactly where Kiev was, except Oz. Captain O'Neil was mucho impressed, right, Oz?"

I shrugged. Geopolitics 101 was the ROTC class, not exactly a challenge. It was the only class Crutchfield and I had together. He hadn't told me he was dating Colleen. Maybe he thought he had good reasons not to. Maybe things had gotten serious between them. This possibility stabbed my stomach hard. I glanced quickly at Colleen. She looked different somehow. When our eyes finally met I read them like the headlines: Crutchfield was screwing her.

I couldn't look at her. Crutchfield dominated the talk at the dinner table. He'd been watching the atomic tests from Nevada on the mornings they televised them. He rhapsodized about the flash of light, the TV screen going ink-black, the fireball pounding up through clouds of smoke like the giant fist of a white genie. "It's so bitchin'," he said. "Like the Fourth of July in hell."

It was easy to see that Crutchfield was in love. I barely touched my spaghetti. Denise had put a big bottle of Chianti on the table, and I drank at least half of it. I wanted to get numb. Now and then I caught Colleen looking at me. Her calm eyes seemed to be observing the dead. She turned her fork slowly, twisting spaghetti into the tines.

"Well, I'd better split," I said, trying to sound bored. I stood up, then sat back down hard.

"Christ, you're *ripped*," Art said.

"Me? Are you kidding?" I stood again, careful to lock my knees this time. I held the back of the chair. Then I let go and raised my arms like wings opening. "See?" I said. "No hands."

"I'm going to take him home," Art said to Denise. "If he gets on his bike he'll wrap it around a light pole."

I held my hand up to him like a cop stopping traffic. "Whoa," I said. "I am fine. I can ride just fine."

"Let Art take you home, Ozzie," Colleen said.

I put my hand on my heart. "I am touched," I said. "But really, gang, I'm okay. I can ride my bike in my sleep."

"I'm going to *put* you to sleep if you keep arguing," Art said.

"Don't be a jerk, Oz," Crutchfield said. "No one wants to see you get hurt."

Crutchfield put a little too much spin on this. It was a slow curveball that breaks in on you and bounces off your head.

"Fuck you, man," I said, moving toward him, bumping the table hard enough to dump some glasses over. At which point Art grabbed me and hauled me out of the apartment.

"It's my house, asshole," he said. "You don't get to act like a horse's ass at my dinner table."

Art drove to Mission Beach, where I puked Chianti into the sand. That made me feel better. I took off my shoes and rolled up my pants and waded into the ebb-tide surf. I washed my face with salt water. The resemblance to tears was not lost on me. I started crying. "You sorry bastard," I said.

The ocean, it occurred to me, was made of teardrops. It made sense, considering all that went on in the world. Cosmic teardrops. I looked up. Sad tears or tears of laughter or both? The black sky's immense silence was part of the long-running joke. I got hold of myself and walked back to the car.

"Guess I fucked up," I said.

"She still loves you, man," Art said. "But I wouldn't let her wait till Christmas if I were you."

"Crutchfield's fucking her, Art," I said.

"Never happen, Oz. She told Denise she thinks Monster is a strange character. Women like Colleen don't screw strange characters."

"And you know all about who women will screw and not screw, right? I mean, it's like you've had thousands, right?"

"Don't piss me off, Oz. I'm trying to help."

We drove into the east part of the county. My window was down and the cool air washed against my face. We were in a dark upper-class suburb. Fat cars sat in the driveways of the smug houses.

"Let's swipe some gas," I said.

Art laughed. "Hey, man, we're not in high school anymore. I've got a job, I can buy my own gas."

"For old times' sake," I said.

I knew he still had a siphoning hose in the trunk. "Okay," he said.

We pulled up beside a cream-colored DeSoto that was parked in front of a big split-level. I got out and unscrewed the DeSoto's gas cap. Art opened his trunk and got the siphoning hose and a five-gallon jerry can. I slipped the hose into the tank, then sucked on it until I got a mouthful of gas. I spit it out and crimped the hose shut until I could get it into the can. We only took a couple of gallons. I replaced the DeSoto's gas cap. The lights came on in the house. Art put the jerry can and the hose into the trunk and we left the scene, burning rubber and laughing like a pair of happy thieves.

15

Stalin confiscated all the saxophones in Russia. He made it a political crime to own one. He was afraid of that second human voice that had been born in America. Someone had played some old-time jazz for him and he saw bad news for dictators in it. He called it western decadence. Those hot licks flipped off despots and made all their propaganda transparent. You couldn't have an obedient anthill society if the workers in it listened to jazz. Uncle Joe heard the message of jazz—*Fuck you, Jack, I'm flying home*—and he cleaned house.

But maybe Uncle Joe *would* allow the ice-cool horns of progressive bop. The ice-cool horns made you sit still and listen. They made you think or worry or fret. You weren't moved to tap your foot or twist the throttle of your bike to the remembered honks and moans and screams of a Big Jay McNeeley or a Charlie Ventura. The ice-cool horns sent you into snowdrifts of stoic contemplation. There was more *I'm fucked* in them than *Fuck you.* I tried to tell Max this, but he didn't buy it.

"There are a lot of squares in *this* country who would collect saxophones and melt them down for paperweights if they had their way, Oz," Max said. "But that's beside the point. Honest-to-Jesus art is always going to piss off tight-assed people whether it's a paranoid dictator or a PTA president. They think any free and unpredictable expression makes them look bad. Which is true, of course."

We were in his apartment, having dinner again. I liked him and had kept in touch with him. His mother didn't feel like eating that night, so Max and I ate alone. He'd made a meat loaf, baked potatoes, cole slaw, and homemade rolls.

Elizabeth had joined her husband, Norbert, in Pittsburgh, and Max had a lot of time on his hands now. They had never gotten all that serious, but had dated once, and sometimes twice, a week. Then Norbert Urquiza came to his senses. He flew back to San Diego and literally begged for forgiveness, which Elizabeth was ready to give. Max had helped her through a hard and lonely time, but she had never become attached to him.

Max looked sad and seemed older now, but he had great resilience. He called it his Rubber Boat Blues Band mentality. "Here's survival rule number one, Oz," he told me. "Stay afloat, because help will come."

We listened to a Miles Davis album while we ate. I could hear the beauty of individual notes, I could hear the brilliant accelerations through the scale, I could even hear the piercing loneliness of the voice in that trumpet, and maybe that's all I needed to hear, but I still could not understand or like it. I quoted something that Louis Armstrong was supposed to have said about progressive jazz: "That stuff is modern malice. There's no melody to remember and no beat to dance to."

"Look, Oz," Max said. "Real artists are always going to shake folks up. They're out there on the edge, by themselves, and what they see is not what the people who aren't there see. Uncle Joe would take Miles's horn away from him once he saw that a lot of Russkies were digging it. You don't have to stomp and holler to worry the Thought Police. Louis Armstrong was on the edge once, too. One of these days someone will come along out of nowhere blowing notes that will make Miles seem part of history. That's how it goes. And let me tell you something else, Oz. Miles wouldn't have it any other way."

Max and I had been to a Dave Brubeck concert that afternoon at San Diego Junior College. The Brubeck Quartet wasn't all that hard to listen to, but it was *brainy*. It was like all progressive jazz: You had to figure it out so you could congratulate yourself when you did. But I couldn't figure it out. Brubeck's rhythms were so strange they made you want to laugh. It was like a waltz and a rumba and a Sousa march mixed together. I imagined dancers trying to move to this confusing rhythm. I saw dislocated hips and sprained backs, people being carried off the dance floor on stretchers.

When Paul Desmond stepped up to solo on his alto sax, the audience went crazy, because they thought they were finally going to be rescued by some out-of-control cat who was going to blow the walls down. They stood up and began to clap a familiar rhythm, overriding the drums and bass, yelling, Go! Go! Go! But Desmond didn't go anywhere except to some monkish landscape inside his high-domed head, and the audience sat down humble and embarrassed because they now realized they were definitely *not cool.* They were what *was* and this music was what *would be.* It became clearer and clearer that the bespectacled alto man who looked like a math professor was not talking to them but to himself and to the other players. Where were the hell-raising, go-for-broke, every-man-for-himself sax men of old? What careful new world were we slipping into now?

But neither one of us was in a mood to argue music. Max brought out a bottle of Johnnie Walker Black and poured straight shots. Then he put on a Mezz Mezzrow album. "This guy breaks my heart," he said.

Mezzrow played "lugubrious" clarinet, Max said, but he meant every note. And that was something. It was true. You could hear Mezzrow inside every note, a personal declaration of the blues. He was no Benny Goodman or Buddy De Franco, but you could hear the extremes of his life in every phrase. "He's real, and he's honest," Max said. "Sometimes that's all you need."

I filled my shot glass to the brim with the Johnnie Walker, raised it to my lips, knocked it back, gritted my teeth against the knot of black flame rising up from my guts.

"Maybe you ought to take this stuff a little more slowly," Max said, his mournful eyes big and red-streaked.

I shrugged. The blues were kissing my brain stem. I downed the

shot, poured another to the brim. "You put the bottle out, Max,"
I said.

"The thing is," Max said, "you don't have enough miles on
you to want to get fucked up."

I thought he meant Miles, and that made me laugh a little. But
he meant miles, as in distance traveled, and I remembered the
endless cross-country trips in the Packard. "I've got ten thousand miles plus," I said. "When do I qualify?" But he just stared
into his drink and I saw that he was feeling down. Mezzrow's
lugubrious clarinet had temporarily sunk the Rubber Boat Blues
Band, and the only help in sight was in the big bottle of Johnnie
Walker.

What Max had really meant was that *he* had a genuine reason
to drown his troubles because his luck was running out and I, at
eighteen, had the whole bright highway of my life in front of me.
Which pissed me off. I poured myself another fat shot of whiskey.
What did Max know about me? What did my being eighteen have
to do with anything?

"It's your life, man," he said.

"So they tell me," I said.

I left Max's drunk and lugubrious. I rode my bike out to the
nearest beach, the Silver Strand. It was deserted, but a quarter-
moon turned the sand silver, just as advertised. I stripped and
ran into the surf. The water cure. I couldn't afford a hangover.

Tomorrow Captain O'Neil was taking a group of us cadets flying in a C-45, a twin-engined Beechcraft the ROTC department
kept at Lindbergh Field. I got out behind the breakers, then

swam north and south, doing laps on an imaginary course, until I got tired. Then I caught a good wave and rode it in, but if there was a philosophy in it that put my life into perspective, I could not find it.

16

Captain O'Neil took the cadets flying in groups of four. Crutchfield and I were in the same group. Some perverse fate kept throwing us together. By the look on his face I could tell that Crutchfield blamed the coincidences on me. I probably had the same look on my face.

We had to get parachute instructions before we went up because of Air Force regulations. We put on the harnesses, then Captain O'Neil showed us how to clip the parachute pack to the front straps. We took turns crouching in the doorway of the parked C-45. One by one we yelled "Geronimo"—the cadets' idea, not Captain O'Neil's—and hopped out onto the tarmac.

We were told to count to ten before yanking the D-ring. "You fall at thirty-two feet per second per second, minus air resistance," Captain O'Neil said. "So in ten seconds you've fallen less than sixteen hundred feet. You've got to figure the plane is coming down too, so those ten seconds, while they may seem like eternity, are the minimum you need to clear the aircraft.''

It was a solemn moment. We pictured ourselves falling through space as the disabled C-45 spun out of control. The captain paused; we held our breath. "If anyone is unclear on this procedure, now is the time to speak up," he said. We answered him with stiff-jawed military silence. "Fine," he said. "Let's do it." We climbed aboard. The first thing we did was toss our harnesses and parachute packs into a careless, unsortable pile at the back of the plane.

Crutchfield got to sit up front with Captain O'Neil during take-off, while the rest of us—two others and myself—took seats in the back. The C-45 could hold about eight people, but the captain didn't want the little plane crowded. We headed north, toward Oceanside, climbing to ten thousand feet. When we passed over Camp Pendleton, the Marine base, Crutchfield came out of the pilot's cabin. "Oz," he said. "Captain O'Neil wants you next."

Crutchfield and I hadn't been able to say much of anything to each other since the dinner with Art and Denise. The tension between us made phony chat impossible. In the few instances when our eyes met he probably saw the bitter surface of my jealous, scenario-creating mind, and I saw the self-justified finders-keepers, losers-weepers challenge of his.

The awful scenarios ran constantly in the projection room inside my skull: Crutchfield and Colleen at the beach. Crutchfield and Colleen at the drive-in. Crutchfield and Colleen necking out at Torrey Pines or Sunset Cliffs, or driving up to the top of Mount Palomar on a moonlit night. Crutchfield having dinner at the Vogels'. Crutchfield completely at home with cold soup, fancy salads, and place settings with five or six silver-plated utensils. And the worst: Colleen's gradual yielding to Crutchfield's pressure, the gradual erasing of me from her thoughts—an erasure I had asked for and had deserved, but which now made me sick with jealousy.

I didn't understand any of this. I would look at myself in the bathroom mirror and believe I could see a face beneath my face, an emerging face I did not recognize. This second face was gaunt and needful and weak, like a starved refugee, a bohunk in rags. Who was this? Why was he so screwed up when he thought he was so hip?

I bodysurfed almost every afternoon, looking for the confident calm the ocean once had given me. On the cosmic scale of things I was a grain of fretful sand on the infinite beach. The gods had to be laughing. And if there were no gods, then I ought to be laughing. It seemed so obvious, but there was no relief in the idea.

Where was the problem-drowning power of the surf? Where was perspective? Riding a giant twelve-foot comber in, I saw them playing on the beach—chasing each other, falling down and rising up, kissing. And if it was night and the beach was deserted, I saw them make a nest in the dark sand and take off their bathing suits. The wave hammering me shoreward became less substantial than the tidal waves produced by the seismic disturbances of my ugly runaway imagination.

I didn't answer Crutchfield. When he sat down I unbuckled my seat belt and went up front to the pilot's cabin. "Santee," Captain O'Neil said. "Aim the airplane at China."

"How do I do that, sir?" I said.

"Take the yoke in your hands and turn it counterclockwise." He pointed at a black dial. "Put that indicator on two hundred and seventy degrees. You won't need any rudder. She'll slip around."

I turned the yoke and the left wing dipped.

"Don't be afraid of it," he said. "And quit trying to sit up straight. Go with the airplane."

I realized that as the wing dipped I was compensating for it by trying to keep myself vertical. I had been in a plane only once before, a dollar-a-ride Ford Trimotor that had come to Fort Worth during a county fair. Wes Caulkins paid three dollars for the three of us and we cruised like an airborne snail around the city at about one thousand feet. The Ford had huge hardwood control wheels that had probably been designed as steering wheels for Model T trucks. The old plane vibrated hard in the bumpy springtime air as it yawed and pitched and sank. The pink lemonade, cotton candy, and hot dogs I'd eaten earlier climbed up my guts. "Looky there!" Wes Caulkins said. "There's the SMU ballpark!" But I couldn't look up from my shoes, which I was about to cover with bright pink puke.

The twin radial engines of the C-45 were picking up RPMs. I could hear them revving as if the plane were diving.

"Keep the nose level with the horizon, Santee," Captain O'-Neil said. "We lost some lift when you dipped the left wing. Didn't I mention this phenomenon in class last week?"

I pulled the yoke back, and the engines began to labor.

"Too much," the captain said.

We were heading straight west now. I turned the yoke clockwise until the bubble indicator showed that the plane was flying level. Then I put the nose squarely on the horizon. The engine roar sounded normal again.

"That's it," the captain said. "Now hold this heading until I tell you to change it." He yawned and looked at his wristwatch.

I was a little hungover but the air was smooth as glass, which was good news to my stomach. Bumpy air would have been hard to deal with. I still felt a little drunk and queasy from last night. I liked this make-believe flying and wondered if I'd ever be a real pilot. It didn't seem likely. I sneaked glances at Captain O'Neil. He looked good in his blue uniform and combat ribbons. A hero straight out of every war movie I'd ever seen—confident jawline, sharp hawklike nose, the unblinking fidelity of his steel-gray eyes. He'd been a bomber pilot in the war, and had flown over forty missions in the European Theater, including the first low-level daylight raid over Germany, in which half the bomber group was shot down.

He looked as if nothing ever got to him. I wondered if that was true. Did that uniform give him some kind of protection against emotional turbulence? Was he above the world not only when he flew, but also when he had both feet on the ground? If his wife started going out with another man, would he still have this same calm look of high purpose in his gray eyes, this *pilot* look, as if he were ten thousand feet above the futile crowds of earthbound humanity?

The engines were laboring, had been for some time. I checked the horizon and couldn't see it. The line where the blue sky met the ocean had fallen below the nose. I pushed the yoke forward and the engines began to race. When the horizon came back up I leveled out. But then the horizon kept coming up until it filled the windshield and I was looking at whitecapped water. The engines kept racing, their building roar indicating that we were in a shallow nosedive. I pulled back on the controls and found the horizon again, only to have it drop away steadily until I couldn't see it. The engines moaned as they struggled to pull the C-45 upward. This seesawing continued. I couldn't figure out what I was doing wrong.

Then Captain O'Neil sat up and chuckled. "They're messing with you, Santee," he said.

"Sir?"

"Your buddies in back. They're moving back and forth, changing our center of gravity. It's an old trick."

The plane was diving again. This time I let it. "The sons of bitches," I said.

Captain O'Neil gave me a sharp, cautionary glance. "Easy, son," he said. "It's all in good fun." He took over the controls. "Send Gilman up here."

I got up and stepped through the passageway between the cabins. Crutchfield and the other two were crouched in the rear of the plane, next to the pile of parachutes.

"Assholes," I said, and they laughed. "You're next, Gilman," I said. Gilman looked about fourteen. Small and skinny, with horn-rims and zits. But he had a private pilot's license and was superior about it. After the rest of us were seated again, the left wing dipped steeply as Gilman made a professionally sharp left turn.

"At least Gilman knows what he's doing," Crutchfield said.

"Why don't you just go fuck yourself, Monster," I said.

He looked at me. His eyes were flat. There was no friendship left between us. Whatever strange bond had held us together through four years of high school was less than a memory now. I didn't know him. He didn't know me.

"I don't *have* to fuck myself," he said. He leered at me to make the message even more obvious. I got out of my seat and he got halfway out of his, but I landed the first punch, a right to the nose. He roared at me and put his head down and butted my chest. The aisle was narrow and the low ceiling made us crouch and our punches were blocked half the time by the seats. I hit the other cadet once, a quiet neatly groomed kid named Pearson. It was an accidental rabbit punch to the neck that knocked his hat off and ungroomed his hair. Pearson stuck his head into the pilot's cabin and yelled for Captain O'Neil. The captain came into the back, leaving Cadet Gilman to fly the plane in circles. Crutchfield and I were on the floor, each holding the other in a headlock, our free arms driving punches into each other's ribs.

"Attention!" Captain O'Neil commanded.

Both Crutchfield and I waited for the other to let go first. I finally did. Then we got up. I was spattered with blood from Crutchfield's nose. My lip was cracked, and I'd bitten my tongue.

Captain O'Neil looked at us without speaking. His calm, impersonal eyes sized us up—what we were now, what we'd be in the years to come. Unremarkable fuckups. A weariness in his face suggested that the world was already overpopulated with legions of such rejects.

The moment had staying power. It seemed to last for minutes. This was godly judgment from the wild blue yonder. One long look from those lofty, cloud-gray eyes said it all. Getting kicked out of ROTC was the least of our problems.

"Good luck in your new careers, boys," Captain O'Neil finally said.

I skipped the rest of my classes that day. I went home, changed out of my bloodstained blues, took a shower. I put on a pair of flannel slacks and a clean shirt.

Mitzi was in the kitchen working a crossword puzzle. I sat down at the table opposite her. "I need to borrow twenty dollars, Mitzi," I said.

She looked up, studied me for a minute. "And I need a seven-letter word meaning 'enmesh.' Why twenty?" she asked. "That's a lot of money. What happened to your face?"

"I'm going to buy a ring. For a girl. 'Entwine.' I took a spill on my bike."

"You're going to buy a *what*?" She started to smile, as if this was the beginning of a joke. But she saw my face then and knew it wasn't. She frowned at her puzzle. "What girl?" she said. "You don't have a girl. 'Entwine' fits, but it messes up thirty-four down."

I tapped a cigarette out of her pack, lit it. She was probably right. "Yeah, I do," I said. "I guess I've never mentioned her.

Thirty-four down is probably wrong then.''

''Mention her now. Who is she? Is she pregnant?''

''No. Her name is Colleen Vogel. Her dad owns the Vogel-Darling Funeral Home.''

''Rich people. What kind of ring do you think you're going to buy a rich girl for twenty dollars?'' She bit her pencil, gazed despairingly at her puzzle. ''Thirty-four down is 'Yankee Clipper.' That has to be 'Joltin' Joe,' doesn't it?''

''I'll put twenty down, and put the ring on layaway. It could be 'trade ship.' Or *'Cutty Sark.'* One of them was named that.''

''No it couldn't. 'Entwine' is wrong.'' She shoved the puzzle aside, lit a new cigarette. ''Ozzie,'' she said, ''you're only eighteen. What do you want to get married for?''

''I'm getting engaged, not married.''

''Engaged,'' she said. She picked up the puzzle. ''That fits.'' She started erasing then stopped. ''Oh shoot. It's past tense.''

''I mean, I'll finish school first,'' I said, but I was improvising now, maybe even lying.

''So what's the big hurry?''

I shrugged. I didn't have the nerve to say it: *I love her.* If I said it out loud it wouldn't be true. It was barely true unsaid. But I wasn't sure of that either. I wasn't sure of anything. I just knew I couldn't stand thinking of her with Crutchfield, or anyone else for that matter. Could that be love? Is that all it came down to?

''Are you in love with her?'' she said, staring at her puzzle again as though my mind was readable in the clues.

What did Mitzi know about love? Her life with men had been like a guerrilla war—hectic dirty combat with long boring periods of stalemate. She was a combat veteran who understood the tactics of the fight but nothing of the war's long-range strategy or purpose. Her question irritated me. It implied motherly concern. She was over her head, and had been from the day she was born.

"Yeah," I said. "I guess."

She looked up from her puzzle. Our eyes met for seconds, as if by looking at each other we would be able to *see* each other. Her life and my life were light-years apart, and there was not enough familiarity in this rare exchange to address the mystery of motive—hers or mine or anyone's. Why does a chicken cross the road? To get to the other side. That summed it up. That was all anyone knew about it. Period.

Nerve failed us and we both looked away. She returned to the solvable puzzle before her.

"What's a six-letter word for 'bud'?" she said.

" 'Blossom,' " I said.

The shining city, marching its white houses down to the rim of the sea! Perfect city, perfect sea, under perfect skies! This is it, this is what we've been searching for. What great things are in store for us! We are home at last, the place we've been drifting toward for years. Our town forever, our special place. No more wandering unwelcomed into dead ends, no more half-baked attempts at transplanting our lives. From now on we'll know where we are and we'll know how to belong. We are not fugitives—we want to belong. From now on we will be able to see clearly what is best, what is second-best, and what to avoid. We will live as people were meant to live, happy and safe in the salt-washed air, among groves of bright oranges and velvety avocados.

We took all the quaint back roads, sampling the countryside. We came from the east hills, through the little towns of Julian, Santa Isabel, and Ramona. Then down into the eastern suburbs of the city. We stayed in a motel for a week and then Mitzi found the ideal house, a house made of redwood that had once been a one-room schoolhouse. Six thousand dollars the owner wanted, and Mitzi flirted with him until he came down to five. She had almost a thousand in cash for a down payment, and the bank gave her a twenty-year mortgage for the rest. It was official. We were home. It was Day One in the brand-new world.

The past was a fading dream that couldn't fade fast enough. I remembered only fragments, bits and pieces that were indelible, but the rest was buried for good. The past

*lost its false authority and its power to hamstring the
future. It was dead as a maple leaf in winter.*

*We're home, Fred. But Fred, as if he is beginning to lose
interest, doesn't answer. I look out the front window and
see a troop of kids my age go flying by on bicycles, a cloud
of dust billowing in their wake. The sun is a white flame
fusing the tops of date palms across the street. I am outside,
sitting on the fender of the Packard, leaning against the
hood. The engine ticks as it cools, the time between each
tick increasing, like a failing clock.*

*I am thinking: Clocks lie, clocks die. This place is
clockless as paradise. I can almost taste this idea in the
bougainvillea-drenched air. I can almost read it in the
blank blue sky.*

17

Benedetto di Coca was arraigned by a federal prosecutor under the McCarran Internal Security Act. This new law required Communists and Communist-front organizations to register with the federal government as foreign agents. Art was subpoenaed as a prosecution witness. There would be a preliminary hearing sometime before Christmas. It was ridiculous—Benedetto a foreign agent!—so no one was really worried, but given the government's obsession with subversives these days, anything was possible.

Art told me this over the telephone. I'd called him the day before I bought the ring to see what he thought about my chances with Colleen. I also wanted him to tell me how tight Crutchfield and Colleen had become. He wasn't helpful.

"The worst thing that can happen is she'll tell you to stick the ring up your ass," he said. "Then you're out twenty bucks at most."

I didn't want to hear that. But his tone of voice made it clear that he had other things than Colleen's emotional attachments to think about.

"You think he got into her pants, Art?" I asked, hating the rising pitch of my voice.

After a few seconds he said, "Jesus, how the hell would I know something like that?"

I got the quarter-carat solitaire at Zale's jewelry store. It was a two-hundred-dollar ring. I thought the store would want to hold it on layaway, but the manager said I could take it with me for twenty dollars down if I was able to make regular payments of nineteen dollars a month for ten months. This was good news. Now I could take the ring to Colleen, rather than the two of us having to drive downtown to Zale's just so she could see the evidence of my commitment.

I needed a job to make the payments, and I found one without much trouble. It was a good part-time job at an electronic supplies wholesale store on Kettner Boulevard, downtown. I saw it advertised in the *Evening Tribune*'s want ads. They needed a stock boy who knew how to read the designations on vacuum tube boxes. I'd talked to the manager on the phone and convinced him of my technical knowledge, and after a face-to-face interview, he offered me a dollar an hour. I could work afternoons and weekends, and easily make thirty dollars a week.

Colleen didn't seem all that eager to see me. She talked about Benedetto and Art, how awful Benedetto's arraignment was, but

I figured this was a diversion. She wanted me to sweat. I couldn't blame her. I'd been acting like a jerk for weeks, and she needed to let me know that my behavior had given her a lot of grief.

"I want you to be my girl again," I said.

"I don't know," she said. "What will I tell Brian?"

I felt my heart stiffen in my chest. I wanted to tell her what she could tell Crutchfield, but managed to stop myself. I shrugged.

"But I love you, Colleen," I said. I heard myself say it again in memory. It sounded believable, it even sounded true. I watched my lips move, saw the righteous insistence in my eyes. Not a single twist of duplicity in that honest face.

We were on the front steps of the Vogel home, her mother's pale face ghosting the front windows. Not the ideal place to declare eternal love. Cars crept by, their tires whispering piously. Passing a funeral home with speed and noise was thought to be bad luck by most people. They crawled along, the drivers facing straight ahead as if they were afraid of being singled out for difficult nightmares by the lingering spirits of the dead.

"What makes you think *Brian* doesn't?" she said. "Just last night he said exactly the same thing."

"He did?" Once again the little movie theater in my skull reeled off nasty episodes.

"But words are easy, aren't they?" she said. "Boys think they can get anything they want if they use the right words."

She looked away from me, eyes dark with specific hurt. Her cute lips were drawn thin by a sharply bitter memory. I took this as a hopeful sign. It looked like Crutchfield had done something to wreck his chances with Colleen. I'd never seen this darkly vexed expression before. I was sure I wasn't responsible for it. At the same time it pissed me off. What sleazy thing had Monster done to merit such a look? I shut the movie off before it had a chance to show me.

"But I've always loved you, Colleen," I said. "Before Crutch-field, before anyone. I've been acting like an idiot, I know. But I think I'm over it, whatever it was." This didn't seem completely true, but on the other hand I had no idea what was. The only thing I knew for sure was that I couldn't stand thinking of her in someone else's arms.

I took the box out of my shirt pocket and showed her the ring. Her face brightened. Then the tears came. I knew I was home free.

"Oh my *God*, Ozzie!" she screamed. I slipped the ring on her finger. She studied it for a moment, then threw her arms around my neck. "It's so beautiful! I *love* it, honey!"

We admired it for minutes as Colleen, face wet with tears, held the diamond to the light to find its brilliant colors.

"So, what *are* you going to tell Crutchfield?" I said.

"Tell him?" she said. "I was just kidding, honey. I don't have to tell him anything. We were just going out, that's all. Did we make you jealous, you big bad bear?"

She gave me a sly sidelong look and a teasing smirk, as if to make me realize that her fling with Crutchfield had just been a plot between the two of them designed to make me come around. I wasn't convinced. The bitter look she had had on her face moments ago had not been an act. But I was willing to let it go at that.

We went to the beach. It was like old times. I dug a hole and she buried me playfully in the sand. "You're mine, you big old goofus," she said. She gave me butterfly kisses from chin to forehead. She stopped to admire her ring. Then she teased me again with her quick lips and darting tongue. This went on for a while, her excitement building.

It was late afternoon, cloudy and humid, and the beach was almost deserted. Another couple half a mile away gazed at the gray horizon, cheek to cheek. Colleen tickled my nose with a fingernail. I swung my head from side to side, trying to escape.

"Okay," I said. "Enough is enough. Dig me out."

"Not till you convince me," she said.

"Of what?"

"Of your *love*, silly."

"I thought I already did."

"I need to be sure. I mean, it's only fair, don't you think?"

"Okay, but I can't do that just from the neck up."

"Yes you can." She touched my nose again with her tickly fingernail.

I made up a pretty speech. "Oh darling," I said. "My world is empty without you, my life would be like a dead starfish on the beach, dried up and stinking, without you."

She shut me up by crawling over me and covering my face with her damp breasts. I tongued her salt. She made ragged cooing sounds until her violent breath reduced them to moans.

"When are you going to dig me out?" I said.

"Maybe never, honey."

The surf was huge and dark in the failing light. She saw me

looking at it. Her face against the evening gloom became years older. Like the face of a woman who had already lived a tiring and dissatisfied life. A woman leaning toward a single desperate act.

"I may wait until the tide comes in," she said.

It was going to be a big tide, but it wouldn't come this far up the beach. Even so, the thought was not pleasant.

"Don't kid around, Colleen," I said.

She picked up a fistful of sand and let a slender thread of grains sift through her fingers, as if from an hourglass.

"It would be a romantic way to die, wouldn't it, honey?" she said.

"Dying isn't romantic."

"Oh but it *is*! Dying can be very romantic!"

"In the movies, maybe."

"Not just in the movies."

"Colleen, for Christ's sakes!"

"I'm just teasing you," she said.

"Then dig me out."

"Are you afraid?" she said. "Are you afraid of me, darling?"

It was harmless teasing, but her eyes glittered strangely. No one knows anyone else. My heart tapped against the cool weight of the sand. I imagined the first wave sliding over my face. I closed my eyes and waited.

In this way I did penance, while the dark ocean roared.

18

The Vogel backyard was a huge exotic garden. It was easy to imagine Adam and Eve here, wandering hot with innocent lust among the vines and leaves. Raised islands, surrounded by a lush ocean of bluegrass, blazed with flowers. Banana trees, orange and lime trees, avocado and fig trees, pomegranates, magnolias, birds of paradise—all were randomly spaced as if they found themselves together here by coincidence. Centered in this planned jungle was a wide, trellised gazebo, top-heavy with bougainvillea. A seven-foot stone wall knitted with woody vines shielded the garden from the outside world. Hummingbirds, more than I'd ever seen at one time, hung suspended in the air in front of several feeders that dangled from the patio roof.

A mockingbird in a silver-leaf eucalyptus tree ran through its copycat repertoire over and over, which made me think that charlatans are part of nature. And on the heels of this idea, another: that dishonesty wasn't a failing among human beings but was a common tool of nature. The twig-mimicking praying mantis, the background-repeating chameleon, the leopard's spots tricking the zebra, the zebra's stripes confusing the leopard. Double-edged deception was everywhere you turned. Those delicate-looking meat-eating flowers that trap insects in a sticky poison nectar that turns them into digestible paste. The anglerfish, waving a fake worm from its head—an actual *growth*—to lure in curious suckers. And then there was skunk cabbage, high with shit-reek, seducing clouds of dung-loving flies to broadcast its spore. Honesty and straightforwardness turned you into food for cagier animals. Deer and grouse and ducks and spawning salmon—they almost beg to be centerpiece dishes. The tricksters are the heroes of evolution. They are the happy, well-heeled survivors.

I sat at a wrought-iron table amid this thriving garden, drinking a Pepsi Mr. Vogel had given me, waiting for Colleen. *From Here to Eternity* was playing at the State Theater and she wanted to see it. She thought Montgomery Clift was the handsomest and sexiest actor in Hollywood. She told me that I looked like Clift. Not as elegantly slim, certainly not as *sensitive* or *noble* ("You rat!"), brown eyes instead of blue, but otherwise I could pass for his less sympathetic younger brother.

She said Crutchfield looked too much like Robert Mitchum for her tastes—the bent nose, the sleepy eyes. Robert Mitchum had eyes you couldn't trust. Or you could trust them to do the wrong thing. I didn't ask her what she was talking about. She said Art looked like a young John Garfield and that Denise looked like a blond Donna Reed. Colleen had started a subscription to a movie magazine and tended to think of ordinary people in terms of how much they resembled, or failed to resemble, Hollywood actors. (Her dad looked like Edward Arnold, her mom like Barbara Stanwyck, Mr. Flooding—embalmed and in the ground now— like an overweight Zachary Scott with even less of a chin, and so on.)

All this was harmless enough and easy to put up with. "What star do you think I look like?" she asked me once, and before I had a chance to think about it, she warned, "If you don't say Piper Laurie, don't say anything." "Piper Laurie," I said, and when you looked at her for a while you could see that she did look a little like Piper Laurie. Bigger breasts, finer features, but close enough to say the resemblance was there and mean it.

One night, up on Palomar, she said, "Call me Piper." I did, and she called me Monty. Monty and Piper made love like rising stars under the giant night-searching dome. I wanted to ask her if she ever called Crutchfield Bob, but thought better of it.

As I sipped my Pepsi the idea that deception was the rule rather than the exception snowballed. Nothing was as it seemed. And that was necessary. If you could strip away all appearances, you'd be left with nothing but the horror of emptiness. We *had* to deceive each other, not just to be successful in the world but to protect ourselves from a truth too electric for the mind to handle. We were two-legged anglerfish, dangling bait, bringing in the suckers. And sometimes we fell for our own lures. I *liked* being thought of as a less sympathetic younger brother of Montgomery Clift. I even began to see that resemblance in the mirror, a resemblance I cultivated. I changed the way I combed my hair, I shaved my dumb mustache. I even practiced that soulful look Montgomery Clift was famous for.

When I arrived to pick up Colleen, Mr. Vogel offered me a part-time job at the mortuary. ("Now that you and Colleen are engaged, you should start learning the business.") He gave me a tour through the "slumber room," where the deceased were put on display all made up to look as if they were only napping. Relatives and friends of the family could sit in this room with the departed and witness, firsthand, their peaceful repose. Mr. Vogel said it was the closest thing to a religious experience most people would ever have, because it gave them an image of death they'd never forget, and that image was one of tranquil beauty and eternal rest. Beneath the painted lips and rouged cheeks and stiffened hair were the wires and clips and pins and sutures that held the wrecked body together, but that was a reality no one, other than the mortician, would be asked to face. It was a deception everyone benefited from. "The forest of emotions requires a careful chameleon," he'd said mysteriously. What he meant didn't sink in until I came out to the backyard alone, where I had time to mull it over.

"We'd start you off in sales, I think," Mr. Vogel had said. "You're a tactful young man with a sense of compassion."

"No I'm not," I said. I imagined Montgomery Clift's honest unblinking eyes, his heartfelt way of expressing himself.

Mr. Vogel looked at me over his cigar as he drew flame into it from his lighter. "Even if I believed that, Oz, it wouldn't matter.

You can learn these things easily enough. We have a few standard tricks that produce the desired effect.''

We toured the casket selection room. The caskets were arranged in no particular order—or so I thought. It seemed as if they had just been unloaded from a truck by careless furniture haulers, but Mr. Vogel told me that the caskets had actually been carefully laid out. The pattern was designed to disarm the customer, to suggest the idea that confusion in a casket showroom was a virtue akin to humility. But there were specific "avenues" among the caskets through which the families of the deceased were led by the salesman. The families were shown the cheapest caskets *first*—untreated pine boards with nail-down lids. They were made to understand by the salesman that these caskets were for wretched indigents or the venomous few who had little or no love for the departed. The next set of caskets on the tour were the Cadillacs—fine hardwoods, plush interiors, brass fittings—well beyond the means of most people. And so the families were relieved to see that the final group of caskets were in the midpriced range, and they almost always bought one of these, usually one of the higher-quality ones. "Everyone wins, nobody loses," Mr. Vogel said, puffing his cigar. "The family feels they have done very well by the deceased. The death is finalized and the families can walk away relieved of all residual guilt. And our salesman walks away with a tidy little commission."

I said I'd have to think about it. We went into the kitchen and he gave me a Pepsi. "Well, Oz," he said, "that's what I want you to do. Think about it. And while you're at it, think about this.

You'll make at least double what you're getting at the electric shop."

I took my Pepsi out to the backyard and waited. I heard Colleen, somewhere in the house, singing "You Belong to Me," a song we both liked. I strolled around the fantastic garden, caught up in the perfumes of the flowers and Colleen's sweet voice. I imagined Montgomery Clift selling a casket to a widow. How could she resist? Clift seemed like a mourner, not a salesman. He seemed crushed by the enormity of grief, not someone who had a satisfying life to go back to.

I sat at a wrought-iron table and thought about the Garden of Eden, about deception, and my part in it all. The forest of emotion requires a careful chameleon. I thought I understood this now. A big king snake slithered by in the carpet of grass. I smiled. The smile didn't stop. I kept smiling until I felt my face crack. A wave of hilarity washed over me. I started laughing out loud.

Alone in the Vogel's backyard I roared with laughter. Tears and snot spilled out of my distorted face. I got up and found cover behind the gazebo where I could fall apart unseen.

19

I was doing no better in college than I'd done in high school, even though I enjoyed being on the college campus. Now that we'd been kicked out of ROTC, Crutchfield and I never saw each other, and that made the campus even more enjoyable. I guess I was just a lousy student. The sight of a thick textbook made me want to listen to music. If I actually opened one, I felt a sinking sensation in my stomach. Every paragraph seemed dense with labored ideas and special vocabulary that needed to be memorized even before you understood exactly what it meant.

Intro to Psychology was a wilderness of such paragraphs. It wasn't that I didn't care about the subject, it was just that I wasn't sure what the subject was. Watson's refutation of Thorndike's law of effect, and his own ideas of frequency and recency, just would not sink in, even though I read them over and over.

On the other hand, the concepts of "satisfiers" and "annoyers" seemed so simple-minded I was sure I'd missed the point. All this made human beings seem like mildly interesting gadgetry, like something you'd read about in *Popular Mechanics*. But the writers of *Popular Mechanics* would have made it a lot easier to read.

"Watson," the professor said, "became confused about human thought processes."

Join the club, daddy-o, I wanted to say.

"One cannot allow the idea that thinking is nonphysical into a behavioristic system," the professor said. "For the strict behaviorist, there are no abstract human properties, such as mind or soul."

"This is kind of like what the Commies believe, right, Professor?" someone asked.

The professor hesitated before answering. Things were a little tense on campus. One professor had been fired because of his socialistic views. Another one had been fired for refusing to sign the loyalty oath. *"Eso puede ser, es posible,"* the cagey psychology professor said, dodging the issue. He gave the rest of his lecture in a mixture of Spanish, French, Latin, and British English. The girl sitting next to me fell asleep behind her book. I watched a silver thread of saliva unspool from her sleeping lips. I walked out and didn't come back.

I was doing a little better in my English class, although I'd only turned in one paper. Clive Carrington, the one-eyed ex–RAF pilot, scratched "Jolly good" on it, adding, "though a trifle scatter-brained."

He missed class now and then. Sometimes he came in drunk,

though he never gave himself away by acting drunk. But his movements were too controlled. If nothing else, I knew a drunk when I saw one. "The English language is a damned mysterious thing," he once said. "You won't master it. It can't be mastered. At best, it will adopt you. If it does, consider yourselves kissed by the angels."

This sort of instruction left the class bewildered. Carrington had gotten his job because he'd published a novel. The English department liked the idea of having a real writer on its faculty. But for a writer he didn't have much to say about *writing*, except things like "Bloody strange business. Don't know why anyone would want to do it for a living." Instead of talking about grammar he talked about his boat, his love of the sea, the kind of women he'd been with since becoming maimed. He never told war stories. Though he sometimes talked about war's stupidity.

"Are you one of these pinko 'Better Red than dead' people?" a grinning, no-neck, burr-headed football player asked him once.

Carrington didn't hesitate. "Yes, I am," he said, thumping the floor emphatically with his cane. "No political system will survive another war. Nuclear war would provide a variety of horrors beside which hell would look like teatime in Coventry."

Some of the students, those who liked Carrington, squirmed in their seats. Talk like that would lose him his job. But he'd lost a leg and an eye in the war, and so losing a low-paying job in a small American college was not probably high on his list of possible personal catastrophes.

I saw a handmade poster on a bulletin board near the administration building that said:

A wise man's heart inclines him toward the right,
But a fool's heart toward the left.
—Ecclesiastes 10:2

Wake up, college students! Don't be misled by
Your Godless Professors!

Even the Bible was preaching anti-Communism, it seemed. Someone tore it down after a few days, but then duplicates appeared in other locations, one on Carrington's office door. All this amused him, but in a sad way. "The only bright spot in all this is that you Americans probably don't know what you're doing. If, like Mussolini's Fascists, you *did* know, then I suppose I'd be less sanguine toward this remarkable country."

Carrington got fired before the semester was over. The official reason was "unprofessional and substandard performance," but most of us in his class believed his political ideas made people too uneasy. His replacement was a stiff disciplinarian who wore a flag on his lapel. He warned us on day one that he would tolerate no political discussion, and that he was a grammarian first, last, and always. "Ask me about commas, not Commies," he said. He looked as if he expected people to laugh. When the class got around to realizing this, they did. I quit showing up for that class, too.

A week later I dropped the rest of my classes. Nelson was unhappy about it—not because I'd wasted his money on books and fees, but because he thought it signaled a downward trend for me. "The future is going to be here before you know it, Oz," he said.

"You're going to wake up one day and find that you're thirty-five years old and still waiting for something to come along. By then it may be too late. Nothing might come along."

We were sitting out in the Packard again under a fine drizzle. I'd been coming out to the Packard a lot lately. It was my lifeline to the past. It felt good to sit in the backseat, to smell the mildewed mohair upholstery and to recall my fourteen-year-old self. I tried, by looking backward, to see ahead. It made sense, and it didn't make sense. Making sense was not a priority. Making discoveries was.

But I didn't make any discoveries. The future looked about the same as the past. Nelson had trailed me out to the Packard. He was a good stepfather, and wanted to see me become a decent grown-up man. "You're supposed to do something with your life," he said. "It doesn't have to be a great thing. It just has to be *some*thing. I'm a blueprint maker. I'm a good blueprint maker. And that's enough. That's how you get along in this life. You find something to do, and you do it as well as you can."

It seemed like the world's weakest argument, even though it was the world's *only* argument. I couldn't answer it. No one could. He was absolutely right. And he was absolutely wrong. I shrugged. "I guess," I said.

"Don't guess, Oz. Believe it."

He'd never been this forceful with me before. It occurred to me then that there was something else on his mind. I felt a small wariness.

"I was wondering how you'd feel about moving into your own apartment sometime," he said.

This came as a true shock. Nothing had prepared me for it. "*Why?*" I said.

"Because if you got out on your own, I think you'd see things more clearly. Things will come into focus. Your mother and I agree on this."

As if on cue, Mitzi tapped the window. She climbed into the front seat. She lit a cigarette. "Jesus, it's cold out here," she said. "Why don't you two come inside and eat something?"

"When?" I said to Nelson.

"Well, not right away. But soon. We'll help you find a clean place."

I looked at Mitzi. She didn't blink.

"Getting rid of your bastard brat at last," I said.

"Don't talk like that, Ozzie," she said. "No one's kicking you out. It's up to you. But Nelson's right. If you were more independent, you might pull yourself together and find something to do with yourself."

"We'll help you out," Nelson said.

"I guess I should have stayed in school," I said.

"No, it would have just put off the inevitable," Nelson said. "You're not a good student. You need to find a trade."

I felt closed in. Four walls and a ceiling had been moving in on me for some time, and now I could see them. They made a seamless box. I was trapped in my own limits. A fear like claustrophobia surged through me.

I felt them but I could not stop them: tears. Nelson saw them and got misty too. Mitzi took a long drag on her cigarette and turned her face away.

"Come on, you two," she said, her voice trembling. "I've got some nice center-cut pork chops in the pan."

I grabbed a pork chop and rode my bike over to Art and Denise's. I asked them if there was anything available in their apartment building.

"There's a furnished room in the basement," Denise said. She was at the sink doing dishes. "It's only forty a month, and right now it's empty. It's hard to rent because it doesn't have any windows."

"I don't need windows," I said. "Besides, it'll just be for a while, anyway."

Art got the key from the manager, and we went down to the apartment. It wasn't much, but I liked it. The walls were crusty yellow, like dried mustard. The furniture was old and worn-out. There was an old-style fridge with the compressor on top, and an ovenless two-burner gas cooking stove. "It's fine," I said.

We went back up to Art's place. Art gave me a beer. We sat at the kitchen table. "They putting the screws to you, man?" he said.

I shrugged. "I guess. They want me to get off my butt. I don't blame them."

He nodded. "You want to apply at Convair? They're hiring more apprentice welders. Riveters, too."

"Mr. Vogel wants me to go to work for him," I said.

"Cool. Take it. You're going to be working for him pretty soon anyway, right?"

An image of Clive Carrington's boat came to me. I saw it pulling out of San Diego Bay, heading into wide open sea, rising and falling with the swells. I wanted to be on it.

"Right," I said.

"Why don't you ask Art how his dad is?" Denise said, turning from the sink. She looked unhappy, grim-faced. Her belly was round under her apron. "For your information, other people have problems too, Ozzie."

"Shit. I'm sorry, Art. How is Benedetto doing?"

Art shrugged. "They're taking their time. They don't really have anything on him. He's never been a card-carrying Commie. He's too ornery to belong to a club. Especially one that gives a lot of orders. They're checking out his naturalization papers, shit like that."

"Why would they do that?" I said.

Denise untied her apron and joined us at the table. She was about four months along and was putting on weight. Her arms and legs had plumped up and she had a small, sweat-glazed jowl. "For your information," she said, "they threatened to deport him. But they need an excuse first."

"Jesus," I said.

"Won't happen," Art said. "He's a citizen like you and me. You don't deport your own citizens."

"No, you put them in federal prison," Denise said.

"Knock it off, Denise," Art said. "Pop isn't going to prison."

"When do you have to testify?" I asked.

Art shrugged.

"And if Art lies, *he'll* go to prison!" Denise said.

"Jesus Christ, Denise. I said knock it off. Nobody's going to prison. I don't have anything to lie about.''

"They'll back you into a corner," Denise said. "That's what they do, isn't it? They'll force you to say something awful about your dad under oath, and if you don't say it, they'll call you a liar. For your information, they'll put you in *jail* for perjury!''

Art banged the table with his bottle. "Will you shut the fuck up, Denise?'' he said.

Denise's face got severely red. "Oooh! *You!*'' she said. She got up and ran into the bedroom. Her ankles were thick, her calves cluster-veined. Art and I watched her, then watched the closed bedroom door as if her water-bloated image was imprinted on it.

"Dumb bitch," Art muttered. "Let's go out.''

He grabbed a six-pack from the fridge and we headed north in his Merc through Rose Canyon, drinking beer. This was a dangerous stretch of road—it held the county record for head-on crashes—but Art kept the speedometer on eighty. We stopped in Escondido and had hamburgers at a drive-in.

The argument between Art and Denise hadn't been about Benedetto. Something else was going on. I'd had enough beer to get personal. "So, what's with you and Denise, Art?''

Art slammed the rest of his burger into his mouth and flooded it with beer.

"Fuckin' marriage, man,'' he said, chewing ferociously, his jaw muscles lumped like rocks.

I didn't think it was a good idea to ask him what he was talking about, or to remind him how he'd argued for marriage a few months ago.

He calmed down after a while. "Denise is okay," he said. "It's just that she gets on my nerves sometimes, you know?''

I believed I did. "Does she say that a lot?"

"Say what a lot?"

" 'For your information.' That would drive me up the wall."

He shrugged. "Never noticed. What drives me up the wall is she won't fuck. Afraid of hurting the baby. I guess I get on her nerves too. We both need to blow off a little steam every once in a while. Like tonight."

I nodded. I wondered how Denise was blowing off steam.

"Let's get shit-faced," Art said.

It was a Friday night. He didn't have to go to work the next day. I did, but I could put away electronic stock in my sleep.

"Where?"

"Anyfuckingwhere," he said.

20

La Cantina Solaz, just off Avenida Revolución in TJ, was loud
with sailors and Marines. We'd crossed the border after hours of
aimless driving. San Diego after midnight was dead, except for
the sleazy joints on lower Broadway that specialized in robbing
raw recruits from Sticksville, USA.

TJ at that hour was just coming alive. The Avenida was ablaze
in neon, the sidewalks thronged with men in uniform, teenagers,
and tourists. Art parked on the busy street. He gave a half-dollar
each to two kids to keep an eye on his car. If anyone started
screwing around with it, the kids were to come into La Cantina
Solaz and get him. He promised them another half-dollar when
we got back.

We found an empty table at the far end of the bandstand and
ordered a pitcher of margaritas. The band was Cuban, two saxes,
two trumpets, guitar, drums—congas and bongos—bass, clave

sticks, and marimba. They played blood-heating music, a blend of jazz and Cuban rhythms, the kind of music that could animate stone. It made drunk Marines and sailors—some of them Midwestern types who looked like they'd never danced anything but regional two-steps and polkas—stand up and hop like rebel marionettes trying to jerk loose from their strings. They crashed around the dance floor, childish and lewd, yelling and laughing. Some held women, some held wishful air. Fights broke out, but the bouncers stopped them, often before the first punch was thrown.

The music, like Benzedrine, lit a match under the brain. Tequila fanned the flame. Tequila didn't have the heaviness of whiskey. Whiskey slowed things down. Tequila speeded things up. Whiskey and the blues—tequila and Cuban jazz. Whiskey pulled you inward and down, tequila outward and up. Whiskey made you feel sorry for yourself, tequila made you feel sorry for the guy drinking whiskey.

Two women sat down at our table. They acted like they owned it. The table could have been in their kitchen and we could have been their guests.

"You boys alone tonight?" one said.

"No, we're with our mothers," Art said.

The whores laughed. They were good-looking, in their midthirties. One was short and dark, more *indios* in her lost history than Spaniards. The other was tall with hennaed hair and heavy crimson lips. Both were sweating. It had been a busy night.

"You mama give you five *dólares* for me?" the dark one said.

A Marine staggered sideways into our table. "You stole my money, cunt," he said to the tall whore.

He slid into her, bumping her chair back. He righted himself and hammered the table with his fist. The drinks jumped. The whore screamed Mexican curses at him. Blood-damaging curses, old when hurled at Cortez. He started to swing, but Art caught his arm.

"Get lost, fuckhead," Art said.

The Marine squinted at Art. He tried to organize the numb muscles of his face into a threatening sneer. "Ya fuckin' punk," he said. He put his opened hand on Art's face and shoved. Art stood up and decked him. One of the Marine's buddies came over, but by then the bouncers, a pair of soft-spoken, three-hundred-pound Apaches from west Texas, froze everyone in place with their lead-filled leather saps. No one wanted a cracked skull. And the band played on. I grabbed the hand of the dark whore and took her out onto the dance floor. We twitched to the machete strokes of the clave.

"So, *chico*, you have five or no?" she said.

"I've got it," I said.

"*Bueno*. You want to dance or to fock?"

"To fuck," I said.

Except I all at once liked dancing with her. I couldn't dance to Cuban music, but it didn't matter. I held her hips and she held mine and the music did the rest. I felt the rhythmic flex and swell of strong muscles under the rocking hips. A pleasure that was not just sexual moved me.

I could have stayed on the dance floor for hours. A woman you could dance with was a woman you could love. This seemed exactly true. The whore and I were in synch—a proper condition for love. She was a five-dollar TJ whore, but that didn't mean the idea was wrong. The bones had to like each other first, then the muscle and blood. After these requirements were met, the head couldn't help but follow. *That* was love. Then her hand slid to my crotch, reminding me that money ruled the planet, not love. "Enough dancing," I said.

"Ya basta el baile?" she said, her grin sly, her eyes flat black but scorching.

"Sí, basta."

We went up the rickety stairs. Art and his whore had already gone up. When I came out of the narrow room ten minutes later, he was waiting for me.

"There's a window at the end of this hall," he said. "We're going out that way. That asshole I hit and his buddies are waiting for us to leave."

We climbed down an iron fire escape and found an alley that led back to the dark street. We jogged to the Avenida and the car. The two boys were still standing guard. Art paid them, and we headed out of town. But Art wasn't ready to go home yet.

We headed east out of TJ toward La Rumorosa, a dinky pueblo halfway to Mexicali. We stopped at an adobe cantina there and drank straight tequila, chewing lime wedges and licking salt from our wrists between shots. The cantina was dimly lit and only a few farmers were in it. The walls were decorated with papier-mâché skeletons in honor of El Día de los Muertos, the day of the dead.

Drunk skeletons, skeletons arguing with skeletons, cowboy skeletons riding skeleton horses, skeleton dancers, skeleton lovers—a
cartoon festival for the dead. It wasn't meant to be depressing—
just the opposite—but Art began to sink into himself.

We were at a small table shrouded in gloom. One of the farmers, a gaunt man in a straw hat, came over. *"Con permiso?"* he
said.

I nodded. *"Seguro*, why not?'' Art wasn't company anyway.
His chin was on his chest. He wasn't out, I could hear him muttering something, a cracked lament of some kind. Denise, Denise,
he'd say, then hiccup something like a curse or a growl. We
weren't going to get home that night, that was for sure.

The farmer had very little English. I understood about a tenth
of what he said. He was drunk and that didn't help. His brother
Baldemar figured prominently in whatever he was saying. I
bought him a drink. He bought me a drink. Art by this time was
facedown on his arms.

"Vamos," said the farmer, then rattled off something about
Baldemar. *"Tú* come *conmigo, quiero* for you to see *mi car-
nalito,"* he said, splicing languages.

''I'll be right back,'' I said into Art's unconscious ear.

We went outside. The farmer headed for his truck, a fairly new
International. He opened the door and pulled out a bottle of mescal from under the seat. We both had a swig. Then he tucked the
bottle under his arm and we walked down the unpaved street.
The moon in its last quarter dusted the countryside in tarnished
silver. We turned up a narrow, heavily rutted road. The field
around us was lumpy, as if it was a nesting ground for giant ants.

We left the road and stumbled around among the anthills for a while, eventually becoming separated. I tried to follow his voice. He'd started singing, the tune splintered with feeling.

"Where the hell are you, *hombre*?" I said.

He sang louder. I saw moonlight yellowed in mescal, and then him, a wistful phantom squatting on the hilly ground. He held up the bottle and I took it. He took it back and waved it like a maestro's baton. "*Canta!*" he demanded. "*Cantemos!*" Singing blind, I croaked approximations in bad Spanish. It didn't matter. It was the singing that counted, not the song. The music was the body's music, crusty wails and shuddering squeaks, a song from the bones.

He offered me the worm. I took it and crunched it honorably. He began a new song, but it had too much sad spirit in it and I collapsed. I listened to his bleak lullabies for a while, then to grainy whispers that could have inched out of the ground itself.

When I woke, the farmer was gone. The sun was a red uncompromising ball that held earth and all its creatures accountable. I pushed myself up. Dirt fell out of my hair. The lumpy field was a graveyard, decorated for El Día de los Muertos. Orange flowers and red ribbons hung on rickety crosses. Picnicking families groomed the mounds and chatted. A child approached me and gave me a sugar-candy skeleton. I accepted it and thanked her.

I stood up, still drunk but not yet sick. The bottle of mescal sat at a jaunty tilt against the dirt mound I'd slept on. There were still a couple of drinks in it. But they were for Baldemar. I shook dirt from his grave out of my clothes. "So long, Baldemar," I said, patting the grave. I felt I knew him. I'd kept him company all night, the night the Mexican dead come back to say hello. We drank mescal and told astonishing Mexican lies.

Mexico and the U.S. labored under the same hard sun, but slept under different moons. I felt small chills race up my legs, my back, and into my neck hairs. Who was to say for sure that Baldemar hadn't fetched me out of the cantina, disguised as his drunk brother? His thirsty singing had sounded like it came from a throat long filled with dirt.

Crazy thinking, this. I trotted away from those graves.

21

Mr. Vogel looked me up and down. The pleased tailor stood back. I turned to the left, then to the right. Each three-quarter profile was slick in the full-length mirror. I looked as sharp as I'd ever look: blue serge suit, black wing-tip shoes, black socks, off-white silk shirt, navy tie with tiny violet diamonds, gold tie clip, white carnation in the lapel. Here was the king snake in the garden. I was ready, thanks to Mr. Vogel, to receive the grieving.

"Doesn't he look splendid, Colleen?" Mr. Vogel said.

"He's gorgeous," she said. "He looks thirty years old."

Her enthusiasm was undiluted. She'd finally gotten over my little Mexican adventure with Art. She'd heard all about it from Denise. Art was still in the doghouse, two weeks later. Neither one of them knew about the whores. I was sure of that. But we didn't get home until the following Sunday. We'd gone from La Rumorosa to Mexicali, then down to the fish markets of Puerto Peñasco. We

came home with a load of shellfish packed in ice. Art had wanted
to bring something home for Benedetto and thought a basket of
giant prawns and abalone would please him. The old man's case
was coming up soon, and the di Coca household was tense. Art
figured a seafood feast would cheer things up.

Mr. Vogel sent me to be measured for a new suit after I accepted his job offer. I had no choice but to accept. I'd been
canned for missing work the Saturday Art and I were roaming
around Baja. In any case, I had committed myself to Colleen,
which meant that sooner or later I would be Mr. Vogel's apprentice. All the arrows pointed in one direction. I was on a one-way
street—no turnoffs, no stops, no U-turns allowed.

Mr. Vogel paid the tailor. Colleen and I got into his Cadillac
and he took us to our next surprise stop. The Dodge dealership in
La Mesa.

"What are we doing here, Daddy?" Colleen said.

He made a mysterious little clucking sound, then winked. We
got out of the car and he led us to the showroom. A salesman in a
checkered sport coat greeted us. "Ah, Mr. Vogel," he said. "I
believe she's ready."

The salesman went into his office and picked up a telephone.
He spoke briefly to someone, then came out of his office, beaming. He started to rub his hands together briskly—the universal
feeding signal of car salesmen—but had the good taste to stop
himself.

"We're all set, Mr. Vogel," he said. "If you'll come into my
office and sign the papers, Frank will bring the car out front."

"Daddy!" Colleen said. "What *are* you up to?"

Mr. Vogel made his little clucking noise again, winked, and went into the salesman's cubicle. Colleen and I went out to the lot. A kid about my age drove a blue Dodge station wagon up to the showroom door. The car glistened from a recent wash. It had wood side paneling, fat whitewall tires, and a steel sun visor that hung above the windshield like the wing of a small airplane. The car looked big enough to hold a family of seven, a big dog, and a quarter ton of luggage.

"Are you thinking what I'm thinking, honey?" Colleen said.

Before I could answer, Mr. Vogel and the salesman came out. "What a sweet little number!" Mr. Vogel said. He handed Colleen the keys. "Now that you kids have set a date, the car is all yours!"

Mr. Vogel looked at me. He expected stunned gratitude. I did my best. In fact, I did feel a little stunned. "You didn't have to do that, Mr. Vogel," I said.

He slapped his forehead and rolled his eyes like Milton Berle, then gave me a little shoulder-punch. "I'll give you *such* a shot in the head, boy! It's a family car, a car I'd expect a son-in-law of mine to drive. It's economical, and it's *safe*. You can get rid of that noisy deathtrap you call a motorcycle now."

Something in the pit of my stomach hardened and sank. There was no room in the equation for my old BSA Victor. I felt sick.

Mr. Vogel saw my face sag. "Wouldn't look proper, you see, for a mortuary employee to be rattling around on a motorbike," he said.

I nodded carefully, as if embracing the good sense of his argument, but my gut was screaming *no no no*.

Colleen interrupted this tense moment by throwing her arms around her father and squealing, "Oh, Daddy! It's fantastic! Thank you! Thank you!"

We all stood speechless, even the salesman, as if overwhelmed by a sudden tide of warm human feelings. I hid in the Dodge, not wanting my panic to be detected. I opened the glove box and studied the owner's manual. But this depressed me even further. The Dodge Coronet Sierra Station Wagon had an L-head in-line six. It displaced 230 cubic inches and put out 103 horsepower at a windmilling 1,200 RPM. It had a 3.25-inch bore and a long, 4.625-inch stroke. Its high, bottom-end torque was more suited to pulling up stumps than rocketing down the highway. But the torque was compromised by a mushy Gyromatic transmission—half automatic, half manual. This had to be the most boring car ever produced. I switched on the ignition and then the radio. The Patti Page hit "How Much Is That Doggy in the Window?" came blaring on, completing the package.

Mr. Vogel tapped on the window. I rolled it down. "Why don't you and Colleen take her for a little spin? But come home before five. We have some wedding plans to make over dinner!"

Colleen got into the station wagon and slid over next to me. "Isn't it simply *grand*?" she said. "Can't you picture our children sitting in the back?"

"It's terrific," I said. "Really terrific."

I drove it off the lot, then out onto the boulevard. I kept going east until the boulevard became Highway 80, the border highway that went all the way to Florida.

"I didn't know we'd set a date," I said.

Colleen pressed her head against my chest. The car was lumbering toward sixty. "Don't be mad, snookums," she said. "I had to tell them something. I mean, after you gave me the ring and all."

"So what *is* the date?" I said. I spun the radio dial, but couldn't find anything but Patti Page. The same station and the same song seemed to be everywhere on the dial.

"January fifteenth," she said.

"Two months from now."

The speedometer needle wobbled against sixty-five. In two months it might hit seventy. The engine must have been turning over all of 950 RPM, an unleashed tornado. It would bore a grandmother into a terminal coma.

"Aren't you supposed to drive it slower, snookums?" she said. "To break it in?"

"You couldn't hurt this car with a howitzer. Don't call me snookums, okay?"

She sat away from me and pouted. "I thought it was cute. I like nicknames. Don't you have a nickname you'd like to call me?"

"Like what?"

"Like lovums, or bunny."

"I don't think so," I said. "Colleen is good enough for me."

I drove all the way to Alpine. The wagon lumbered up the mountain grade, the irritating Gyromatic shifting back and forth between high range and low range.

We stopped at a roadside café for Cokes. People turned to gawk at me in my mortuary suit. They gawked without a bit of self-consciousness. The hill country east of town had been settled by dust-bowl refugees. They'd stopped thirty miles short of the Pacific Ocean, figuring that was far enough from Oklahoma and Arkansas. They hadn't changed much since the 1930s. I guess I must have looked like a banker to them. I heard muttering, quiet laughter, a halfhearted curse. A big man in bib overalls came over to our booth.

"Excuse me, mister," he drawled. "We was just wonderin'. Is it Jefferson or is it Ben Franklin on a hunnert-dollar bill?"

"Fucked if I know, Abner," I said.

Colleen's eyes got very wide. The man filled himself with air as if he was getting set to blow me away like so much dust. He back-tracked to his booth and consulted with his friends. They were all wearing bib overalls, too.

"Let's split," I said. I got up. Colleen wasn't moving fast enough. I took her hand and pulled her out of the booth. When we got to the front door a beer bottle exploded on the wall next to my head. We ducked out and ran to the car. I started it, stomped the gas, and popped the clutch. The Gyromatic whirred and the big rear hips of the car sank down and we waddled out of the parking lot. Something exploded against the back bumper, an-other beer bottle I figured, but by then we were on the highway and picking up speed. I started laughing.

"It isn't funny," Colleen said, her teeth on edge. She sat as far away from me as she could, arms folded. There were tears in her eyes.

"Yes it is, lovums," I said. "It's funnier than hell."

"Why are you acting this way?" she said.

"It's the suit," I said. "I feel kind of like a banker in it."

"You're not acting like a banker," she said.

I left the highway and took an old country road that snaked up into the mountains.

"It's the suit. And the car. Maybe it's the combination."

"You're not making sense," she said.

I turned the car into a dirt road that skirted a small canyon. I stopped in a wide spot and switched on the radio. Patti Page was gone. Al Martino was overpowering some ballad. I spun the dial. The pickings were slim. It was either Al Martino or Johnny Ray.

"I love this song," Colleen said. Johnny Ray was singing "The Little White Cloud That Cried."

I held my tongue. Colleen snuggled up against me.

"I guess it *was* kind of funny," she said, giggling a little. "Those Okies were so *dumb.*" I kissed her as Johnny Ray started to pour on the sobs. "Promise me you'll be a good boy from now on," she said when we broke for air.

"Promise," I said.

"No more trips to Mexico. No more acting crazy."

"Promise," I said.

I slipped my hand under her sweater. Lifted her bra up to her collarbones. We kissed again. She put her hand on my blue serge crotch.

The Coronet Sierra front seat was wide as a sofa.

"Not here, Ozzie honey," she said.

"Here," I said.

I got my belt loose, she unzipped my pants. Her eyes narrowed and went dim. I liked her eyes when they did that. Like a power greater than either one of us was pulling the strings. My necktie

fell across her face. I watched my cufflinks wink in the gray No-
vember light. My suit coat was still buttoned. Like a banker in his
office with his secretary. I felt the power of my suit. She bit my
tie. She jerked her head back again and again with my tie in her
teeth. I watched my cufflinks, tried to admire them. In an effort
to hold back. It was working. Gold rectangles. About the size of
postage stamps. With my initials on them. O.S. Mr. Vogel was so
generous. He liked me. What a prince. How lucky I was.

"Maybe it *is* your suit," she said, later.

I took that to mean she approved. I didn't ask her to explain.
She did anyway. "It was a lot . . . *better*," she said. "Better than
ever."

I didn't mean to ask, but the question walked through my lips
anyway. "Better than Crutchfield?"

She slapped my face and burst into tears. "*Yes*, better than
Crutchfield, you son of a bitch!"

I got the car turned around and back on the main highway. I
kicked the accelerator into the firewall but the fat-assed Dodge
wouldn't cooperate with my anger. It hummed along like a well-
behaved citizen.

The Dodge cooled me off. It set a fine example of model behavior. The Detroit car industry, with its wide-beamed, softly sprung
machines, was setting the example for the American people. Be
steady, be accommodating, be compliant, be gentle, be likable, be
inoffensive, be a good neighbor.

"I'm sorry, Colleen," I said, slowing the big friendly wagon
down to sixty. "I'm an idiot, honey."

She slid across the seat and sobbed on my shoulder. "Don't

ever mention Brian to me again, Ozzie. Promise me."

"I promise."

"I love you, honey," she said.

"And I love you, honey," I said.

I listened for the hollow note in my words. Either it wasn't there, or I had forgotten what it sounded like.

22

"Speak softly to the bereaved consumer. Be sympathetic but not saccharine. Don't, however, go overboard and fall in love with him. His situation is not unique. We all must face the death of loved ones, sooner or later. Remember your job is to provide a public service *and* to make a profit. We are not merchants of death. We did not invent it. We are facilitators at the disposal of the living. Think of yourself as a member of a transition team. You assist in the crossing over. You are an artist specializing in the Final Adieu. It is a noble task. Not many are called, not many have the mental facility to guide the bereaved toward a substantial expenditure. It is a delicate task, one requiring consummate merchandising skill, an interest in financial self-improvement coupled with essential human decency, and utter loyalty to Vogel-Darling Inc. These requirements are never in conflict with each other. Seen correctly, they augment, support, and complement each other. Remember, your goal is to relieve the bereaved of his pain by providing him with a product *in an appropriate price range* that assuages residual guilt and obviates its prolongation."

I read this page twice but still wasn't sure what it meant. Mr. Vogel had typed it up for casket showroom personnel years ago. I sat behind my little desk among the caskets and potted palms, waiting for Mrs. Haberman to show up. She was already an hour late. Mr. Haberman had died suddenly at the dinner table. He was only forty-nine years old. There had been no warning. He spit out a piece of steak, grabbed his chest, and toppled over dead.

Dickie Corvus, our chief "body-snatcher," found this out from the physician who signed the death certificate at the hospital. Dickie Corvus had been working for Mr. Vogel for ten years. He wasn't bright, but he was strong. A body-snatcher had to be. Hauling dead bodies out of upper-story bedrooms and hospital basements played hell with the lower back. Dickie, who liked to talk, would come by the showroom now and then and tell me stories. He called himself a body-snatcher, but never in the presence of Mr. Vogel, who wouldn't have approved of the term.

Dickie Corvus was about six feet four and weighed at least two hundred and fifty pounds, with no loose fat. He worked with a much smaller man, Irwin Tubman. Irwin was unreliable. He was a drinker and often wasn't able to pick up bodies with Dickie. I had never seen him. He stayed away from the showroom, probably because he didn't want anyone in authority to smell his breath. Strong as Dickie was, he couldn't carry bodies by himself. Not in a dignified way, at least. ("I could drag 'em down the stairs by the heels, but most folks wouldn't go for that.") When Tubman didn't show, Dickie had to find a substitute. Sometimes he hired bums from the rail yards or deadbeat beachcombers. "The thing is, Mr. Santee," he said, "you can't let a stiff lay around for a coupla days collecting fly shit while you roust some boozer out from his hole. Folks will just call up somebody else to do it, and Mr. Vogel, Jesus, he'd roast my nuts on the barbecue if we lost customers like that."

It made sense, his coming to me about the problem. He saw me as someone called "Mr. Santee," who wore a one-hundred-dollar suit and was about to marry the boss's daughter. But I shrugged him off. I didn't think it was my place to complain about coworkers. Dickie looked uncomfortable, talking to me about his troubles. Irwin was his cousin. He wanted him out, but he wasn't about to turn against family. It was a delicate matter. It caused the big body-snatcher considerable anguish.

Mrs. Haberman arrived, along with a younger man. I figured he was her son. She was dressed in black, face held together with an armor of hardened makeup. She wobbled on her high heels, as if trying them out for the first time. Her son was a little older than me, maybe twenty. He was wearing a suit that had been cut for a man forty pounds heavier and a couple of inches taller. He walked into the showroom ahead of his mother, scanning the place, as if making sure there were no traps waiting for her. When I stood up behind my desk he came straight over to me.

"Look," he said. "What I *don't* want is a sales pitch, okay? I want a coffin and I don't expect to fork over three months' pay for it, okay?''

"Certainly, sir," I said. The customer is almost never right but must be allowed, temporarily, to think he is—another line from Mr. Vogel's typed-up list of instructions.

I led the way through the caskets, starting with the unfinished pine boxes.

"These look good," he said. "We want to keep it simple."

"We sell these mostly to the county," I said.

He stepped back and studied the box. "What's that supposed to mean?"

"The county buries unclaimed transients in plain pine," I said. I heard Mrs. Haberman take in breath.

"How much?" her son said.

"Eighty-five dollars. No guarantees, of course."

"What kind of guarantees you talking about?"

"Leakage, penetration by burrowing animals, rot—that sort of thing."

Mrs. Haberman started sobbing quietly. But her cheapskate son had asked for it. I decided to give him the *coup de grâce*.

"How tall was Mr. Haberman?" I asked.

"Six even," the son said suspiciously.

"We might have to break his legs," I said. "These economy boxes come in one universal size, measured for the average five-foot-nine-inch male."

Mrs. Haberman moaned. She staggered sideways. Her son went to her side, held both her hands in his. "We'll look at some

others, Mommy,'' he said. He seemed to be shrinking down into
his oversized suit. His neck looked like a pale stalk in a white
vase. I tried to keep my smile from distorting my well-controlled
face.

They wound up buying a six-hundred-dollar "Eternal Comfort," a plushly cushioned, rayon-lined cherrywood model in the
upper quarter of the mid-priced range. I signed them up for an
underground concrete coffin liner to protect their "investment,"
and a full day of open-casket viewing in the slumber room. The
whole works came to more than twelve hundred dollars. My commission at four percent came to fifty bucks and change. Not bad
for half an hour.

After they left I went back into the cold room to have a look at
Mr. Haberman. He was on a table waiting to be worked on by Mr.
Vogel. I raised the sheet off his face. He had a tall, intelligent
forehead and a long sensitive nose. The delicate nostrils seemed
pinched against a nasty odor. Mr. Haberman, even in death,
smelled a rat. His eyes had been closed but the stubborn lids had
drawn themselves up. The glittering irises, black with dilation,
stared at the dark ceiling. Lip drift gave him a wary grin.

Mr. Haberman looked like he'd caught on to a scheme and had
second thoughts about buying into it. But Mr. Vogel would remove all suspicion from his face. By tomorrow, Mr. Haberman
would wear the expression of a man who'd had a full and richly
satisfying life and was not at all unhappy that it had ended when
it had. But for now, he stared doubtfully into finite space.

I had lunch with Colleen out in the back garden. She'd fixed egg salad sandwiches and chocolate pudding. We ate at the wrought-iron table next to the gazebo. Hundreds of birds raised a din in the trees.

"Daddy says you're doing really well, honey," she said.

"Daddy's right," I said.

"Aren't *we* cocky?" she teased.

"I like selling coffins," I said, biting into a sandwich. "It's just like selling anything else. Only classier."

"Classier?"

"I mean classier than vacuum cleaners or magazine subscriptions."

"I don't think you should compare it to selling magazines, honey. I mean, what you do is so much more *serious.*"

"That's just it. It *isn't* more serious. That's the secret. If you think it's more serious then you get yourself all tangled up in stuff that doesn't help."

"I don't know what you mean, honey," she said. She looked around the yard a little frantically, wanting to change the subject.

"I mean things like, is it right or wrong. Is it good or bad. That type of crap. It's a lot simpler than that. A buck is a buck. Just remember that. Look at what your dad has done for you. And for us. He makes tons of money. He's a happy man. Period."

"Oh look, hon!" she screamed. "A woodpecker!"

The black-and-white bird sat on a branch looking for dead wood.

I hadn't made myself clear. Truth was, I liked the job. It was a little on the shady side, but what wasn't? Selling was selling, and the customer was always going to be on the short end of the stick, whether it was coffins, Chevies, or Mixmasters. Profits had to be made or the whole works would collapse. And to make a profit you had to get more money from the customer than the product was worth. It was that simple. It was Rule One. Profit was the engine, credit was the fuel.

Mrs. Haberman was going to get a short-term loan to pay for her husband's funeral, and that was proper. What choice did she have? She couldn't leave the old man rotting in the garden. She couldn't ask her dipshit son to haul the body to the county dump. Someone had to dispose of the dead. Ordinary families couldn't do it even if they wanted to. There were public health laws about body disposal. Only a trained professional could do the job. What a sweet system! We had the customer by the balls.

After we ate we strolled around the garden. Behind the gazebo I wrapped my arms around her. "I'm a happy man, Colleen," I said. We sank into the lush grass, kissing.

"Not here," she said, yanking at my belt.

"Here," I said, unzipping.

Above us, somewhere in the trees, the woodpecker hammered away at a dead branch and the jackpot of worms he knew was inside.

23

December began with a hot streak. I sold six mid-priced caskets by the eighteenth, plus funeral arrangements. My commissions added up to $266. People were dying like flies. This was a town populated by military and civil service retirees, and that explained the profitable death rate. But younger people were dying at a good clip that month, too. Nothing explained that except rotten luck. Theirs, not mine.

I checked the obituaries in the paper every morning over breakfast the way some people check the weather forecasts or stock quotations. I sat in my windowless one-room apartment and saw the obits as a kind of commodity report on a high-yield-per-acre crop, a crop I wanted a bigger share of. I figured if we got even a quarter of the business in the east county I could make at least eleven thousand a year. Cornering the market was out of the question, but we could do better. Much better.

Billboard space was part of the problem. Mr. Vogel had only
two billboard advertisements—one on El Cajon Boulevard facing
west, one on University Avenue facing east. Not good enough. We
needed two on each street, facing both directions. And we needed
to cover a larger area. We had to have them in the north part of
the county, the beach areas, and the south. But we needed more
than billboards. We also needed a more sophisticated approach.
I suggested radio spots to Mr. Vogel. Maybe even a television ad
during the local news broadcasts.

I showed him something I'd written up. "Dignity and Security,
in an atmosphere of Understanding and Heartfelt Sincerity—*this*
is the Vogel-Darling pledge to YOU."

He put on his reading glasses and looked at the slogan, then he
took off the glasses and looked at me. He cleared his throat.
"Well, Oz. I appreciate your effort, *and* your attitude. Very
commendable. It's just that . . ."

"It should rhyme, right? It's too stuffy, right?"

"No, no. It's fine." He looked uncomfortable. We were in the
living room, waiting for Milton Berle to come on. Mrs. Vogel was
hidden in her huge Hepplewhite wingback chair. Colleen was sitting next to me on the sofa. Mr. Vogel leaned back in his recliner.
He'd been putting on weight. His tired jowls rolled back against
his earlobes. His stomach was mountainous and gassy. He let slip
accidental farts that thundered softly in the deep cushions.

"I could make it rhyme," I said. I closed my eyes a few seconds
to get it right, then said: " 'Vogel-Darling's pledge to *you*—Dignity, Understanding, and Sincerity, *too*.' That would come over
great on the radio, don't you think? Maybe they could put harps

or violins or something in the background, so it wouldn't just sound like a beer ad.''

"Oz, we—the mortuary association—have certain standards. We limit ourselves to billboard advertising. To go beyond that would violate our . . . gentlemen's agreement, you see. Decorum is so much a part of . . .''

"But Mr. Vogel. It's a business. And business is business. Those other guys, hell, they're out to make a buck, too. Aren't they Johnny-on-the-spot at hotel fires and plane wrecks and earthquakes, picking up bodies like they were money bags that fell off an armored car? The dentists in L.A. went crazy when Painless Parker began to advertise, and look what happened. Painless Parker is the dentist king. He ran a thousand un-progressive dentists out of L.A.''

A long exasperated sigh came from the tall serpentine wings of Mrs. Vogel's antique chair. *"Must* you talk business now?'' she said. "We're trying to spend a calm evening together.'' Her tone made it clear that spending a calm evening with me in her living room was not her idea of a great time. And now she was facing a lifetime of such evenings.

She didn't have to worry. If I started making the kind of money I thought I could make, Colleen and I would have our own comfortable house by spring. I squeezed Colleen's hand, thinking about it. She squeezed back, emphatic and horny, her nails digging messages into my palms. The closer we got to our wedding date, the sexier she became. I figured she was thinking about our house, too, and what we'd be doing in it ten times a day, picking a new room each time.

"Perhaps we can add another billboard," Mr. Vogel said. "But we'll talk about it some other time, Oz. Again, I *am* impressed with your . . . ah, zeal, son."

After Milton Berle, Colleen and I excused ourselves. We went out to the kitchen and got Pepsis. She looked at me, her head cocked to one side. "Are you *feeling* all right?" she said.

"I feel great," I said.

I felt like I'd been sucking Benzedrine up my nose for a solid hour. I jumped up and put the flat of my hand on the ceiling. I did a handstand. I dropped to the floor and did twenty one-armed push-ups. I chugged my Pepsi and belched.

"You're red as a beet," she said. She put her hand on my face. "You're burning up, Ozzie!"

"It's hot out."

"No it isn't. It's December. You've got a fever."

"But I'm not sick."

"Let's go upstairs. There's a thermometer in Mother's bathroom."

"*Mother's* bathroom?"

"She likes her privacy."

The habits and preferences of rich people still amazed me. Colleen showed me the upstairs of the Vogel house before we went into Mrs. Vogel's bathroom. Mrs. Vogel not only had her own bathroom, she had her own bedroom, sewing room, and library.

"How come she sleeps in her own bedroom?" I asked.

"Daddy. He stinks of formaldehyde. She can't stand the smell of embalming fluid."

I peeked into the library. Fat leather-bound books with gold-embossed titles on the spines filled an entire wall. A mahogany desk big enough to play Ping-Pong on sat on a thick oriental carpet. An antique grandfather clock ticked in a corner. The time was off by seven and a half hours, a casual disregard of the merciless clock-driven routines that ruled the lives of ordinary working people.

"It's nice being rich, isn't it?" I said, mostly to myself.

"Oh, we're not rich, Ozzie. We're just a little better off than most."

I looked at her, but she was serious. She actually believed it. Somehow, this excited me. I kissed her, wet and sloppy, my hot hands exploring familiar terrain.

"No, not now, not here," she panted. "Let's find out what your temperature is."

Mrs. Vogel's bathroom was as big as my apartment. It even had furniture—a sofa, a chair, a coffee table. Colleen rummaged around in the cabinets under the double sinks.

"Here it is," she said. "Oh dear."

"What?"

"It's a rectal thermometer."

"Uh-uh. Nothing doing."

She rummaged around some more but didn't find anything else. She studied the thermometer, looked at me.

"No," I said. "Never happen."

"Ozzie, be reasonable. We're already mostly married. And you are *sick*, mister." She scolded me like a school nurse, hands on hips, eyes narrowed with matriarchal threat. She locked the bathroom door.

"Colleen, just a damn minute. If you think . . . and hey, what if your mother wants in?"

"She won't. Her favorite program comes on next."

She unbuckled my belt, yanked down my pants. There were other things on her mind than my temperature. This undermined my resolve. She greased the thermometer with Vaseline, then studied methods of attack.

"Get away from me, you pervert," I said, not meaning a word.

"Look who's calling who dirty names," she said, pointing to the distortion in my shorts.

She pulled down my shorts and knelt in front of me. She held my buttocks and pulled me toward her trembling lips. If I had a fever, it had suddenly doubled. She slipped the thermometer into my rectum, then forgot about it. I forgot about it too. "Jesus, nurse," I said, as she took me almost into her throat, her eyes bright with mischief and lust.

I gripped her shoulders and hoped my moans were not roaring around the big house. Locked in the frantic push and pull of her lips, I tried to occupy my mind with other things to dull my over-sensitive trigger. I rehearsed a variety of greetings to walk-in trade.

The greeting can make or break a sale. You've got to select your words carefully. You can't just glad-hand people and act like they're old drinking buddies. You can't tell them this is their lucky day since we've got a big special on the "Rest Haven" cas-ket—buy one now, get another one at half price the next time need dictates. The job demanded a classier approach. "Ah, sir (or madam), I assure you I'm here to assist in every possible way.'' Something like that, but not that. Too Limey-sounding. "This is a terrible time for you, and I want you to understand that I am here for one purpose and one purpose only, and that is to be your servant in your time of need.'' Oily, but not bad. Some oil is required. Oil is a lubricant. Too much gums up the works. A little goes a long way. The idea is to make them believe you give a shit. You can't give a shit, of course, because if you did you'd be a basket case in no time. The grief is theirs, not yours. This is something you have to remind yourself of. The grief is theirs, not yours. The grief is theirs, not yours.

I held back from the point of no return as long as possible, but now it came. I whimpered. Colleen jumped up and rinsed her mouth with Lavoris. When she finished she pulled out the thermometer. She was perky, I was filleted meat.

"Did you like that, Ozzie?'' she said abstractedly, holding the thermometer to the light and squinting at it.

"Jesus yes,'' I said.

Then the ugly thought occurred to me. Where had she learned that little trick and the techniques that went with it? An image of her going down on Crutchfield flashed in my burning brain. Of him urging her to do it, of him showing her how they did it in France, of him holding her shoulders and moaning. Of her sucking the son of a bitch into a blissful slab of filleted meat.

"Oh my God,'' she said. "It's a hundred and four. You're *really* sick, Ozzie!''

"I feel sick,'' I said.

24

I got a shot of penicillin and a prescription for something to knock me out from a doctor in North Park. He said I had a pretty bad strep infection. I stayed in bed for three days, visited by three-dimensional full-color dreams. Colleen came over in the Dodge with thermoses of hot soup twice a day. I'd eat the soup, throw it up, eat some more. Then I'd crawl back into my bed and my VistaVision dreams, and Colleen would go upstairs and visit with Denise.

At night Art would come down with a whiskey toddy. He was in a grim mood. Benedetto was going to be deported. The grand jury had found out from the FBI that he'd lied on his original application for citizenship. He had an arrest record in Italy, but hadn't listed it. It seemed he'd kicked one of Mussolini's Blackshirts off his land before it was confiscated and spent a year in prison for "unpatriotic behavior." ("He has shown, here and in his own homeland, a contempt for plain and simple patriotism, your honor," the prosecutor said.) The Feds also accused him of harboring illegal immigrants. *That* tipped the scales. They threw the book at him. A judge concluded that he had forfeited his rights to citizenship. Benedetto's union provided a lawyer who promised to keep fighting the case, but in the meantime Benedetto would have to go back to Abruzzi, where he had nothing. No family, no land, no prospects. There was a chance he could come back someday, if the government found him "fit for citizenship," but he'd have to "kiss the flag on the White House lawn and sing 'God Bless America' in perfect English with no garlic on his breath before they'd even consider it," the lawyer said. Art was going to have to support his mother and his own fledgling family on his $1.67 per hour.

People by the thousands lined up outside Vogel-Darling waving money at me, begging for caskets. The showroom was crowded with customers. But where were the caskets? I made phone calls to suppliers all over the country, and they assured me that trainloads of new models were on the way. This dream always ended with me having to bar the doors against grousing mobs of casketseekers.

The towering wave blocked the sun. I caught it, happy at first, then realized with horror how big it was. It wasn't going to break on the beach. It steamrolled the city. I dodged chunks of hotels, bridges, cars, zoo animals, and entire flotillas of Navy ships. The mountains east of the city and the wave were going to meet head-on—water and earth, grinding all civilization between them. I woke from this just before the wave broke, my ears hissing with fever.

Colleen on top of me moving with energy, her face unable to reflect light, a dark oval emitting impatient grunts. My early coming was intolerable to her, and she stroked me hard again and mounted, her solid female weight full of strange rage, her energy undiminished, even increasing. Then sponge baths with cool water, lingering at the genitals, the sponge replaced by lips and careful teeth. Her demure sighs lowering into open groans, music from the world's first day. I woke glued to the sheets by a congealed funk of sweat and semen, then slipped back into the interior life that spun continuously from the warped loom of my cooked brain. I found myself alone in the showroom with mobs of casket-seekers. If you listened carefully through the mutter and roar of the greedy crowd, you could hear the rising hiss of the world-ending wave just as it started to break.

"If I had one of those fuckers here I'd beat his fucking head in," Art said. What fuckers? What fuckers? "My old man never did a goddam thing to anyone except help them. Now look." I looked. Benedetto was lying in a coffin, his painted lips fixed, by Mr. Vogel, in a saintly smile. "Fucking pack of rats," Art said. "Fucking slime-licking shit-sucking rats. If I had one here I'd cave his ratty skull in, I'd paint the fucking walls with his brains." Who? Who? But he couldn't hear me; in fact, I wasn't there. It was Art, talking to Benedetto, Benedetto happy and forgiving in his coffin, an "Eternal Comfort" in the upper-mid-priced range.

An earthquake shook my bed. It was three in the morning. I woke cool and hungry. Someone in the apartment above me was yelling, "Did you feel that, Margery? Did you feel that, Margery?" I thought he was talking about sex, but then I smelled plaster, which meant the quake had been real enough to crack a wall or ceiling. I sneezed five times. Colleen had left a bowl of chicken salad in the fridge. I ate it all, at least two quarts. I drank a Coke, then another. I went back to bed and Colleen was there with Crutchfield. "What are *you* doing here?" Crutchfield wanted to know, pushing himself up on his elbows though still attached to Colleen. I woke up then, still sick, still unable to eat. I got up and felt the wall for cracks. A B-36 rumbled through the sky above the apartment building. Then another, and another. My little room condensed the roar. The apartment building was directly under the southeast glide path for Vultee Field. I got back into bed and pulled the pillow over my ears, then woke again to silence. My dreams now were coming in layers. It panicked me to think each waking was unreliable, that I couldn't be sure what was dream and what it was I woke into.

"I dreamed I was better," I told Colleen.

"That's a good sign. That means you're getting well."

We sat at my small table. She watched me eating her soup. Chicken noodle. It was good. I ate with real appetite.

"Tell your dad I'll come in to work tomorrow."

"You'll do no such thing. Tomorrow's Friday, anyway. You might as well wait until Monday. You've lost a lot of weight, Ozzie."

I flapped my pajama top against my ribs. "I'm a shadow of my former self," I said.

"I can't wait to touch your former self, honey," she said.

"But you will wait, won't you?"

"What's that supposed to mean?"

"Nothing." I slurped soup into my big mouth.

"I told you before. I don't want to hear that kind of talk, Ozzie."

"I'm sorry, honey."

"I forgive you. You've been sick."

"At death's door," I said. "At the grave's edge."

"Don't joke about death. It's bad luck."

"Not in Mexico." Shit. I slurped soup into my big mouth.

"Don't you talk to *me* about Mexico, Ozzie," she said, and I hunkered down over my soup, dutifully chagrined.

She took my temperature, this time with an oral thermometer. I was back down into the nineties. I was weak but hungry. I ate another bowl of soup, persuaded her to come to bed with me. We lay naked face to face. But she clamped my investigative hand between her strong thighs. "No, not yet," she said. "We're not going to take any chances with a relapse. We've got plenty of time to poontang, mister. We have all the time in the world for *that*."

Poontang. Not a word I'd ever used with her. But if not me, who? I ordered my inquiring mind to stop right there. I kept my troublesome mouth locked tight. It was a sailor's word, imported from the China Sea. A Marine's word, found in Korea. *Jesus, shut up*, I told myself. "Poontang?" I said.

"*You* know," she said coyly, innocent finger on my lips, sealing them.

"Fuck, you mean. You mean fuck."

"I told you never to say that word, Ozzie. You know I do not like it. It's *horrid*."

"Sorry," I said.

"You'd better be."

It wasn't really a fight, but we kissed and made up anyway.

After she left I cleaned up my gray little apartment. There wasn't much to clean. A few dishes in the small sink, the dust rats that had collected under my three-quarter-size bed. It smelled like a sickroom, but there were no windows to open for fresh air. I put a Willis Jackson record on, and that took the sharp edges off things. I followed it with Mulligan, then with the Charlie Parker/Flip Phillips Machito record, which had great mood-lifting power. And then the ground-zero detonations of Big Jay McNeeley. No taste, the man has no taste, I could hear Max Tbolt saying, as Big Jay, flat on his back, pulled the scream out of his black bowels and launched it through his battered horn.

By evening I knew I was well. I made myself a lunch-meat sandwich, opened a beer, showered, got dressed. I went upstairs to Art's apartment, but he and Denise were gone. Probably to Benedetto's. I tried to sort out what Art had said to me, tried to separate dream from nondream. Benedetto convicted, jailed, deported, dead? None of the above? I went to the carports at the back of the apartment and cranked up my bike. I hadn't ridden it since promising Mr. Vogel that I'd sell it. It didn't start until the tenth kick. It sputtered, caught, then roared. Music to my ears. My thigh was shaking from the effort. I pushed backward with my feet until the bike was out in the alley, then I kicked it down into first and twisted open the throttle. I roared out onto Myrtle Avenue and headed for Balboa Park.

The cool December wind on my face took away the dregs of fever. I gunned it onto the Cabrillo Freeway. Traffic was light, and I pinned the speedometer on ninety and held it there all the way to Mission Valley. I took the Mission Valley Highway east, cruising at a law-abiding sixty-five.

I saw an MG a few hundred yards ahead of me. It turned off the highway in Fletcher Hills and headed into La Mesa. Under a series of arc lamps I saw that it was a red MG. I also saw that the driver had long auburn hair, and I saw that the driver was not alone.

I shut off my headlight and followed them. They turned up Alto Drive. I could see the driver downshift as they started the corkscrew climb up Mount Helix. It was dark here, and I could barely see the road. Even so, I switched on the headlight only when their taillights disappeared around a bend. I did this to orient myself on the narrow asphalt strip that snaked alongside the avocado groves and millionaire houses. But my head was becoming disoriented in its own way. Poontang, she said with such familiarity. A word that slipped through her lips often enough to lose its crude foreign overtones, a word as pleasant and unthreatening as "yo-yo" or "goofball" or "wingding."

The MG stopped in front of Crutchfield's house. The Crutchfield yard was well lighted. The bowsprit goddess that hung above the groves stared into ground-level floodlights. Bad cello music corrugated the night air.

They sat unmoving in the car—talking?—then their heads came together in a brief kiss. The quick peck of parting friends, or the kiss of already exhausted lovers? Crutchfield got out and Colleen drove through the turnaround driveway, waving gaily. She came back down Alto, came close enough for me to reach out and touch her, but I stayed hidden behind a thick oleander. I didn't know what my face looked like, but I knew she would not want anything to do with the derangement of thoughts and images that controlled it.

I went home, slowly, carefully. I undressed and got into bed. My fever was back. I slipped down gravid and weak into new layers of dream.

Max Tbolt seemed glad to see me. "Long time no see, Oz," he said.

"Thought I'd say howdy," I said. In fact, I'd surprised myself by stopping at his apartment. I'd been riding my bike around Imperial Beach on the south end of town Sunday morning, trying to shake a two-day case of the blues. It was one of those ideal December days in southern California—temperature in the high fifties, the salt air hard and astringent, everything in razor-sharp focus. A day made for biking. Even the BSA seemed to sense the perfect conditions. It responded to tiny twists of the throttle with game-hearted eagerness. The front wheel almost came off the pavement once when I kicked it into third at fifty miles an hour. Torque to spare.

"You look a bit tapped out, Oz," Max said. "Coffee?"

He poured me a cup. It was fresh and strong. He pushed a bowl of sugar cubes toward me, I pushed it back. A preacher some-where in the apartment was yelling about the fallen world. It was a radio preacher, coming from his mother's bedroom. She had the volume high enough to rattle dishes in the cupboard.

"Fallen world my aching ass," I said. "It's great out there today, Max."

"God's country," Max said.

"Damn straight."

But he was down about something. It was past ten o'clock and he was still in his bathrobe and bedroom slippers. His face, stub-bled with gray, was creased from uneasy sleep. He looked fifty, even sixty.

"What's wrong, Max?" I said.

He looked at me. "Shit, what isn't, kid." He lit a cigarette and stared off into the smoke. "I've got some bad news. You chose the wrong Sunday to drop by."

I tensed up a little. I'd had a bad night, too. The bike ride had helped. I'd looked forward to seeing Max. But I didn't need an-other dose of bad news.

"You remember Bernie Issel?" Max said.

"Remember? Sure, I remember. What happened?"

"He's dead, Oz. The dumb bastard finally bought it."

"When?" I felt a dryness in my mouth. I sipped my coffee.

"A few days ago. Got whacked. Dropped his pipe and when he bent down to pick it up he stuck his head under the pallet. The crane op dropped a ton of flat steel on his head. Issel's timing was so perfect you'd think the asshole planned it. It was not what you would call pretty."

"The dumb fuck," I said.

"I warned him," Max said. He was staring off into space again. Issel wasn't the only thing on his mind.

"You *did* warn him. I remember. Jesus, you're not blaming yourself, are you? I mean, Max, that guy would've walked in front of a cement truck sooner or later."

Max got up and went into his bedroom. He came back in a few minutes, dressed but still unshaven. He had some papers in his hand. He dropped the papers on the table, poured himself another cup of coffee, then sat down. "I probably shouldn't show these to you," he said, shoving the papers toward me.

They were letters. From Elizabeth Urquiza. Her handwriting was beautiful, large and loopy, like that of an eager third-grader who had just learned the Palmer Method. I imagined her practicing her warm-up ovals on an empty sheet before beginning to write. I brought a page up to my face and smelled her.

She started off chatty—describing the little town she lived in, Moon Crest, on the Ohio River, just outside of Pittsburgh, the cold cold winter, the friendly neighbors—but then her handwriting got smaller and smaller and began to slant off to the right, as if a gravitational force had pulled the words off course. These cramped paragraphs spoke of trouble at home, of Norbert's temper, how he even struck her, not once but on several occasions, and how she blamed herself. I turned the page over and the handwriting started off courageous again—large and round, the looped l's and b's optimistic, each line perfectly horizontal—but after a few inches of this the writing lost its self-confidence and started to decay again, the letters shrinking and huddling against each other, slanting erratically, t's falling over into l's, p's crowding s's, e's closing into undotted i's. She had taken a job at a glass factory, and she had started seeing a coworker, a young man named Lewis Weese. Norbert had found out and had become brutal. He'd beaten Weese badly, not bad enough to put him into the hospital, but bad enough to scare him off. The letter went on and on, praising Lewis Weese for not bringing charges against Norbert, blaming herself for causing the trouble, exonerating Norbert—*and then the kicker:* "I often think of you, Max, your sweetness and generosity, and think that maybe we had something more than friendship, didn't we? How safe and happy I felt when we were together. . . ." And the handwriting blossomed here, became round and huge, innocent as grade school, the sentiments sweet and honest and devastating. I looked up from the letters and Max's eyes were red and wet and his mouth was turned down in a bitter inverted smile and his hand trembled.

"I'm going to Pittsburgh," he said. "To see her."

I didn't have the right to say anything. The look on his face convinced me that anything I said would have no effect anyway. The preacher in the bedroom was half talking, half singing. "You got to *taste* the bitter waters, my friends. You got to *see* old wormwood, flying at your eyes. The pestilence will come like smoke from the *pit*, and you will seek *death*, you will chase *death*, but death will run *away* from you like a bride from an unworthy husband!"

"You hear that? You hear that, Maximilian?" his mother shrieked from the bedroom.

"She's pissed off at me," Max said.

"I don't blame her, Max," I said.

He looked at me. "You think I'm nuts?"

"Sure, man. Fucking certified. USDA-approved *filbert*, man."

He dismissed me by looking away. Then he said, "I'm going to bring her back with me. I'm a fool, I know. You don't have to tell me."

"Norbert will stomp your fat fool ass, Max."

He shrugged. "I love her, Oz. I don't have any choice."

He got up and put a record on. "Prisoner of Love." Perry Como on the vocal. I almost laughed out loud. Brainy old Max was thinking of himself as a prisoner of love. Perry Como, the ex-barber, was too mellow to drown out the doomsday preacher.

"So you love her," I said.

"Haven't you heard, kid? Love conquers all."

Night after night alone you'll find me, too weak to break the chains that bind me, Perry sang.

"Is that what it does?" I said.

"You don't know what I'm talking about?"

I shrugged. Shook my head no, nodded yes. Said, "Sure, I guess."

He didn't scoff. "Then you ought to know how it is."

"I think I'm learning, Max."

Maybe I was, but I couldn't have said what it was that I'd learned.

26

"I came by your apartment but you weren't there," Colleen said. "Where were you?"

"I took a ride up to San Clemente," I said.

"On your motorcycle?"

"No, on my roller skates."

I was sitting behind my desk, waiting for walk-in or phone business. I'd been there two hours. Hadn't anyone died over the weekend?

"Why are you acting like this, Ozzie?"

"Acting like what?"

She sat on my lap. Kissed me. I slipped my hand up her skirt. Too rough. She jumped up. "What's *wrong* with you?" she demanded.

"Nothing."

"You're a damn liar," she said. Angry tears brightened her eyes.

"But I'm not stupid," I said.

This stopped her little act. "What's that supposed to mean?" she said.

"It means I'm not blind."

"You're not making sense." But her confidence was shaken. She was thinking fast. Her eyes twitched as if they were reading headlines.

"Sure I am," I said.

"If you don't stop this right now, I'm leaving."

I shrugged. I was content to let her think about it for a while. She stamped her foot and went into the main part of the house through a door at the rear of the showroom.

A group of people came in just before noon. Two women, a man, and a boy. They were all well-dressed. One of the women was in her sixties. She had a diamond on her finger big as a shelled walnut. The other woman was in her thirties. She looked breakable, like porcelain. She also wore a diamond you could weigh on a bathroom scale. Mother and daughter, I figured. The man, a pudgy guy in a camel-hair coat, had to be the younger woman's husband. I got up and greeted them. I figured right off that they'd spring for a "Sweet By and By," a top-of-the-line solid bronze model with the Aqua Supreme Cheney velvet lining and Auto Adjust foam bed with innerspring mattress. Three grand to people like these was pocket change.

"Welcome to Vogel-Darling," I said. "May I be of service?"

Only the boy looked at me. He was about seven, pudgy as his father, and obviously spoiled rotten. He looked at me with practiced insolence. Then he held his nose between thumb and forefinger and stuck out his tongue.

The adults went directly to the plain pine coffins. "We'll take one of these," the man said, as if he was buying lumber in a hardware store.

"The county usually buys these," I said. They were still acting as if I was invisible. "The county uses these for unclaimed indigents."

"I'm not interested in what the county does," the man said.

I aimed my next remark at the older woman—the widow, I figured. "These are what they use in the pauper's field, ma'am. Bums, unidentified remains, the bodies of people who left no one behind, or they left behind people who couldn't care less about them. That's what these are commonly used for. I'm sure you'd prefer something much nicer. Something befitting the years of quiet intimacy and loving affection between you and your late husband. Something the gophers and moles and those pesky root-borers won't get into."

The woman looked at me as if I had pulled out my dick and waved it at her. "Why is this awful young man speaking to me, Lowell?" she said. Her aristocratic tone of voice made it clear I had committed a breach of the social contract by talking to her directly.

"Maybe I misspoke," I said. "Let's start over, okay? Now, what can I do for you good folks?"

"You can refrain from calling us good folks, for one thing," the younger woman said. "We came to buy a plain coffin for Dad. That's all we want. Dad didn't believe in excessive funeral expenses, and neither do we." She would have been good-looking except for her eyes. They were set too close together and were dull as canned peas.

"You don't have to explain yourself to this moron, Flavia," Lowell said. "Now listen, bud," he said, poking his soft, pink finger into my chest. "See if you can understand this. We want a plain pine coffin. We don't want anything else—no embalming, no cosmetics, no viewing, no funeral procession. The body is ready to be moved. I want you to pick it up today at Mercy Hospital and have it buried by tomorrow. We have a plot picked out at Paradise Gardens. Now, is that clear? Or do you want me to get some crayons and draw a great big picture for you?"

"Embalming is required by the California Board of Health," I said. The boy was standing behind me, stabbing at my ankle with the pointy toe of his shoe.

"Did I say we were shipping the body somewhere?" the man said. "California requires embalming only if we're shipping. But we're not shipping. So don't try these cheap gimmicks on us, buster."

I walked away from him. If he said one more word I was going to hit him. I picked up some papers from my desk, shuffled through them as if they meant something. The kid had followed me to the desk. He ran his shoe into my ankle again. I whispered into his ear, "If you kick me again, you little cocksucker, I'm going to boot your ass so hard you'll have shit running out your ears for a month."

He ran to his mother, screaming.

"What did you say to Wendell?" Lowell demanded.

"I told him to quit kicking me," I said.

"He said he was going to beat me up!" Wendell screamed. Flavia pulled her fat son against her protectively, stroking his hair.

"My God! What kind of mortuary is this?" Lowell said. His face was red. "Do you often threaten the children of the bereaved?"

"Only assholes like Wendell," I said.

The women were already gone, Wendell with them. It was just me and Lowell. "I'm going to report this to the Better Business Bureau," he said.

"Fine. Now why don't you get the fuck out, Lowell?" I took a step toward him. He backed away, turned, headed toward the door at a pace brisk enough to make his fat ass jiggle.

I sat at my desk, more pissed off at myself than at Lowell. I'd blown a six-thousand-dollar funeral. A good salesman would have gotten them away from the pine boxes in thirty seconds. A good salesman would have made the solid-brass "Sweet By and By" look like a fire-sale bargain. A good salesman would have convinced them he was Jesus Christ's designated successor, offering salvation not just to the old dead man but to the whole family. Even to that little prick Wendell.

I twiddled my thumbs for another half hour, then went into the house to find Colleen. She was in the kitchen, fixing our lunch.

"Are you still a bear?" she said over her shoulder.

"I don't know what you mean," I said.

"You could at least say you're sorry."

"I'm sorry," I said. "I'm the sorriest son of a bitch alive."

"Now *see?*" she said, turning from the counter. "There *is* something bothering you. Why don't you just say what it is so we can eat our lunch in peace?"

"Crutchfield," I said. It came out like a bark.

"What do you mean?"

"*Now* who's playing dumb?"

Her quick eyes studied me. I could almost hear her brain spinning.

"I'll make it easier," I said. "I happened to see you and Crutchfield together. In your car. I saw you in front of his house."

"You've been *spying* on me?" she said.

"Not on purpose. I was riding my bike in Mission Valley. I saw your car. So I followed."

She turned back to our lunch. She was mixing tuna salad in a large bowl. "It wasn't anything," she said. "He wanted to go out. I said no. I told him we were engaged. Then he said he wanted to say goodbye in person. We drove around a little, and that was *it*. Believe what you want, Ozzie."

Her voice was steady and a little fatigued. There was something convincing in that fatigue. I'd seen this look before. The older woman she would one day be was visible. It was a privileged glimpse. I saw that her beauty, which was in her glance and in the way she moved, would be sustained.

"I believe you," I said. "I'm sorry."

I understood something about myself then. I understood that I *wanted* to believe her. And that wanting made it true. I took this as more evidence that I was in love. What else could it mean?

"Are you sure?" she said, spreading tuna on slices of bread.

"Sure enough," I said.

"Good. Let's eat lunch."

27

"You got to use your legs, Mr. Santee," Dickie Corvus said. "Pickin' up a stiff can mess up your back real bad, unless you do it right."

We were on our way to pick up a body out in Lakeside. Dickie was driving the old hearse, a 1938 La Salle. The car was used by the mortuary strictly as a "service vehicle"—a body transporter. The processional hearse was a 1952 Caddy.

A woman, thirty-six years old, had died at home of cancer. Her husband was waiting for us. I'd taken the call. He spoke softly, in incomplete sentences, as if he couldn't bring himself to say what he wanted. I almost hung up on him. Mr. Vogel saw me holding the phone away from my ear and staring at it in disgust. He took it from me and managed to get the man to talk.

Mr. Vogel's patience and sensitivity were professional and real. He had class to spare. I was a low-class actor full of strut and cheap style and not much else. I'd made some good sales but I'd never cracked the three-thousand-dollar barrier. People who could pay that kind of money for funeral arrangements were generally put off by my approach even when I managed to soften it. You can't fake class. You can't hide your lack of it behind a one-hundred-dollar suit.

My demotion to body-snatcher wasn't exactly punishment for my latest trouble with rich clients. "I think you'd be more comfortable working in another area of the business, Ozzie, at least for a while," Mr. Vogel had said. "I blame myself. I shouldn't have started you out in such a delicate area."

He thought the humble job of picking up bodies would be better preparation for dealing with the families. The artificial environment of the showroom, he'd said, reduced the bereaved and the salesman to a buyer-seller confrontation that could "atrophy the human dimension." Collecting the deceased, he'd said, would bring me face to face with the reality of loss.

My dream of making big money was on hold. Body-snatching paid by the hour, and we only had four or five bodies to pick up a week. Irwin Tubman's unreliability gave me fairly steady work. I was going to get fifteen to twenty hours a week at $1.10 an hour. So I was back to where I was at the electronics wholesaler. The good news was that this would only be until Colleen and I were married. After that, Mr. Vogel had a surprise for both of us. When he said this he was beaming, so I figured it had to be a pleasant surprise.

Dickie pulled the La Salle up to a frame house tucked against a eucalyptus-covered hillside. This was the back country. The roads for the last two miles had been gravel. There were chickens pecking around in the yard, haphazard ricks of firewood stacked against the side of a weathered barn, a rusted Model A Ford sitting on blocks in tall weeds next to the house. A newer Ford was parked in front. The house itself was in good shape—bright yellow with gleaming white shutters.

"Shit, it's two fuckin' stories," Dickie said. "That probably means the missus is in a upstairs bedroom. That means we got to negotiate a sharp corner at the top of the stairs to get her down." Big as he was, Dickie had a small head and a small-featured face that was permanently etched by suspicion and doubt: He expected to get screwed by life, and life, so far, had obliged him. "You can count on it, Mr. Santee, she's probably a porker."

We got out of the big La Salle. The front door opened before we climbed the porch. A thin, balding man wearing heavy horn-rimmed glasses met us. "It's too warm in the house," he said, as if explaining something. "You're from . . . the mortuary?"

I glanced back at the hearse. What did he think a seventeen-foot black van was, a milk truck? "Yes, sir," I said.

He stood there, the glare from his glasses hiding his eyes. Dickie cleared his throat. "Whereabouts is she?" he said.

"What?" the man said. He looked confused. He pushed his glasses higher on his nose. A hen hopped onto the porch, then hopped off in an unprovoked tantrum of wings.

"Your wife, Mr. . . . ." Seeing that the man wasn't forthcoming, Dickie pulled a folded piece of paper out of his pocket, visibly peeved. He squinted at it. "Mr. Stackpole," he read.

Stackpole held out his hand for someone to shake. I reached

for it. It was a small dry hand that had abdicated any claim on strength it might have had. "She, Vanessa . . . how odd it sounds. I mean, her name now, just to *say* it. Vanessa." He smoothed his thin hair. "Come in, please," he said. He turned his back and went into the house. Dickie looked like he'd swallowed a rusty nail.

Stackpole was a bad housekeeper. The living room was littered with newspapers and magazines and plates of leftover food. Fat bluebottle flies orbited lazily through the room. We went into the kitchen. Stackpole sat at the kitchen table. He raised a cup of coffee to his lips. He sipped thoughtfully. It looked like he'd forgotten us. Dickie cleared his throat again.

"Oh, what am I thinking of?" Stackpole said. He jumped up and got two cups out of the cupboard and filled them with inky coffee. "Cream? Sugar?" he said.

Dickie, pained by all this, looked at his watch. "No thanks," he said. "We're on a tight schedule, Mr. Stackpole. We'd better pick up the missus and be on our way."

"Vanessa," Stackpole said, testing the new strangeness of his dead wife's name.

"Like I said, Mr. Stackpole," Dickie said, "we're behind schedule already."

"Have some coffee. Here . . ." He got up and found a can of condensed milk. "I insist. Please."

A boy of about fourteen came into the room. He looked like a smaller version of Stackpole, except for his thick red hair. "Dad," he said.

Stackpole looked up at the boy. An emotion worked his thin

jaws. I heard the grind of his teeth. "This is . . . John," he said.
"My son. What is it, Johnny?"

"She's been up there two days," the boy said to us.

"Jesus H. Christ," Dickie murmured.

"We'll skip the coffee, Mr. Stackpole," I said. "Can you lead
the way, John?" I said.

The boy took us to a staircase. "Up there," he said. "Down
the hall and to the right." He was a competent kid who didn't
mind demonstrating it.

Dickie went out to the hearse and got the canvas stretcher and
drop cloth. I went back into the kitchen. Mr. Stackpole stood up
and grabbed my arm with his strengthless hand. "I've been
working with inclusion compounds," he said.

I stepped away from his grip. "Uh huh," I said.

"I'm sorry," he said. "I mean, I teach chemistry . . . at State
College. My life has been nothing but these molecular struc-
tures." He lifted his head slowly until his thick-lensed gaze rested
on the ceiling. I figured his wife was on the other side of that ceiling. "She . . . she . . . Vanessa, is, was . . . I mean."

"Inclusion compounds came first," I offered.

Tears suddenly rolled down his face as if a spigot had been
twisted open. "Yes! I mean, I was so . . . absorbed. The architec-
ture of molecules was . . . is . . ." He turned his face as if to spit.
"My life. My whole life."

John stood there, arms folded against his small chest. Now and
then he shot a look at his father. An unforgiving look that he'd
have to grow out of. Stackpole sank into a chair, lowered his head
into his arms. His thin back heaved silently.

The screen door banged. Dickie glanced into the kitchen to catch my eye. His wronged-by-life look was turned up full blast. He jerked his head at me, impatient. I patted Stackpole on the shoulder, and Dickie and I went upstairs.

Vanessa was lying on the bed in her nightgown. She was unusual-looking. A Nordic redhead with heavy Mediterranean lips. Her head was turned as if she had died while looking out the window at something interesting. Bluebottle flies walked in and out of her slightly opened mouth like sightseers from another planet. Her eyes were half open and dreamy. It was warm in the room. She smelled bad.

"At least she ain't a porker," Dickie said. He grabbed a carbon of the death certificate off the dresser, made sure it was signed by a doctor, then stuffed it into his shirt pocket.

We rolled her over and onto the stretcher. The nightgown gathered on her hips. Her buttocks and back were mottled purple from the pull of gravity on uncirculating blood. Dickie strapped her onto the stretcher and covered her with the drop cloth. Then he ran lengths of twine through brass grommets in the drop cloth to tie it down. We couldn't have the cloth coming off Mrs. Stackpole as we maneuvered her down the stairwell and through the house.

"Now don't forget what I told you, Mr. Santee," Dickie warned. "Use your legs or you'll fuck up your back, okay?"

She wasn't a big woman but the weight of the stretcher surprised me. By the time we loaded her into the La Salle I had broken a sweat. Stackpole didn't come to the door to watch us drive off, but his son did. Dickie stomped the gas and the hearse slid sideways on the gravel road.

"What's the big hurry, anyway, Dickie?" I said. "We're through for the day, aren't we? What was all that about us being behind schedule?"

He shrugged. "Nature calls," he said.

"What?"

"I got to take a shit, Mr. Santee," he said.

28

I dusted caskets while Dickie washed the La Salle. It was early Saturday morning and the Vogels were still asleep. The show-room had a six-speaker hi-fi system that played churchy organ music at very low volume. Mr. Vogel had adjusted the player to repeat the same record over and over, an E. Power Biggs rendi-tion of a Bach fugue.

It was unlikely that walk-in customers would show up this early on a weekend morning. So I picked the Bach record off the spin-dle and put on my new Charlie Ventura album. The big-hearted wail of his tenor burned away the reverential hush of the show-room.

Charlie had never sounded this good on my old machine. I kept the volume medium-high for a while, but then the music got to me and I turned it up full-bore. A deaf man could have heard it with

his teeth. The showroom was several walls away from the bedrooms of the big house. I convinced myself the sound wouldn't
carry—at least not enough to wake up the Vogels.

Ventura's band amplified life. Glorified it. Made it supreme.
Death was a showroom full of impressive coffins and somber
music and reverential hush and people weighed down by grief.
Life was crazy human lungs hammering spikes of air into brass
horns. Life was a head arrangement with ecstatic riffs. Death was
the spacing. You had to have the spacing so that the notes
wouldn't fall into each other. No spacing, no music. I heard all
this in the Ventura band's rendition of "Euphoria." It made the
cheap coffins jump. The expensive ones were unmoved.

A customer walked in, interrupting my bebop-inspired philos-
ophizing. I trotted to the hi-fi and pulled the tone arm off my
Ventura record. I put Bach back on and lowered the volume to a
tasteful hum. Here was a chance to make a sale and maybe re-
deem myself.

The customer was a small, muscular man in a T-shirt. "Well
looky there," he said. "You're just a pissant punk." His thick
neck was cabled with veins ready to explode.

"Pardon?" I said.

He'd been drinking. I could smell him from ten feet away.

"I'm fed up," he said.

"You're under stress, sir," I said. Grief did strange things to
people. I didn't want to screw up another sale by a wrongheaded
reaction to a grief-ravaged customer. "This is understandable,
sir. In times of loss . . ."

"Don't mess with me," he warned.

"Sir?"

"I could flatten you like a paper bag."

He danced on the balls of his feet, tucked his chin down like a boxer. "I'm sure you could, sir," I said.

"You've got a smart mouth, you know that?"

"My big drawback, sir."

"Goddamm it, I'll mess you up, you keep on smart-mouthing me."

"Is there something wrong, sir? Dissatisfied perhaps with our arrangements for a loved one?"

"That's it. That's all I'm taking off you, punk." He danced toward me on tricky feet and threw a punch that caught me on the chin. I didn't expect it and so didn't protect myself. I fell flat on my back. Black wind poured into my head. He grabbed my shirt, pulled me up to me feet. Then he threw me against a "Sweet By and By." I bounced off the heavy brass coffin and fell again. He jumped on me and started swinging. I got my hands up in front of my face and caught most of the punches on my arms until he got tired. He let me up and I staggered away from him while he got his second wind. Then he grabbed me again and dragged me to an "Everlasting Joy" and pushed me into it headfirst. I kicked feebly at him, catching him in the chest, but he was relentless. He managed to stuff me down into the innerspring mattress of the upper-mid-priced-range coffin. He tried to lower the lid but I kept a foot on the edge so the lid couldn't be closed and latched.

Dickie came in. "Jesus!" he yelled. He picked the customer up like a small dog gone wild with distemper and threw him aside. The man came growling at me again, but Dickie clubbed him down with fists heavy as flatirons.

"Get out of here, Irwin," Dickie said.

The man climbed up the side of a "Royal Slumber" spitting blood. "This smart-ass here took my job, Dickie," he whined.

"Hell if he did, Irwin. You gave it up your ownself. You can't be depended on, Irwin, so what do you expect?"

"I expect to be treated decent," Irwin mumbled.

"So you come in here and stomp on a boy," Dickie said. "That's how you figure to get treated decent." Dickie shook his head in disgust. Irwin stumbled toward the door. Getting punched by Dickie must have been like sticking your head under a drop hammer.

"I'm real sorry, Mr. Santee," Dickie said after Irwin found his way to the street. "He had no call to do that. irwin's a little nuts. If it makes any difference, I want you to know that I am through with that side of the family, because most of them are nuts." He looked worried, as if his job might be in jeopardy.

I climbed out of the coffin. Felt my teeth. The two front top ones were loose. I spit blood into my hand. "No sweat, Dickie," I said.

"You feel up to makin' a run?" he said.

He'd be up the creek if I didn't. "Sure," I said. "But let's stop at a Safeway so I can get some aspirin and ice."

Out in the La Salle, Dickie looked at his clipboard. "We got three to pick up. One at Mercy, one downtown at the city morgue, one way the hell out in Spring Valley.''

We went downtown first. A three-year-old kid had chased a ball between the back wheels of a semi. He'd passed between sets of wheels, got hung up in them, and was pulped. What was left of him was packed in a rubber-lined carton at the city morgue. Dickie went in to get it while I sat in the hearse with ice on my face. I checked myself out in the side mirror. My left eye was closing and the puffy skin around it was turning dark. My lips were fat and crusty.

After a few minutes Dickie came out with a box in his arms. His little head looked unreal on his bulky neck and shoulders. His usual pained expression was absent. This contributed to the unrealness. He needed to look severely put out to give his small head the illusion of normal size and seriousness. It was a compensation he had learned—like a stubby-legged man who takes long strides to make you think he is taller, or a bony woman swinging her hips to make you think she has them. Dickie looked like a monstrous child, horrified by a sudden realization of his own strangeness.

''Bad, huh?'' I said when he climbed back into the driver's seat.

''Jesus,'' he said. ''I hate to pick up runned-over tykes.''

''Mulligan stew, huh?''

He glanced at me sharply. ''*You* want to take a look, Mr. Santee?'' he said, his familiar sour look safely back in place.

''No thanks,'' I said.

We collected an old man at Mercy Hospital, then drove out to Spring Valley to pick up a woman. Dickie pulled the la Salle into the driveway of a bungalow-style house built in the late twenties or early thirties. He looked at his clipboard. "Mrs. Alice Luna," he said. He ducked his head and looked at the house through the windshield. "One story. That's good. She's probably in a back bedroom. But there's a walk going around the house. This should be pretty easy. Unless she weighs a quarter ton."

Mr. Luna greeted us at the door. He was about eighty and thin beyond frail. His clothes hung on him as if draped on wire hangers. His smile was startling—a pointlessly electrifying flash of perfect dentures that appeared and disappeared in quick white pulses.

"I'm having my dinner," he said.

When he was a young man his smile no doubt had charm. But now his teeth, though they were false, were the only young thing about him. His magnificent teeth mocked him. Mocked the old man in the La Salle. Mocked the mangled child. Mocked mortality.

He shuffled into his kitchen. I followed him. He sat at a small wooden table and resumed eating. "We're running behind schedule, Mr. Luna," I said.

"Really?" he said. "And why are the dead so impatient these days?" He looked up at me, the blinding smile crashing into my eyes. I angled my eyes away from it.

Dickie was hulked in the archway between the kitchen and living room. "We could go gas up the La Salle and come back," he said. "It's riding on empty."

"Splendid," said the old man, the horrible white smile propelling Dickie out of the archway. "Go, go. But you," he said, turning to me, "why don't you stay and have something to eat? You are a young man and young men are always hungry, correct?" He studied my battered face but made no comment.

In fact, I was hungry. I'd skipped breakfast and hadn't felt like eating lunch because of my loose teeth. But the old man was eating black beans and red rice and I could handle that. "Sounds good," I said.

Dickie left and the old man dished up a plate for me. He went to the fridge and took out a beer. "Just what the doctor ordered," I said.

I started scooping beans into my mouth and swilling beer. Then I remembered my manners. "I'm sorry, Mr. Luna," I said. "I'm making a pig out of myself, and you've just . . . well, you know."

He waved me off. His long fleshless fingers were twisted with arthritis. "Don't worry about it," he said. "My sadness is mine, not yours. There is no need to pretend. Besides, Alice is no longer suffering. Soon, I will join her. Eat."

He stared at me for a while, sizing me up, I figured. Then his dentures lit up the room. There was no getting used to that smile. It caught me by surprise. I needed to shield my eyes against it. I bent to my plate and spooned beans and rice into my face.

"Are you afraid of getting old?" he said. It was as if he'd been saving this question for someone, and now here I was.

"No," I said.

"That is because you are young," he said.

I guess he'd seen my discomfort. There wasn't much left of him—tattered flesh on sticklike bones, the old skull papered with tight, liver-spotted skin, the weak eyes rheumy.

"I have advice for you," he said.

"And what's that, Mr. Luna?" I said, my mouth full.

"Do not worry about it so much."

"I'm not worried about it at all."

"That is because you are young. But you will, one day. You will worry about it. My advice is, do not."

"Why not?" I said.

He leaned toward me on his delicate elbows. "Because *this* is forever," he said. He waved his hand in a shaky circle, taking in the entire kitchen, his smile illuminating the walls.

"How so, Mr. Luna?" I said, humoring him. I got up and re-filled my plate at the stove.

"Because we are here and only here. This is the truth. There is no place to go. And there is no time to go there."

"But we die," I said. "Things end."

"A picture ends at the frame but the picture remains. There is the picture, the frame, and nothing else. Nothing is nothing. Is this not correct?"

"Whatever."

He looked at me, poised to smile again.

"Could I have another beer?" I said.

"Help yourself."

I got another one from the fridge.

"Do you understand me, *m'ijo*?" he said when I returned to the table.

"Not really," I said.

He laughed. "Good, good! If you had said yes, then you would

have not understood. You can only understand this by not understanding it. You see?''

"No."

"Hah! Very good!''

Dickie knocked once on the front door, then came in.

"Excuse me, but we got to go now," he said. When Mr. Luna
was not forthcoming, Dickie said, "So where is she, Mr. Luna?''

The old man sighed wearily. He braced himself against the
table and stood up. "In there," he said, pointing a shaky finger
at a door down a hallway off the kitchen.

Dickie went to the door and opened it. He came back. He
looked peeved, like he'd been the butt of a schoolyard joke. "She
ain't there," he said.

"Ah, forgive me," the old man said. "She must be in *there*."
He nodded at a second door farther down the hallway.

Dickie looked in this room and came back. "What the hell's
going on?" he said.

"Mr. Luna," I said. "Where is Alice?''

Mr. Luna reached down to scratch the ears of an old tomcat
that had come into the house with Dickie. "Guapo," he said.
"Did you give a big *chingazo* to that *pendejo* Siamese next
door?''

"Please, Mr. Luna," I said. "Tell us where your wife is.''

"In there," he said, pointing to the first door again.

"No, she *ain't* in there," Dickie said, pissed off now. He
looked into the remaining rooms of the small house. "There ain't
no dead body here at all," he said.

"She is here," the old man said, scratching the ears of his old cat.

"The hell," Dickie grumbled.

"Is, was, will be," said Mr. Luna, shrugging. "Then, now, always. That Siamese next door has no *huevos.*"

I went outside and looked around the front and back yards, just in case. A neighbor watering his lawn was smiling to himself in a way I didn't like.

"You know anything about Mrs. Luna?" I asked.

"You didn't eat anything while you were inside, did you?" he said.

He flopped water into a big oleander that separated his lawn from Mr. Luna's. "What do you mean?" I said.

"Hector's old lady died fifteen years ago. People around here think he poisoned her." He battered the oleander again with a thick rope of water. "With *that,*" he said, nodding at the tough shrub. "You make a brew out of those leaves and it acts like digitalis. You know, the heart medicine. Too much, and bingo. Heart attack."

My heart clutched up in my chest, my stomach rose.

"Cops said heart attack. But, shit. They used to fight like cats and dogs, Alice and Hector. She was Irish, a boozer. He rode with Pancho Villa, according to him at least. He calls up a mortuary every couple of years or so to have someone pick her up. Christ knows why. Some weird type of guilt, maybe. Most places charge him twenty bucks and let it go at that. He's nuts, but I guess you figured that out by now."

I felt sick. He looked at me, laughed. "Hey, don't worry, if he gave you any oleander tea you'd be on the ground right now twitching like a sprayed bug."

Dickie slammed out of the Luna house. "Goddammit! I am sick and tired of crazy people!"

He bellowed this sentiment into the quiet streets of the neighborhood, as if his complaint would receive universal sympathy.

29

Christmas Eve. Mr. Vogel was putting away the rum punch like
there was no tomorrow. Mrs. Vogel cleared her throat every time
he refilled his cup. I joined him at the punch bowl. My eye was
still black but the swelling had gone down. I told people who
asked that I'd been playing catch with a friend and had taken my
eye off the ball. I told Colleen the truth. She wanted to call the
cops and have Irwin jailed, but I talked her out of it. "The jerk
has enough trouble as it is," I said. I didn't believe that—Irwin
probably deserved all the misery that would come his way—but I
didn't want Mr. Vogel to find out. A brawl in the showroom
would have been the last straw, no matter who started it. He'd
begin to see me as a magnet for trouble, a reputation I'd have a
hard time shedding.

Mr. Vogel filled my cup, spilling some on the carpet. Mrs. Vogel
choked on a cake crumb. But her sound effects didn't have any

effect. Mr. Vogel aimed to get drunk no matter what. I guessed it
was a yearly thing, a tradition.

There were about fifteen guests in the Vogel living room, a few
more in the sitting room. The spindle of the Vogels' record player
was loaded with Morton Gould records. Sedate music for well-
behaved people who were spilling over with self-esteem. It grated
on my nerves. The rum punch helped.

Colleen looked great in a white strapless dress and high heels.
She looked like a wife, greeting people, welcoming them, offering
refreshment, laughing politely at their little witticisms. "This is
it," Mr. Vogel said. He collared me in the crook of an affectionate
elbow. "This is the pinnacle, my boy. You work hard, you play
your cards right, and this is the reward." He meant it, but he
said it with a slight wince, as if he'd sipped pure grain alcohol
instead of sweet rum punch.

"Don't drink too much of that, Ozzie," Colleen singsonged
through her social smile.

"Too late," I said, smiling back.

"I *mean* it," she said, and drifted off to greet new guests.

"Just like her mom," Mr. Vogel said fondly.

I looked at him. He was serious. I had to ask: "How so, Mr.
Vogel?"

"She's a cutie. A cutie always gets her way."

Mrs. Vogel a cutie? I glanced at her. She looked like the embit-
tered queen of a barren domain, sitting stiffly in her tall wingback chair, nodding graciously at arriving guests, the guests dutifully seeking her out to pay their respects before moving quickly
on. Frail and regal, dispensing approval in rationed, abstract

smiles, wielding total control of her domestic realm—reserved,
preserved, frozen. A cutie? Definitely not a cutie. I tried to see
her as she must have been twenty years earlier, but failed. She
was exactly who she was—rich, important in the community, uncompromising, always right.

"She's wrong about you, though," Mr. Vogel said, as if reading my mind. "I think you have what it takes to settle down and
enjoy a life of responsibility. You're going to work out just fine,
Ozzie."

"But Mrs. Vogel doesn't think so?"

"She tends to think poorly of most young men these days. You
know—the music, the fast cars. Things were very different during the Depression. What she doesn't understand is that character is a constant. Things may change radically, but character will
always make itself known. The basics don't change. The basics
are the basics. Birth and death, happiness and grief. Love, of
course. Love is, should be, a basic. The bad things—hate, spite,
selfishness, greed, intolerance, cruelty—these are character is-
sues."

I took this as a rambling compliment. "Thanks," I said.

He looked at me, puzzled.

"For the vote of confidence," I added.

"You're a clever boy," he said.

I wasn't sure this was another compliment, but I said,
"Thanks, Mr. Vogel," anyway.

"Come with me, Oz," he said. "I want to show you something."

We carried our punch cups back into the cold room. This place was so familiar to me now that it had lost its exotic eeriness. The dead were as common as the living, the main difference being the dead couldn't spring surprises on you.

He led me to two tables that had been placed side by side. "I'm going to show you the world's best-kept secret, Oz," he said. "I'm going to show you what love is."

He pulled back the sheets from the faces of the two bodies. They were old people, a man and a woman, well into their eighties, gray skin like parchment. He hadn't done cosmetic work on them yet. They'd been embalmed and he'd put in the hardware to keep their eyes closed and lips together, but they were essentially unchanged from what they'd been in life. He gazed at the old couple for a while. I sipped my punch.

"An old man dies," he said finally, "and his wife follows him a day later. He of heart failure, she of grief—which is another form of heart failure."

Tears without warning fell down his expressionless face and onto the dead. He didn't seem to notice.

"Hard to figure," I said.

"Not hard to figure at all," he said. "There's no mystery in this. Their lives were intertwined. No, not simply intertwined. Grafted. Their lives had grafted onto one another, becoming the same life. They were a single living organism. One could not survive the death of the other. Simple as pie. As rare as . . . no, there's nothing as rare as this."

His tears kept falling. It was all very touching, but he was going overboard. I blamed the punch. He got drunk once a year, and that obviously wasn't often enough. He needed practice so that he wouldn't cut loose with embarrassing ideas and sentiments. A practiced drinker cuts loose what he wants to cut loose.

"So what's the world's best-kept secret?" I said.

He looked at me, frowning, as if he'd misjudged me. "You're looking at it, son. *Love.* This is the secret. People don't know what it is. But this is it. The grafting of lives. It doesn't happen overnight. Most of the time it doesn't happen at all."

I tried to picture Colleen and me ten, twenty, thirty years down the line. No sustainable image occurred to me.

Mr. Vogel let out a ragged sob. "You wonder why I am weeping. I'll tell you. I am weeping for myself, Oz. I've never had what this old couple had. I'll die alone. Most people do. They live alone, they die alone. They never graft themselves to another. Cannot or will not. It comes to the same thing."

"Another character issue," I said. Blame the punch. I bit my lip.

Mr. Vogel looked at me sharply. Then he smiled. He slapped me on the back and laughed. "I'll give you such a shot in the head, you wisenheimer! Pow! Right in the kisser!" Milton Berle to the rescue.

He covered the two old folks and took out a pair of cigars. We lit up and smoked over the bodies for a while, not talking, honoring the old lovers with a small impromptu ceremony in the half-light of the cold room.

It occurred to me that he didn't know anything about the old couple. How could he? He hadn't lived with them for the last fifty years. It was possible they despised each other. No, he had invented their grafted lives as a kind of ideal that had eluded him.

He was unhappily married, period, and didn't know what to do about it except mourn for himself. I found this more touching than his revelation of the world's best-kept secret. He may have been right about the old couple. But a bigger secret had to be the weight of disappointment that even successful people like Mr. Vogel carried with them day after day, year after year. They plodded through their lives stubborn as mules under a cruel load. The mystery, if there was one, was *why*.

We rejoined the party. Mr. Vogel headed toward the punch bowl. Mrs. Vogel watched her husband dip out a full cup, drain it, fill it again. Her lips were a thin pale line, inviting as a knife edge. I looked around for Colleen. She was in the kitchen helping Mrs. Larson slice up fruit cakes. I pulled her away. "Your pop is on his ass," I said.

"He does this every Christmas," she said. "Don't worry. He'll keep it up for another hour or so, then disappear into his bedroom to sleep it off."

"How about you and me disappearing into your bedroom?"

"I've got a better place," she said, thrilling me.

We went out the back door, found our way in the dark to the garage where the hearses were kept. There were stairs on the outside of the garage that led up to a second-story apartment. This was the apartment we were to live in after our wedding. We climbed the stairs to the landing. I waited impatiently as she fumbled a key into the lock. Then she pushed open the door and turned on the lights. *"Voilà!"* she said.

It was a newly furnished two-room apartment—kitchen and bedroom. The kitchen was large enough to hold an Early American dinette set. The cabinets were stacked with bright white plates, saucers, and cups with blue Pilgrims etched on them. The bedroom was claustrophobically cozy. There was a plump four-poster bed in it with a bright blue ruffled spread. The chest and vanity and night tables were also Early American.

The unblemished creamy walls of the apartment smelled of new paint. The bedroom window, skirted with crisp blue-and-white gingham curtains, looked out to the street. The window in the kitchen, also covered with the same crisp gingham, looked out into the backyard. The smell of brand-new carpet, along with the paint, made me a little woozy.

All this could have been a display in a corner of the furniture section of Sears—"Domestic paradise on a limited budget!" This was happy newlywed furniture: upbeat, cheerful, optimistic. Dark thoughts didn't have a chance in these sweet surroundings. Everybody in the land was under one mandate: Be happy! I broke a sweat.

Colleen had thought of everything. There was even a reusable plastic Christmas tree—the latest thing in seasonal technology from Sears—in a corner of the bedroom. The was a present under it. She saw me looking at it. "Go on," she said. "Open it."

I picked it up and tore off the wrapping. It was a blue bathrobe with my initials sewn into the breast pocket along with a pair of flannel pajamas, also blue. A pair of leather slippers lay flat in the bottom of the box.

"Put them on, dear," she said.

She opened a chest of drawers and took out a frilly pink night-gown.

"I'm going to change in the bathroom," she said. "You change in here."

She opened a narrow door in the wall at the foot of the bed and went in. I closed the shades of both windows and got undressed. I pulled the straight pins from the pajamas and put them on. They smelled of sizing and itched my skin from ankles to neck. I shoved my feet into the slippers. Then I put on the robe and cinched the belt. I looked in the fridge, praying for beer. It was empty.

She came out, a vision in pink. Her breasts lifted the gown with each breath, nipples playing peekaboo behind the dainty folds.

"Merry Christmas, darling," she said, turning out the lights.

We kissed. It was a long intricate kiss, a summary of all the passion of the last few months. But my heart wasn't in it. The crisp hiss of my flannel robe on her nylon gown raised blue coronas in the dry December air. Then she broke it off and turned the night-table light on. She pulled back the bedspread and blankets and smoothed out the sheets. Her efficiency and sense of purpose made my toes curl. She climbed into bed and patted the smooth sheet beside her. I took off my robe and slippers and got in. She cuddled against me.

"At last," she said.

I tried to digest this. "At last what?" I said. It wasn't as if we hadn't been screwing like minks for the last few months.

"Don't be dense, honey," she said. "At last we're in our own bed, in our own home. Isn't it just scrumptious?"

We kissed again, then got down to business. But a certain key figure wasn't present.

"What's wrong, dear?" she said.

"I don't know," I said. "Maybe I had too much punch."

She got on her knees and bent down to my reluctant dick, gripping it in her fist. She applied friction, like a confident Scout urging flame from leaves and twigs. She generated heat but no campfire.

"What should I do?" she said.

"Let's wait awhile," I said. "It's probably the rum."

We waited.

"Are you being mean to me, darling?" she said.

"No."

"Don't you know you're making me unhappy, dear?"

"No."

"No? Is that all you can say? 'No'?"

"No."

She got up and turned on all the lights. I lit a cigarette. She picked up her clothes and went into the bathroom. She came out, dressed. "I don't want you to *ever* drink rum again, Ozzie," she said.

"I promise."

I didn't believe it was the rum any more than she did.

We went back to the party.

"Announcement! Announcement!" Mr. Vogel yelled when he saw us. He was drunk as a lord, a shower cap on his head and a champagne bottle under each arm. Mrs. Vogel was still in her chair, looking old and tired and aggravated by the sight of her increasingly festive husband.

"I am a mortician!" Mr. Vogel announced loudly. "I am proud to be a mortician! I am a very good mortician!"

There was scattered applause. A few men whistled. One man said, "Hear! Hear!"

"And now my son-in-law-to-be is about to follow in my foot-steps!"

Colleen squeezed my hand. I looked at her. Something was up, and she knew about it.

"I was going to save this until after you two were married," Mr. Vogel said to us. "But after all, it *is* Christmas, and Christmas is the time for bestowing gifts on our loved ones."

The crowd applauded again. They formed a circle, surrounding me and Colleen.

"So, my dear children," Mr. Vogel said. "Right after your wedding, you will honeymoon in San Francisco, where Ozzie will attend the Golden Gate College of Mortuary Science, my old alma mater. Children, you will have six glorious weeks together in that wonderful city—all expenses paid—after which Ozzie will be thoroughly prepared to work as my full-fledged apprentice!"

"The mortician's apprentice!" someone yelled.

"The mortician's apprentice!" echoed another.

"A toast! A toast!"

"A career is launched!"

Mr. Vogel uncorked one of his champagne bottles. The cork rifled across the room, and the bottle, which had been given a hard shake, sprayed us all.

3 0

That could have been my life. But things happen. For instance, Mitzi and Nelson split up. Just like that. Just when everything seemed to be going well between them. It wasn't another man this time. It was something in her, some inner directive that said it was time to be alone. Nelson was crushed, but understanding. He moved out gracefully and graciously, and took an apartment in Kensington, closer to work.

Dickie and I picked up a green man in Lemon Grove. He'd died of cirrhosis. He'd been a heavy drinker and his liver was wrecked, which explained his over-jaundiced skin tone. His widow, Cassandra Cudahy, was a drinker too. "I get edgy," she rapsed. "I like to take the edges off." She could only speak on the intake of breath, which made her every utterance sound like a swamped swimmer's cry for help. She was an attractive woman in her mid-thirties. She had coal-black hair and milk-white skin and judgmental blue eyes. She spooked Dickie, but she interested me. The attraction was mutual. I went back to her house one night on my motorcycle. We drank bourbon and water and played her late husband's Guy Lombardo records, which made her aggressively sentimental.

"What am I doing?" I said. "I'm getting married."

She had an attractive scowl. It was one of the things I found interesting about her. "You're corrupt," she said, her wide unblinking eyes nailing me to the wall. "You have few scruples. There is no stink of sanctimony about you. My husband was a church sexton, a pillar of righteousness. You are an indecent piece of male ignobility. You have the ideals of a tapeworm."

Her sense of humor was subtle as a blackjack.

She was Catholic to the core. Where Colleen treated sex like cake icing, Cassandra Cudahy knew she was prying loose the hinges of hell.

This drove me on, ignobility and corruption rampaging in my blood. She groaned and writhed in bed, not with pleasure but with something beyond pleasure, as if licked by tongues of hellfire. This made me want to add to her torment. Coming, she would scream backwards—the wet and windy groan someone would make if stabbed through the lungs.

"Oh God, Cassandra," I said, after one such session. "I think I'm in love with you."

"Don't talk nonsense," she said. "Humans can only love God. Generally speaking, they are disasters to one another."

"You can't believe that, Cassandra."

Her dry, air-sucking laugh clattered about the room. "I can, and I do," she said.

That, in some unimaginable way, could have been my life, too. But things happen. The world in 1954—the year before the advent of automobile tail fins—seemed to be picking up speed, like a freight train that had lost its brakes on a downgrade.

A man and a woman decided to cross the Pacific Coast Highway on foot. They were drunk and not paying much attention to the thrust and momentum of the world around them. They were holding hands but had begun to argue. She leaned away from him and into the lane of traffic. He saw the Buick coming and tried his best to pull her back with his strong grip but failed. The man was left standing on the median holding the woman's arm, which had been torn from her shoulder by the speeding sedan. He had walked for miles in a daze, still holding her disowned arm. Dickie and I picked up the woman at the city morgue. The severed arm had been returned to her. It lay unblemished on her shattered torso, athwart the buttocks. It was an obscene practical joke, played by ungoverned events.

A new bomber manufactured in Seattle, the B-52, had suddenly made the B-36 seem like a clumsy hybrid—half World War Two, half World War Three. The B-52 was pure World War Three. It could fly as far and as high as the B-36, with the same bomb load, but half again as fast. Convair had already begun to lay off people. Art was nervous about his job, but things happen.

He suddenly had a lot more to worry about: he'd received his draft notice.

"The fuckers have it in for me," he said. He believed that the draft notice had been arranged by the Feds in retaliation for his uncooperativeness on the witness stand. The irony was that Benedetto had been cleared by an appeals court and was not going to be deported after all. He wasn't even going to get jail time. Things in the di Coca household went back to normal. Benedetto's cronies came over every Saturday to play music and drink strong wine. The FBI cars still parked in front of his house. The agents seemed more bored than ever with their assignment. But Art was going to be a soldier, perhaps sleeping in his own shit in Korea.

"You'll still be my best man, won't you?" I asked him.

"Sure," he said, glum with disinterest.

We were in his apartment drinking beer. Denise looked big enough to be carrying twins. She was understandably bitter.

"He'll only be gone for two years," I said helpfully.

She turned her bitterness on me. "Why didn't they take *you*? What's so special about *you*?"

I agreed with her. It didn't make much sense. But Art insisted the government was punishing him, especially now that orders for new B-36s had stopped. The production line in Ft. Worth had practically shut down. Art, who had no seniority, had already been notified of probable layoff.

Art and I went out. We took a pint of Seagram's and a case of beer up the coast and drank them on the beach south of Oceanside. Art passed out. The water was cold this time of year, so I hit the surf fully dressed except for my shoes. I lay in the cold foam,

letting the waves break over me. Then I waded out to neck-deep
water and rode a wave back in. But this wasn't a good surfing
beach. Two ocean currents met off this part of California and
produced complicated waves that shouldered into each other at
oblique angles and broke perplexed in a froth of confusion.

I walked down the beach. The bloated oblong sun squatted on
the west rim of the world like a colossal cosmic mistake. I passed a
packing crate that someone had dragged onto the sand. An old
man stuck his weathered head out of a gap and cackled at me. He
was a beach bum, a "nature boy." His greasy gray hair hung
past his scrawny, sun-blackened shoulders.

This was a common enough sight, so I kept walking.

"Hey you," he said.

"I don't have any money," I said.

"Money!" he crowed. "You got money on the brain! I don't
want your money! Come talk to me, boy."

I shrugged, walked up to his crate.

"Come on in."

He made way for me. The crate was big enough to hold two
people. He had it supplied with cans of food, a few bottles of li-
quor, tin dishes, an assortment of junk. Pictures were tacked to
the walls. Magazine cut-outs of circus animals, a fading snapshot
of a happy family, a shocking pencil drawing of a crucifixion—
shocking because it had the passion and honesty of an unskilled
but determined hand. Probably drawn by the beach bum himself. The crucified figure was a bespectacled man in a business
suit. A briefcase dangled from the thumb of his nailed hand.

"Bitchin' drawing," I said.

"Me," he said. "I used to be an exec in a big New York company. Had a wife, big house in Great Neck. Two Duesenbergs and a Rolls. The works." I looked at him. His fat porous nose was mapped with gin blossoms. His bleary eyes were unfocused. "There are a lot of ways of making your way through the world, all of them bad. I rejected them all."

"Right," I said.

"Believe what you will. You want a drink?"

"What've you got?"

"That's the wrong question, son," he said.

"Whatever."

It was vodka, or grain alcohol mixed with water. It burned going down and it had no flavor. We drank out of tin cups.

"None of my business," he said, "but what makes a kid like you willing to drink with an old-timer like me?"

"That's the wrong question, sir," I said.

He laughed, a creaky, dry-rust wheeze. "So what's your story, son? I've told you mine."

I told him about my upcoming marriage, my job, my career.

"Whew!" he said, lifting his tin cup.

"Easy for you to say," I said.

He tugged his beard. He searched through his junk and came up with a pair of wire-rimmed glasses. The lenses gave him owl eyes. "Here's the deal," he said. "You're swimming in a riptide older than the hills. It takes a while to figure this out." He looked like a doctor who'd just made a comprehensive diagnosis.

"I think I already had that figured," I said.

"But you're still going to play out that loser's hand?"

"Call me Dumbo," I said. "I mean, I could be living the good life, just like you."

He took off his glasses, sipped his strong brew. "You're a nasty boy," he said.

"I don't mean to be, Pop," I said.

Things happen. A week before the wedding, my draft notice came. At first, Colleen was angry. She seemed to hold me responsible. I guess I wasn't upset enough.

"You act like you *want* to go into the Army! Don't you care about us, darling?"

We had just returned from Catalina. We'd taken in a Stan Kenton concert, and the music was still electric in my brain. Vito Musso, Kenton's baritone sax man, had knocked the crowd out with his raspy solos. The amazing big-band music filled you with a kind of helium. You felt like you were floating away with it.

"Sure I care, honey," I said. "I mean, who wants to go into the Army?" I heard myself saying these things, knew I believed what I was saying, but even so, I wasn't unhappy. "Two years isn't a big deal. It'll go by in an eyeblink. We'll get married as soon as I get back."

But this only made her sob.

"Maybe I'll get some soft clerk-typist job stateside. Then we could be together a lot sooner than two years."

"Do you think so, Ozzie?"

It took me a few seconds to answer her, because in my mind Vito Musso was still blowing down the house and my foot was tapping happily to his gutty, death-defying solo.

"I think so," I said.

"Don't lie to me, honey. I couldn't bear that."

She took my hand in hers and kissed my knuckles. I was ashamed of myself. Yet this improvised fiction kept falling out of my mouth. "We can probably get off-base housing, and a living allowance. The Army does that for people."

We were in my underground apartment, drinking from a jar of Benedetto's dark red wine. I put on a record Max had given me, lugubrious jazz by Mezz Mezzrow. Our moods deepened and darkened in the dingy room. "I just wanted to be happy," Colleen said. "Was that too much to ask?"

Maybe it was. I took her into my arms, protective and consoling, but Mezzrow's blue clarinet took us someplace else, someplace bittersweet and unbearably confined. Her eyes darkened with an abstract melancholy, and in that mood we went to bed. We had a night of exhausting exploratory sex, letting our imaginations lead the way. She improvised heroically, with shocking energy, as if imprinting me with a searing memory, a carnal tattoo.

In the early morning she got up and made coffee. She sat in a ratty armchair and sipped from her cup. She looked around my apartment—at the empty mustard-yellow walls, the little two-burner gas range, the worn-out brocade of the sofa. She ran her fingers along the pitted chrome legs of my small dinette table. "This is what you really like, isn't it?" she said, mystifying me. She looked as if she were seeing, for the first time, the warts on my soul.

I shrugged. "It's tolerable."

After a moment she sighed and said, "It's over, Ozzie, isn't it?"

I started to protest, but she came over to the bed and put her finger on my lips. "Don't," she said. "It's okay. Maybe what we had was all we get."

Then I saw *her* as if for the first time. Her beauty was merciless. An adult wisdom had been sealed in her, and now that seal was broken.

"Jesus, Colleen," I said, suddenly frantic. "Let's go to Yuma and get married this afternoon. Then—"

"No. I don't think that would be a good idea."

"I love you, Colleen," I said. "I really do."

Her sad smile tore my heart out. "I'll write to you," she said, but her eyes were distant. It was her turn to invent charitable fictions. "I'll write to you every week, my darling."

"Our children," I said, grabbing for straws. "Deirdre, Rosemary, William, and Peter."

"Postponed," she sighed.

No-names locked in the black ring of eternity, I thought, but would not have said.

Yet I saw them in my mind as Colleen and I held each other, perhaps for the last time. I saw us all—happy and strong, a solid little collective, touring the fantastic world in our sturdy blue Dodge. I could hear their small, wonder-filled voices, too: *Daddy, what's that? Daddy, where are we? Daddy, when will we get there? Daddy, why . . . ?* And I would have enough answers to make things interesting. Some of them would even be true.